Jesus Lives in Trenton

Jesus Lives in TRENTON

A Novel

Christopher Klim

CREATIVE ARTS BOOK COMPANY
Berkeley ✦ California

Jesus Lives in Trenton is published by Donald S. Ellis
and distributed by Creative Arts Book Company

For information contact:
Creative Arts Book Company
833 Bancroft Way
Berkeley, California 94710
1-800-848-7789

Christopher Klim
c/o Hopewell Promotions
P.O. Box 11
Titusville, NJ 08560-0011

ISBN 0-88739-418-3
Library of Congress Catalog Number 2001097455

Printed in the United States of America

Without the unyielding support and inspiration of my wife Karin and friend Robert Gover, this book would not exist.

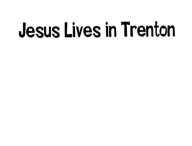

Jesus Lives in Trenton

PART 1

CHAPTER 1
Miss Record Exposed

In the beginning, before Jesus appeared, before someone claiming to be Boot Means' biological father showed up, Boot was attacked by two naked women in a Trenton hotel lobby. He knew how to defend himself, having grown up in foster care, but as an emerging photojournalist, he expected a scuffle with a political mob or a ghetto riot, not a gang of bathing beauties gone wild.

As Boot hit the lobby, the girls were waiting. He loathed direct attention, and thirteen women in bikinis glared at his approach. They formed a jagged line, throwing judicious elbows like jostling men at an airport luggage carousel. A few checked their skimpy attire, stealthily plucking the swimsuit thongs from their asses. Boot pretended not to notice.

A tall brunette cracked her knuckles. "You're late."

"I can read the time." Boot quietly cursed his Pinto's cranky carburetor. He envisioned his rusting car crushed into a tidy cube in the demolition yard.

"The paper said 7:00 P.M."

"I know what it said." Boot had typed the advertisement as part of his assignment. GIRLS WANTED 4 DAILY MISS RECORD CON-

TEST. Some journalists at the *Trenton Record* reported on local sporting events. Others covered breaking news from the state capitol. Boot held the lowest staff position above janitorial help. He languished on Page 6 with its smattering of gossip and skin—slightly better than cleaning toilets.

He dropped his best disinterested stare on the brunette. "You don't have to wait."

She snorted and turned back into the line.

The room paused for Boot's next move. He darted onto the mock lanai near the tiki bar, pushing aside the rattan furniture to clear space. He unfurled a fake backdrop of surf and sand, then plugged in the standing lamps, but his camera tripod had a stripped wing nut, and it telescoped to the floor like a terminal drunk.

He knelt down, binding the legs with electrical tape. The women grumbled. Hair mousse loses its pouf within an hour, even faster beneath the lights.

"Just a minute." Boot fumbled with the roll of tape. Perspiration moistened his collar. The whines and sighs of women riffled at his back, an alien language to him.

"Having trouble?" The brunette's sarcasm sizzled through the air.

"Nothing I can't handle." He stood up and slapped on his portrait lens.

"Need a bobby pin or something?"

"It's under control." He eyed the latest batch of contestants. What did the great journalists see when they faced a crowd? Where did they find inspiration? This group resembled a carbon copy of the previous week: phony blond bombshells, counterfeit Marilyn Monroes. They'd been coddled their whole lives, raised on the cushy lies of mommy and daddy, salved with hairspray and insurance policies. Boot understood reality. He'd been abandoned as a baby, raised in a disjointed collection of families, and schooled in urban survival and a patchwork of religious hogwash. Guts and hard work created success. These women owned a greater chance of being sucked into a jet engine, than realizing fame.

He retreated into the safety zone behind his camera and opened the flood gates. The end of logic appeared at hand. "Let's have the first lady, please."

She strutted into the lights, wielding a hot pink strapless suit and thighs like blue ribbon hams. Boot spotted shadows in the dimples above her knees.

He checked the clipboard, reviewing her essential data: name, age, measurements, likes, and dislikes. "Under dislikes, is that broccoli?

"Yes, brocli."

Boot penciled in the correct spelling. "Alright turn to your left, please."

"This good?" she asked.

"How about your other left." He guided her with a pointed finger. Contestants often confused his left with their left and stutter-stepped like running backs avoiding an open field tackle.

She blushed. "This good?"

"A little more," he said. "Stop right there. Thank you."

She twisted her neck and struck a raffish pose, evoking the centerfold of a porn magazine. "Boot. That's an interesting name."

"It's short for Booth."

"Is it a family name?"

He didn't want to get into it. The facts he'd gathered about his family fit on the head of a pin. His mother, it was assumed, scribbled 'B. Means' on the hem of his nursery blanket and deposited him behind the Macy's cosmetics booth in Manhattan. The sales clerk dubbed him Booth, and the name stuck like the punch line to a bad joke. That was all he knew. The rest he made up to suit the moment. "I'm the great, great, great, great grandson of John Wilkes Booth."

"Did people tease you a lot?"

"Only in history class." He squinted at her cheesy legs. She'd never make the cut. The boys in the newsroom rested coffee mugs on prettier portraits.

"Why don't you sit down," he suggested.

The brunette yelled from the line. "Hey Bud, can we break up the gab session here?"

Boot grimaced. What was her hurry? There was nothing to do downtown after dark, except drink. Trenton boasted no discos, strip clubs, or bowling alleys. Like a strung-out whore standing in the rain, the city longed for action.

"You'll get your chance," he said.

The brunette had muscular limbs. She raked a brush through her kinky hair, as if she could tame it into a different style. "Can you move it along? She hasn't got a prayer."

He eclipsed her from view with his Nikon. He pressed the shutter release and called for the next woman.

"Tell chunky to clear the decks." The brunette forced her way to the front.

The women ahead of her bristled, and the bleached blond at the start of the line blocked her path.

"Out of the way, blondie." The brunette poked a hairbrush into the blond's belly ring.

The blond shoved back. "Wait your turn like everyone else."

Boot ignored them. He wanted to shoot and run, get back to the office before the final press deadline. Since Sheldon Storch bought the *Record* and slashed the payroll, the newsroom resembled a deathwatch. Everyone waited for the next body to fall. Journalists felt compelled to stand witness.

The brunette poked harder. "What are you going to do about it?"

The blond squared her shoulders. "Get in line, bitch."

"Oh yeah, you peroxide shitbrain?"

"That's right, pug face."

Boot froze. Two Miss Record hopefuls circled on the Downtowner's worn carpet. They looked to be inventing an exotic new dance, until they collided, forming a less convivial arrangement. They pawed each other like rabid cheerleaders, grasping hair by the handful, making a hateful pompom of each other's head.

The brunette took down the blond, straddling her chest. She aimed for cosmetic adjustments, smearing makeup and applying bruises, but when her bikini top sprung loose and shot across the room, her polished fingernails dug into the blond for keeps.

"Ladies." Boot crept out of the safety zone. He looked to the others for help, watching them collect like mannequins in a closet.

He stood over the brawl. The women looked evenly matched in style and spite. He held out his hands to stop them, yet with all of those body parts flying out in the open, he feared handling the wrong one.

"Ladies, please!" He snatched the blond's arm in mid punch, but the brunette grasped for her rival's hoop earring. She swung her arm, taking out a lamp stand. The long metal rod crashed to the ground. The bulb flickered, then shattered with a sickening pop.

Boot cringed. That cost twenty bucks to fix.

His temper rose to the fray. He latched onto the women, twisting their arms, working them like the sticky clutch in his Pinto. "Damn it! Cut it out."

Each woman waited for the other to squeal first. Heated glances raced toward Boot. The blond puckered her lips to spit, but the brunette stopped cold, her expression sober, as if suddenly recalling the focus of her rage.

With a crude groan— the kind truck drivers release when pushing away from the prime rib special on the Turnpike—the brunette thrust a stiletto heel behind Boot's knee. His leg collapsed under him.

"Keep your mitts off me, you son of a bitch!" She stabbed him again in the small of his back, and pain surged up his spine.

The blond flashed angry tan lines and fists to match. She rammed a full set of turquoise rings into Boot's mouth, and he bit into his tongue.

Boot clutched the spiny arm of a rattan lounge chair, fighting to reach his feet, but the brunette with the lightning heels wriggled behind and mounted his shoulders. She pinned his head between her thighs, squeezing the blood into his ears, pounding his head.

As he pried at the brunette's knees, the blond lunged at his waist. Her arms encircled him, the knob of her shoulder jabbing his kidneys. Every ounce of her underfed frame landed on target, driving his chin to the rough carpet.

Sharp blows pummeled his back. The smell of sweat and body cologne hit his nostrils. His contact with women was limited to singles, and the force of them banded together surprised him.

A crowd gathered around. The other women cheered. The hotel manager hollered. Two husky security guards leered over the struggle, dictating the action over a walkie-talkie.

Boot covered his head, hearing sordid remarks crackle over the airwaves. People wanted to see the fight before it broke up. Moe from maintenance was racing down in the elevator; Thelma from housecleaning too. Boot pressed his face into the shabby rug. He'd take on the world alone, dividing it into frozen images, defining it in newsprint, but in an instant, he'd found himself on the wrong side of the story, his camera out of reach.

CHAPTER 2
The Golden Donkey

They were laughing when Boot entered the newsroom. Heads poked above cubicles to stare. At 9:30 P.M., those polishing stories for the morning edition paused to stand on their chairs and applaud. Not since sports writer Jimmy DiLorenzo got loaded at a Christmas party and insulted the mayor did the newsroom find occasion to jeer. That was seven months ago, over a half year of abuse for Jimmy D. Boot felt the mantle settling on his shoulders. Wisecracks shot past his ears like shrapnel. News people knew how to stick it to you.

He pressed a cold can of soda to his swollen lip. He no longer worried about modesty. He swallowed a little blood, thinking of his idol, the Pulitzer Prize winning photojournalist Eric Pulvermann. Did Eric ever deal with this crap?

Boot watched the chief editor march toward him. Art Fontek carried a heavyset frame, and his nose hosted a mole accented by three wiry hairs. A hardcore journalist since the 60s, Art's wide ties and blunt sideburns seemed frozen in 1973—a time when Nixon resigned and the country's notion of news coverage changed forever.

Art stopped Boot in the center of the newsroom. He shook Boot's hand as if tugging a heavy chain. "Congratulations."

Boot lowered the soda can to his belt. "How did you hear?"

"The hotel manager called. He wasn't happy."

"Did he mention a busted up lounge chair?"

"I took care of it, although I can't say as much for you."

"What?"

Art flicked a finger toward Boot's mouth. "Nice lip."

A woman shouted from two cubicles away. "You should have seen the other gal."

People chuckled. Boot quietly burned.

Jimmy D shuffled up with his hands behind his back, donning a huge grin. He handed Art the trophy—a gold-plated horse's ass on a pinewood stand.

Boot felt as if he'd been punched in the kidneys again.

Art raised his hand to address the office. His voice rattled the dusty plaques on the walls like an overjuiced PA system. "This is a sad moment. Many of us enjoyed Jimmy's tenure as the village idiot. It was a good run. Who could forget last year's Winterland Ball and his immortal words to Mayor Karl Voss ..."

Others chimed in as Art recalled Jimmy D's famous fumble. "Hey, that green bow tie and cummerbund makes you look like a fag."

"Not even Jack Daniels," Art continued, "was quoted with such candor."

He held forward the golden donkey as it was known. "Before us, we have a young man who holds that spark of greatness. Tonight, Boot Means proved his mettle, placing his butt on the line and quite literally getting it kicked."

"Don King is on line one," a man in the back yelled. "He wants to know when Boot plans a rematch."

The floor broke into laughter.

Boot considered walking away and never returning, but he was glued to this spot in the world. His student loan and credit card bills piled higher than the phone book. If he quit, he might land in the Sears Photo Center at the mall, a photographer's worst excuse for living. A daily flogging was better than staring down an endless parade of computer-generated backgrounds and drooling children.

He dipped his chin and accepted the golden donkey, amid a plethora of cheers. He understood office politics—a shade different than the rules governing foster homes. Once in a while, someone took a hit just to make everyone else feel better. This ceremony offered a welcome distraction from constant layoff rumors and the screaming red ink on the *Record*'s financial logs.

Jimmy patted Boot on the back. "Welcome to hell, son."

"Now onto business," Art said. "Rico, the police raided the Race Street apartments for drugs again. We missed it. Get your butt down to the station and find out what happened. When you're finished, get your butt in my office and explain why we missed the story. You have until midnight."

Rico Torrez grabbed his coat during Art's instructions and bolted for the stairwell. The elevator took too long.

"All of you keep forgetting," Art said, "there are two other papers in town."

Art looked to his left. "Teresa, the statehouse is debating auto insurance proposals tomorrow. I hope that's at the head of your list."

A demure woman with deep black hair kept her eyes on her computer terminal. Her fingers moved furiously over the keys. "It's in my book. I'm as good as there."

Boot backed away with small steps. He gripped the donkey in one hand, and with the other, he touched the soda can to his mouth. The salty aluminum stung his cut lip.

Art took a slip of paper from his suit pocket. "Finally, Jesus was seen in town."

Sarcastic groans rose from the gallery, although Boot noticed Teresa cease typing.

She looked up. "Jesus?"

"Stop the complaining," Art said. "A woman saw Jesus on a billboard on Jefferson Avenue."

Teresa smirked. "Was it a church ad?"

"No, an ad for Smythe's Diner." Art held the slip of paper above his head. "Who wants it?"

For the first time since Boot strolled into his own public roasting, he saw people retreat. They ducked into their cubicles like soldiers in foxholes.

"If I don't get a volunteer," Art said, "it's dealer's choice."

Boot studied the tops of the office cubicles, praying no heads popped back up. He glanced at Teresa, unable to gauge her interest.

He stepped up to Art, his boss, everyone's boss. But did his fate rest with Art or Sheldon Storch? Art was tough but fair, the kind of man Boot might admire as a father. Storch sported the nickname Neutron Shel. If he showed up at one of his numerous companies and disliked what he saw, all of the people disappeared.

Boot's palms felt sweaty and a knot formed in his throat. "I'll take it."

Art ignored Boot's approach. He scanned the newsroom, a pilot searching for an open landing strip. "You've had enough fun for one day."

"Please, I can do it."

"Go away, Boot."

Teresa returned to her computer keyboard. "Let him have it. No one else wants it."

Art stabbed his nose in Boot's face. "You think you're ready to graduate?"

"Give me the chance."

"Recite rule Sixteen."

The question fazed Boot, until he realized the point. Art insisted that his writers memorize Strunk and White's *The Elements of Style* from cover to cover. When Boot first saw Art quiz a feature writer, Boot rushed to purchase a copy. He waited for the moment when Art came to him, and in two years, this was the first.

"I'll give you a hint," Art said. "It's one of the Principles of Composition."

"Clarity," Boot replied.

"Recite the rule."

Boot closed his eyes, conjuring the black and white text in his mind. "Use definite, specific, concrete language."

"That's what I want from you."

Boot wanted to leap out of his shoes. "I can have the story lead?"

Art nodded. "I want one clear and concise sentence."

"You mean you want a caption line for the photo."

"I know what it's called. Camera jockeys think it's an invitation to a freeform essay."

"Thank you."

"Don't thank me yet. That picture and sentence has to be mighty interesting to get printed."

"I'll do my best."

"Her name is Emily Phibbs. Here's her address." Art slapped a scrap of paper in Boot's hand. "Find out what she means by Jesus. Separate the facts from fiction. I'm not running a bulletin board for Trenton Psychiatric."

"Yes sir."

"And those Miss Record proofs better not be late either."

"Yes sir."

CHAPTER 3
Dander Demons

Boot Means stood on Jefferson Avenue, searching for Jesus. He stared through a length of razor wire fence, sizing up an abandoned box factory. The windows were shattered, and the lot was overgrown and littered with a half dozen rusting cars. Even if the Jesus story never panned out, he didn't mind the other writers laughing at him. He knew how to survive on scraps. One day, he'd salvage one of their rejects and make them see his worth.

The street curved with the Raritan Canal, and a stale odor wafted from the slow-moving water. Boot aimed his camera at the factory, spotting the suspect advertisement for Smythe's Diner near the roofline. A faded and peeling mural stretched across the pitted bricks, tempting the neighborhood with a steaming meal of roast beef and biscuits. Dark gravy flowed over the plate, dense and speckled, swirling with patterns like dirty motor oil. It hardly evoked Boot's appetite, much less the image of Jesus Christ.

"Hey snapshot, got a smoke?"

Boot spotted a young woman standing across the street. She wore a blue and white body suit that reflected the incessant neon light of a liquor store window.

"Cigarette?" She asked.

"Excuse me?"

"A smoke. You got one?" She propped her hands on her hips. Her dyed auburn hair showed streaks of pink, pulled straight and slicked to her scalp. "You don't know me?"

He recognized her as a hooker from the train station. He often passed her at night, while canvassing Trenton with his camera. He followed the steps in Eric Pulvermann's book, *Fifty Ways to Capture the Universe*. Pulvermann's Law #1: You have to be there to get the shot.

"I've seen you around." Boot prepared to rebuff her proposition.

He watched her cross the street. He owned plenty of photographs of her from a distance, but up close, her strange lip appeared to be a long thin scar from her mouth to her ear. One cheek lifted above the other, which was why she turned her head to the side.

"You're giving me a weird look," she said.

"I'm sorry. What's your name?"

"That's better."

"I'm Boot Means."

"Call me Christine. Got a smoke or what?"

"I used to smoke, but I'd rather save the money." He offered her a stick of bubblegum.

She glanced away. "Why you staring at empty buildings in the dark?"

He scanned the skyline. Yellow streaks dashed above the capitol's golden dome, and the cathedral bell tolled across town. "It's almost morning."

"That doesn't change it. People going to think you're crazy."

He resented her snap judgment, but then he'd already formed a few of his own. He thought that people like her took the easy route. "I'm doing research."

"You know they're going to tear the thing down?"

"I can see that." Boot read the public notices posted along the fence. The demolition date already passed.

"So what are you looking at?"

He pointed his finger. "The sign up there."

"If you're hungry, that diner's around the corner."

"Don't you see anything in the sign?"

"Nothing fancy, snapshot. A greasy plate of food, like the other stuff they serve."

"Look harder."

She squinted her eyes. "What am I supposed to see?"

"A face."

"A what?"

"Jesus." He watched her reaction, a slight parting of her lips.

"Jesus?" she laughed. "You are crazy."

"I'm on assignment for the *Trenton Record.*"

"So you're a reporter, snapshot."

"Yes." He liked the feel of his new title.

She walked by him, tossing a dismissive hand from her side. "You of all people should know. There ain't no Jesus in Trenton."

At sunrise, Boot sat in Mrs. Emily Phibbs' living room on Belvidere Street, hoping she held a clue to the Jesus image. He fidgeted in a musty corduroy armchair. Something about her house bothered him. He didn't mind the neighborhood, even though the homes on either side stood burnt out and boarded up. He rubbed his eyes and scratched his nose. The smell of the place caught in his throat, like a mouthful of sour milk.

"I hope you like Chamomile." Mrs. Phibbs poured yellow tea into china cups. She was a big-boned black woman with silver hair. A green cotton dress hung over her frame like a drop cloth. "I think it's dandy in the morning."

"I drink whatever's around the newsroom." He didn't say that he sometimes ate whatever was around the newsroom as well: abandoned donuts, leftover pizza, homemade cookies. It saved time and money.

She waddled toward the front window and threw back the heavy drapes. Sunlight fell over the wooden bookcase and floorboards.

For the first time, Boot realized they weren't alone. Cats lurked everywhere. He counted enough furry critters to jolt him into an allergic coma. Three gray Siamese laid tucked within the open spaces on the bookcase. A fat tawny curled inside a basket by the TV, and a shaggy ragamuffin pawed the cassette door to the VCR.

Boot held his breath, but already he felt his eyes water. He first discovered his cat aversion at the age of ten. He'd been placed in a foster home for just a few hours, when his nose started running and his eyes swelled shut. His new family faced a choice between him and the family pet. It was hardly a fair contest. In the end, he sat on the curb with a box of tissues, waiting for the agency to pick him up.

"I don't read the *Record*," Mrs. Phibbs said. "I read the *Times*."

"You did speak with Art Fontek?"

"Who?"

"Art Fontek?"

"Well, the other papers wouldn't return my calls."

"The *Record* is interested in all community happenings." The sense that he wallowed on the bottom end of journalism felt stronger than ever. He heard Jimmy D cracking a whole new line of jokes.

"I was expecting someone not so young. Are you sure you're with the paper?"

Boot pulled the camera from his bag. "I need to ask you a few questions about the sign."

"My nephew will be home any minute."

"We can speak on the porch if you like."

"That won't be necessary."

Boot scraped a tear from the corner of his eye. Sludge formed in his sinuses. He breathed through his mouth.

"Are you alright?" Mrs. Phibbs asked.

"Yes. Ummm, the sign. When did you first see it?"

"I'll get you a tissue."

When she left the room, Boot rushed to the window and stuck his face to the screen. Tiny hairs shimmered on the fine aluminum grating. He sneezed hard enough to pop his ears.

A three-footed heather cat emerged from beneath the couch. It had matted fur and one eye scarred shut. The hideous feline bounced up beside Boot, unfurling its tail like a probe. It prodded and poked the cuff of his jeans until it seemed satisfied. Boot wanted to put it out of its misery with the heel of his shoe.

"Beat it," he whispered. "Go on. Beat it."

It looked up and grinned with the typical ambivalence of the species.

"I think she likes you." Mrs. Phibbs held out a box of tissues.

"What happened to it?"

"My car."

"You ran it over?"

"She likes to crawl under the hood. It's warm in the winter, and when I started my car one morning ... well, my nephew had to cut her free from the fan belt."

Boot scrunched his nose and reached for a tissue. "Thanks."

"My babies have been such a comfort to me since my husband's taken ill."

"What's the matter with him?"

"Angina. It gives us a scare now and then."

"Sorry to hear that." Boot wiped his nose.

"You should take better care of yourself. You look like you've been in a fight."

He knew to leave his eyes alone but ground his knuckles into them anyway. "I'm on a tight schedule. Can we discuss the sign?"

"I drink Echinacea tea whenever I feel sick. Do you know what that is?"

"No."

"It's a flower. It's good for you."

He started to wheeze. His skin felt ready to crawl from his face. He fought back a wet cough. "Please, Mrs. Phibbs, I need to get back to the newspaper."

"Young people are in such a hurry." She waddled to a chair and sunk her ample backside in the cushions.

"I'm sorry," Boot said. "Can you tell me about the sign?"

"Did you see it?"

"Yes."

"What do you think?"

Boot wondered how to reply. He was not a religious person. He never prayed for miracles, like other people. "It was dark. I couldn't make it out."

"But you'll go look again?"

"I have pictures."

"It's obvious. I was walking to Handy's Market. Do you know where that is?"

"On Calhoun."

"I go every Thursday to play the lottery." She put both hands over her heart. "I just looked up and saw Him. I've passed that building a thousand times, but there He was."

"Who did you see?"

"Jesus, His face, clear as day."

"I don't understand." Boot opened his notebook and added his commentary. *She saw Jesus.*

She pulled two ticket stubs from the end table. "I won the lottery after that. Five thousand dollars."

"You think the sign was responsible?" *Coincidence*, he scribbled.

She peered down over her glasses, as if no other possible explanation existed.

He considered rephrasing the same question but realized the futility. He returned to his notes. *She actually saw Jesus. Lunatic.*

The three-footed cat hopped on Boot's lap, working its crooked tail beneath Boot's chin. He wanted to hurl the sorry beast across the room, but he would have to touch it.

"She does like you," Mrs. Phibbs said.

The cat shook its head, raising a cloud of dander to Boot's face. Boot sneezed, startling the creature to the floor. It tumbled on its bad leg and righted itself once more.

Boot put both hands to his eyes, rubbing them until they were aflame in their sockets.

"You have a cold, don't you?" she asked.

"I need to get out of here." He swallowed hard. "One more question. When you look at the sign, how exactly do you see Jesus?"

"Like I said, He's up there clear as day. My neighbor's seen it too."

"That blabbermouth bitch!" Doris Francis swept past Boot outside her Belvidere Street home, four doors down from Mrs. Phibbs'. Doris clutched a red umbrella and a paper lunch bag. Her varicose legs pounded the sidewalk, beating a testy path to a blue Chevette by the curb.

Boot sniffled, then discretely hacked up phlegm into a tissue. He felt as unsociable as Doris. He'd volunteer to drive every cat into the river with a flamethrower. "Mrs. Phibbs told me about the sign. She says you're her friend."

"Friend." She stabbed her keys into the car door.

"Is there a problem between you two?"

"Not until now."

"Did you see Jesus too?"

Her eyes opened up like the aperture in his fattest camera lens. "I told her about it."

"Did she see it before winning the lottery?"

"I told her about the sign. I saw it first."

"Did anything unusual happen to you?"

She plopped inside the Chevette and glanced up at Boot. She appeared ready to spill her story but just gnashed her teeth. "If she's going to behave like this, I can't wait for them to tear the sign down."

She slammed the car door and sped off.

CHAPTER 4

Neutron Shel

Boot approached the *Record*'s home office in the city war zone. A helicopter circled the complex, like a relentless silver bird aiming to drop its load. He ducked inside the building and crossed the lobby. He intended to present his Jesus piece to Art and show his boss what he produced from a thin story lead.

Jimmy D stood by the elevator, a copy of *The Sporting News* tucked beneath his arm. His eyes lit up at Boot's approach. "Good morning, golden boy. How's our star reporter?"

"Just passing through." Boot wanted to avoid the newsroom since the golden donkey debacle, but there was no surer way to reach Art. "What's with the helicopter?"

"Storch patrol."

"Sheldon Storch?"

"The one and only."

"Is he going to land?"

"Eventually. He likes to observe the building to see who arrives late." Jimmy D checked his watch. "And by my calculations, you just missed screwing up this one."

Boot stepped inside the elevator with Jimmy D. The floor numbers rose with his blood pressure. Sheldon Storch wasn't visiting to hand out bonuses. Heads would roll. Boot wondered if he'd make it to sundown.

When he reached the third floor, three people from Human Resources nearly bowled him over in the hallway. He let them march past and into the newsroom. A security guard lagged behind, humming a dull tune.

Boot watched the icy foursome plod into the editors' conference room, the place where the top brass met to hash out the headlines and feature stories. The inner sanctum had a long mahogany table and glass walls that faced the main floor. Writers never looked in that direction, for fear of jinxing the fate of their stories, but today, journalists peered above their cubicle walls to see inside. For once, they longed not to be the topic of discussion.

Lingering by the coffee maker, Boot staked out the conference room. He spotted two senior editors and an entertainment writer named Ivy Innocente. The security guard sat in Art's chair, twiddling his thumbs.

Boot heard Jimmy D call out. The slick sports writer stood outside Teresa Ringley's cubicle, mouthing words of doom. He raised a hand to his neck and made a deliberate slicing gesture from ear to ear.

"What's going on?" Boot asked, walking in that direction.

"The Leisure Section." Jimmy D clutched a mug of coffee.

"They fired the entire Leisure Section?"

"Downsized is the accepted terminology. Rumor has it we've replaced it with a serialized column. That's five dead soldiers by my count."

Boot shuddered. If the paper released Ivy after thirty, thirty-five years, they'd wipe him away like a sneeze. "But Ivy's been here forever."

"She'll get ..." Jimmy D looked at the conference room. "... a nice severance package, I hope."

"Don't count on it," Teresa said. "I heard in Philly, Storch sent them packing with just two weeks pay."

"Well I'm in no trouble," Jimmy D said.

"How's that?" Teresa asked.

"Thank God for local sporting events. Who else in the world would cover Trenton Thunder baseball games?"

"The *Trenton Times* ... the *Trentonian*."

Jimmy D's smug expression sunk into his coffee mug.

Boot considered his own resume. Other newspapers might wonder what he did for the last two years. He envisioned his rapidly approaching future behind the counter of a camera store. *And how many rolls of film can I get for you today, sir?*

"Don't worry, Boot," Teresa said. "I think you're safe."

"For now anyway," Jimmy D added.

"The blood letting is probably over."

"Do you think?" Boot asked.

"I think so."

"I guess," Jimmy D said.

They paused, an odd moment when three journalists dug deep for words. Boot almost wished for a Jimmy D quip to fill the void.

Rico Torrez broke the silence. He stomped up to them, the skin furrowing upon his brow. "They axed three from the pressroom."

"No shit," Jimmy D said.

"And two from Accounting, and one from Human Resources."

Jimmy D set his sights on Boot. "I'd pack my bags if I were you. Unfortunately, you'll have to leave the golden donkey behind."

"They're pissed in the pressroom." Rico licked his lips. "I let them know the writers union is talking about a strike."

"Writer's union?" Jimmy D nearly coughed his java through his nose. "I only hear those two ugly words when it's time to collect annual dues."

"Jimmy's afraid a strike's going to disrupt his lifestyle," Teresa said.

Rico turned to Boot. "The photographers say they'll support a strike too."

Boot kept his mouth shut, wiping his nose with a tissue. He could afford to strike as much as he could afford to lose his job, and besides, the *Record* hired him as an apprentice photojournalist. He should have been voted into the writers union from day one, but they never put his name up for nomination. Now they wanted him to support a strike?

"I'll try my hand in New York." Boot refused to let them think he held no options.

"You have something cooking?" Jimmy D asked.

"Maybe."

"Are you going to join us if we strike?" Rico asked.

"I don't know." Boot studied everyone's face. He rubbed the scab on his tongue against the inside of his cheek.

"I trust him." Teresa put her hands on her computer keyboard and started typing. "He'll do the right thing."

To Boot, the right thing involved getting himself off of Page 6, but he possessed little to persuade his boss. He gripped the Jesus assignment in a manila folder. It contained the sketchy testimony of two women and picture proofs of a building advertisement that depicted Jesus no better than an ink blot resembled a Van Gogh masterpiece.

"I'll talk to you guys later." Boot walked away, eyeing Art's office near the conference room. The conversation did more than scare him; it summoned his courage to charge through Art's door.

He found his boss seated behind his desk and glued to a computer terminal. One of the three TVs was switched on and tuned to CNN. Scenes of an African riot zipped through Boot's peripheral vision.

Art bit into a headcheese sandwich. The gelatinous slices of meat jiggled over the edges of rye bread and plopped onto a crinkled sheet of paper. "What do you want?"

"I heard Sheldon Storch is on his way."

"Do you have something to say?"

"I need ummm ... I have the Jesus piece."

Art studied Boot up and down. "I don't believe it. You look even worse than last night."

Boot's voice was clogged and sticky, and his nostrils felt plugged with cement. "I'm allergic to cats."

"What did you do, roll in a litter box?"

"Mrs. Phibbs owns dozens of cats." Boot placed the Jesus proofs and notes in front of Art and backed away.

"The cats would have made a better story. It's a shame you suffered for this one."

"Why is it a shame?"

"Let me take a look." Art glossed over the Jesus piece, scooped it up, and tossed it on the windowsill behind his desk. "Are you finished with Miss Record?"

"I stuffed everything in your mail slot." Boot didn't want to be around when Art reviewed his Miss Record work. Because of last night's mishap, he recycled rejected proofs from earlier shoots.

"It's in my mail slot?"

"Yes."

"Can I see what you have?"

"I'll get it." Boot dashed to Art's mail slot and returned with a short stack of Miss Record candidates and their bios.

Art counted the sets. He kept a close eye on Page 6. Boot loathed the special attention. Art usually clipped and rewrote pieces on the computer and sent them straight to the copy editor over the office network, but for pet projects, he perused the hard copies, hand delivering caustic commentary when needed. He seemed to enjoy scribbling red ink over the pages and photos, dropping them on the admonished journalist's desk like grenades. He tacked the worst critiques on the newsroom bulletin board.

"You somehow managed to get this done," Art said.

"If you've done it once, you've done it a million times," Boot replied, sheepishly.

"Not according to Sheldon Storch." Art placed the set on a pile of approved stories for the copy editor. "Which leads me to my next subject. Storch wants to start a contest: Miss Record at the Beach. We're posting entry forms in tomorrow's paper."

"How is this different?"

"Storch thinks we're not getting everything we can out of Miss

Record. The beach is supposed to generate excitement."

"I don't think the setting is the problem."

"Save it. I already know what you're going to say. It's Storch's baby, so it's nonnegotiable."

"I see."

"A photo shoot is slated for Seaside, and that's your department."

Boot struggled to manufacture enthusiasm. "I know."

"Good." Art faced his computer terminal. On TV, the Secretary of Labor announced unemployment figures for the last business quarter. The trend was up.

Boot sat quietly, amassing his nerve. He cleared his throat. "What did you think?"

"I'm sure they'll be fine," Art replied without looking.

"They will?"

"We'd print a chimp in a bathing suit if that's what signed up for Miss Record."

"I mean the Jesus story."

"There's no story there."

"Two people said they saw Jesus in the sign."

"I bet they were convincing."

"They believe they saw Jesus."

Art swung his computer terminal for Boot to see. "Look at this."

Boot skimmed the articles about to appear in the *New York Times*: trouble with the IRS, Indonesia balks at trade restrictions, gunfire in the Gaza Strip. The *Trenton Record* could purchase these articles if needed.

"You want stories?" Art punched the screen. "These are news stories."

"I'd like to cover a piece like that."

"We all would." Art sounded bitter, not sardonic as usual. The walls in his office were plastered with pictures and awards from his forty year career. Boot knew Art started as a beat writer in Baltimore and hustled for a correspondent's position at the White House. Before the *Record*, Art edited a seventy-year-old paper in Cincinnati, until it went under.

Boot grabbed a stick of gum from his pocket and popped it in his mouth. With his nose plugged up, the gum tasted like dirt.

"What do you want from me?" Art asked.

Boot shrugged, expecting another fatherly jab to come his way. He often hung out by the coffee maker in the morning, until Art ribbed him about his hair or the black clothes he always wore.

"Shit, OK." Art slid the Jesus proofs off of the windowsill and into his lap. "Let me see this. I guess you have to start at the bottom before you make the headlines."

Boot watched his boss study the photos of the Jesus sign on Jefferson Avenue. He'd tinkered around in the darkroom, forcing Jesus' image from the negatives of Smythe's billboard ad. It was a rough outline, but if he stared long enough, if he squinted his eyes just right, a face appeared inside the plate of Smythe's famous biscuits and gravy. "Do you see Jesus?"

"It doesn't matter."

Boot hedged his bets. "I'm not as certain as the women."

"It doesn't matter if you see Jesus either. That's your lesson for the day." Art shut the folder again. "We'll try to push it on Page 6."

"It won't fit the Local section? I can add more text."

Art's pit bull demeanor resurfaced. "Sure, I'll drop it right next to the Mayor's re-election campaign."

"Alright, Page 6 is great."

"A picture and one line is all you get."

"I can follow it up with a ..."

"Boot, get out of my office."

"Yes, sir."

"Go get those chimps in bikinis. Make us all proud."

Boot stopped himself short of asking again. He'd earned a fresh piece of real estate in the paper, no matter how insignificant. He backed out of the office, before Art changed his mind.

CHAPTER 5
Stacy's Hair

"I saw your article in the *Record*." Mrs. Ohm emerged from the dark. Boot's landlady was a chunky woman with thick wrists and ankles like softballs stuffed into stockings.

"Good evening." Boot stood beside the dumpster, emptying her garbage cans in the bin. He was a month behind with the rent. He thought to stop his car and haul her trash down to the dumpster. He used to do it often, especially in the days after her husband died.

Mrs. Ohm appeared breathy from the walk from her house. Managing the trailer park by the river seemed like more than she could handle alone. "I look for you every day."

"Oh?" He hoped it wasn't because of the rent. He had to fix his car last month, although it didn't run like new as promised. He'd get the money to her.

"Page 6," she said. "I look for you every day."

"Miss Record?"

"I saw your article about Smythe's billboard."

"It's just a picture and a few lines." Boot played it down, yet when he first saw it in print, he tore it out and stuck it in his wallet for good luck. He had a taste of the real thing and wanted more. He needed something impossible for Art Fontek to refuse.

"I guess you'll be off Page 6 soon," she said.

"Maybe."

"Have you been promoted?"

"Not yet."

She massaged her swollen wrist. "Did you forget the rent?"

"I've been meaning to talk to you." He glanced at his car. The engine sputtered beside the dumpster.

"Do you think I can have it soon?"

"Yes, soon." He refused to say much else, not wanting to tip the scales the wrong way. He used to be her favorite tenant, the pet of the trailer park. After cancer took her husband, Boot lent a hand, lifting heavy objects around her house, changing the water in her fish tank, listening to her ramble on about the old times. They'd shared a few meals, and once after a half bottle of Chianti, she called him her adopted son.

"When you find the money," she said, "you'll let me know?"

"Right."

Boot jumped into his Pinto and sped off. He eyed his trailer at the end of the third cul-de-sac. He wanted to pop on a blues record and relax, but his girlfriend was waiting for him. *Damn, an unannounced visit.* Stacy's bright red Corvette was parked beside the stoop, and the windows of his ApacheStar 208 glowed like a supermarket at night.

A touch of anxiety slowed his pace toward the door. The brightness of his trailer repelled him. He rarely used the lights, tacking black felt over the windows to guard his negatives from the sun, and if he was not developing pictures, he preferred the gray blue glow of the stereo or the shaded beam of his book light. Stacy liked to flick on every bulb, including the neon strip beneath the wood laminate cabinets. That way she saw everything, as if he hid something in plain view and the lights exposed it.

Outside the door, he heard water blasting in the little kitchenette sink. She probably scrubbed the coffee pot or polished the stainless steel countertops. Sometimes she rifled through all three cabinets, arranging canned food in alphabetical order or the mismatched glasses according to size. Boot let these intrusions go without a word. It was a lot like dealing with Mrs. Ohm. If he let things slip past, he could deny everything later.

Boot walked inside. Stacy huddled over a chrome contraption with a stubby black nozzle. Her soft brown hair draped down like a perfect ream of silk. The condition of her hair often reflected her attitude.

"You're here," he said.

"How come you never used the espresso machine?" Stacy's full lips gathered into a pout. "It's still in the box."

"Espresso keeps me up at night."

"I thought you worked all night."

"You have to stop bringing presents."

"It wasn't expensive."

"It's not the money."

"My grandmother gave it to me. Alright? And I already have one. Think of it as a loaner."

Boot observed the tall chrome device on the counter. "I don't have room in the kitchen for it."

"You don't have room in here for a can opener. When are you going to move out?"

Boot didn't want to say how soon. If he skipped the rent again, he'd be living in his Pinto. "The rent's cheap."

"And everything else about it."

He decided not to reply. A rich girl would never understand.

When the machine finished spitting foam and the tiny cups steamed full, she placed two chocolate chip cannolies on a paper plate. Boot recognized the green and red tape on the box. That bakery closed hours ago. She must have waited for him all night.

"So," he said.

"So." She blew the steam back into her cup.

He watched her navigate through the narrow kitchen and shimmy into the breakfast nook by the door. She wore a brand-new suede skirt and heels. He didn't think she dressed the same way twice. Her closet overflowed with the designer threads that her mother bought for her.

"You didn't mention you were coming by," he said.

"I didn't."

Boot joined her at the table. The pungent odor of chocolate and espresso crowded his nose. "Did you have some kind of meeting tonight?"

"No." She pressed her mouth to the cup edge. The lights on the Trenton Makes Bridge flashed red in the distance.

"Dinner at the club?"

"No."

"What then?"

She opened the *Trenton Record* to Page 6 and spun it around to face him. She smacked her finger on Boot's tiny story about the Jesus sign. "Is there another B. Means at the *Record?*"

"It's me."

"Congratulations. When were you planning to tell me?"

The pieces fell together: her surliness, the surprise visit, the newspaper article. They jogged an old promise loose in his brain. He once swore to propose marriage, as soon as he settled in at the paper. He recalled the exact words used to assuage her. 'When I do something other than those damned Miss Record photographs,' he said and forgot about the matter until just then.

"Well?" She glowered.

He searched for a quick rebuttal, watching her barren ring finger tap the enamel table top. She'd probably buy the damned diamond for herself if he gave the nod. "Stacy, let's not rush into anything."

"Let's not rush?" A renegade strand of hair fell over one eye, and she blew it back into place.

"I mean, let's see what happens."

"What's going to happen?"

"Things are so uncertain at the paper. I could lose my job any day."

"I have money."

"That's not the point."

"A job's not important."

"It is to your father." Boot understood her father's dedication to work. Mr. Bizzotti headed a large trading firm. He raced overseas more often than home to dinner.

"It would take a year for Daddy to figure out you weren't working, and by then, you'd have another job."

Boot glanced around the trailer for a new topic. His eyes locked onto the refrigerator door. She'd rearranged his portrait collection.

"What's the matter?" she asked.

"You moved my pictures." Her meddling irked him.

"They were scattered."

"I liked them as they were." He kept a hierarchy, sort of an imaginary family tree, torn from newspapers and magazines. He told Stacy he saved them merely for their artistic value. He wanted to get up and put them back in their proper order.

"Don't change the subject." Stacy took his hand. "I know you're nervous."

"I'm not nervous."

"It's a big step."

"You're telling me."

"We'll take it slow."

Boot scanned her face. She scrunched her nose whenever she grew impatient. He could agree or send Stacy packing. In truth, neither felt right.

"I can't afford a wedding," he said finally. "I can't even buy a ring. You know what the *Record* pays."

"I'll take care of it. The bride's family is supposed to pay."

"Not for everything."

"We've discussed this." She rose from the table.

He watched her unbutton her teal silk blouse. She was kind and giving, and she never raised her voice with him. Why shouldn't they marry? He treated her with respect and somehow pleased her just by paying attention. She could do a lot worse. He could too. He needed to get over the money thing. He hated when rich people behaved like they owned the world, although she never did. She seemed embarrassed by her wealth.

As she made her way to the back of his trailer, her clothes dropped carelessly to the floor. He studied her sleek figure made hard and tight from hours of aerobics and dance classes. A year ago, she'd never think of disrobing with the lights on, much less perform a subtle striptease act.

She turned and rolled her lower lip into a sexy pout, teasing him with a moist bit of her sensuous mouth. "Are you joining me?"

He recalled when they met. The newspaper had volunteered one thousand hours to the Recording Center for the Blind, and as he wandered into the downtown studio to do his part, he found Stacy behind the soundproof glass of the front booth. Her lips massaged the words into the mike. He never revealed how long he studied her—twenty minutes, maybe longer. He wanted a picture. He supposed she dictated poetry, putting her own spin on a classic. He learned later that she recorded the first three chapters to a calculus textbook, and she never understood a word.

She waited with the sheet yanked up to her breasts. Boot undressed himself and laid next to her.

They began stroking each other with the confidence of knowing what each other liked, until she grabbed his thigh. He noted the change, unlike the beginning when he coaxed the passion from her with a foot massage or a caress of her neck. Lately, there wasn't any interest in those matters.

When he reached for her foot, she pulled it back. "What are you doing?"

"I thought you'd like a rub." He worked the tenseness from her arch, moving up her ankle and calf, searching for a spot to claim anew.

She pulled him to her mouth, kissing him hard and hungry. This excited him, as if she came to exploit the rewards of a battle finally won.

They joined as they always did, with him on top. He moved inside her with a faster rhythm than he hoped. She pushed back, forcing the pace higher. He tried to slow her down. He wanted to make it special, a new landmark in their lovemaking, but her hips grew rigid, squeezing forth the mystery of her pleasure. She was quiet and lost to him, then he disappeared himself.

Boot woke to the sound of thunder. When lightning struck the Delaware River, it whipped across the water like a snaking chain. He felt Stacy's hair tickle his arm. She insisted on clinging to his side. He shifted against the trailer wall and waited for the rain.

The storm raced down stream and hit the ApacheStar's aluminum veneer like steel pellets dropping from the sky. If it rained too much, the cops forced everyone from the trailer park, fearing a rapid rise in the river. Before the concrete storm drains, the city streets swelled with rainwater like Venice, but today, they only worried about the trailers.

Boot listened to the initial storm burst, until it settled into a steady patter. Thunder crashed and echoed off the windows. Lightning flashed phantom patterns of daylight. Stacy wriggled closer, and Boot let her reclaim a familiar position on his shoulder. He stared at the ceiling, trying not to name his troubles.

CHAPTER 6
The Dove Network

wo weeks later, the last thing on Boot's mind was meeting some-one famous. He stood in his office, screening phone messages and shuffling through photographs. He was the beat reporter for the 'Jesus of Trenton.' He'd invented the name, partly as a joke and later as a means of separating the dozens of calls jamming the *Record*'s phones. The response to his first article confounded him. Whenever Jesus became involved, everyone grasped for a piece of the action, and the *Record* was no exception. Boot chased one outrageous claim after another into a daily Page 6 slot.

The room started to shake, and the papers on his desk rustled like leaves. Boot grabbed the edge of his chair, waiting for the tremendous roar to bellow up from the floor.

"What was that?!" A pretty redhead froze in the doorway. She spread her sandaled feet apart, holding onto the door frame.

Boot laughed. The noise once startled him too. His office sat in the old print manager's loft above the pressroom floor, and whenever the huge photocomposition machines fired up, they rumbled like a fleet of trucks emerging from a tunnel.

Without looking, Boot reached to save his coffee mug from vibrating off his desk. "Welcome to the wonderful world of newspaper production."

She took a cautious step, testing the floor, expecting it to swell like the deck of a ship. "I'm Julia Sherowich," she yelled above the noise. "You must be Boot Means."

"That's me." He sized her up as another believer. He'd seen and heard just about everything regarding the Jesus sign: a postal worker who conversed with it, an eighty-year-old lady who grew a new set of teeth after seeing it, and a band of artists that camped outside it to protest its slated demolition. So what was next?

He studied the approaching redhead. She wore khaki pants and a tight cotton top that tugged at her chest. Her lips were painted bright pink to soften the hard corners of her mouth. He imagined the unusual combination of Miss Record and Jesus seer.

"I've been looking for you," Julia said.

"You've found me."

"Barely. People weren't too friendly in the other building."

"I know what you mean." Boot appreciated his isolated office in the printing plant, far away from the newsroom. Since the layoffs, tensions between management and the writers union simmered near the boiling point. "Can I help you?"

"I hope so." Julia's eyes roved over his photographs. She stopped at the golden donkey trophy, which Boot employed as a paperweight. "Someone important wants to meet you."

He took the lunacy in stride. "Jesus?"

"Not today."

"Who then?"

"Melanie Dove is interested in your work."

Boot recognized the name from her hit gospel records. One of his foster parents played them incessantly, and for that reason, he remained indifferent about her career, losing track of it when she switched to preaching. "Doesn't she have a TV show?"

"Every Sunday."

"Right." Nothing bored Boot more than that crap littering the airwaves.

"You are familiar with the Dove Network?""

"Vaguely."

"We've come to Trenton to expand the ministry."

"What does that have to do with me?"

"Miss Dove has seen your reports in the paper."

"Melanie Dove reads the *Trenton Record*?"

"I think someone in the Network faxed it to her."

"How can I help you?"

"Miss Dove wants to explain. Would you like to take a ride?"

After a short trip across the city, Boot followed Julia Sherowich up to the Downtowner Hotel's penthouse suites. He'd never visited a hotel room as lavish: fresh flowers, large comfortable furniture, shiny walls with golden fruit and leaf patterns. It reminded him of the living room in Mr. Bizzotti's Titusville mansion. He didn't know any place like it existed within the city limits.

Julia poured a glass of sparkling water into a crystal glass and handed it to Boot. Her eyes panned the room, including an arrangement of makeshift desks with scattered audio and video recording equipment. She nodded as if everything laid just in the right place, then winked at Boot and disappeared through a side door.

Boot wandered to the corner window, absorbing a panoramic view of daytime Trenton. From twenty floors high, the bombed-out city center presented a friendlier face, almost cleaned up in parts. He understood why people preferred to live high above it.

Melanie Dove burst into the room. Boot immediately recognized her from TV, although her height surprised him. She stood about six feet tall, taller than him anyway. Her straight blond hair fell in a blunt cut upon the shoulders of her pin-striped suit. The deep blue jacket material overpowered her light features.

Boot met her on the oriental throw rug in the middle of the room. She held his hand like a man, firm and without reservation. Her pale blue eyes laced into him, and her trademark dimple puckered below her left cheek.

"I already know everything I want to know about you," she said, "but you can tell me more."

Boot felt the twinge in his stomach one gets when approached by a celebrity. If anyone else entered the room, Boot didn't notice. He braced himself. He planned to tell her very little. She was going to do the talking, cough up something useful for his column. He envisioned a feature article for the People section in Sunday's pullout magazine.

"Nice to meet you," he said.

"I'm glad you came. You must be very busy."

"Jesus has me booked up."

"Was that a joke?"

"A small one." He felt his face flush.

"I haven't a lot of time." Dove released him and sat down in a white Victorian chair with a peach floral pattern. "Have a seat and tell me about yourself."

"I thought you already knew everything." Boot sat opposite her and put his glass on the adjacent table. Copies of *Plain Truth* and *Rolling Stone* magazine fanned away from his glass.

She folded her hands together as if to pray yet shook them toward Boot. "I'm learning that you're very suspicious, which is not surprising for a journalist."

No one ever referred to Boot as a journalist, not without him first stating it. It was so much more professional than 'reporter.' "I'm curious why I'm here."

"And I'm curious why you came."

"I heard your name, and I wondered why you were in town."

"Didn't Julia explain?"

"She mentioned something about increasing your membership in Trenton."

"Everyone deserves to hear the word of God."

"I guess."

"And don't forget Trenton State Prison and the youth correctional facility in Bordentown."

Boot knew both places. The prison had old stone walls, like the Revolutionary War monuments in center city, and the juvenile center looked like a farm, with its sprawling fields and grazing cattle. But inside, they both exuded the same existence: iron bars and rules far short of self-reliance. For most of his youth, he felt a step away from hard confinement.

"I know," Boot said. "You do the jail thing."

"The prison ministry is an important arm of the Dove Network."

"So why approach me?"

"You know about the Jesus of Trenton. No one else is covering the story."

"The other papers don't think it's newsworthy."

"But you do. I understand you cultivated this story on your own."

"I didn't paint the sign." He tried to figure her angle. Anyone can phone the *Record* and track him down, but how did she know the story's history? Was it a guess? Or did she speak with someone at the paper?

They talked for forty-five minutes. Dove explained her mission to bring people to God, while Boot related a few unprinted stories surrounding the Jesus of Trenton. He found her to be polite and curious, and he respected her forthrightness. In his limited interview experience, so many people attempted to misguide him, either by malice or ignorance. This exchange was refreshing, and he thought of the various ways to write Dove into his column. On the next professional level—the place where he hoped to thrive—Dove was the type of person that he needed to impress.

"I like you," Dove said. "Let me see what I can do for you."

"I was hoping for a picture." Boot wanted more quotes, enough to flesh out a full-length article for an interview magazine. He imagined his first big sale, a real stringer piece. He might skip the baby steps at the *Record* altogether.

"Please let people know that my ministry is open to all."

He whipped out his Nikon, judging the light striking her portion of the room. It lent a nice luster to the cherry wood trim of her chair, good for a black and white exposure. "Are you comfortable with this pose?"

"How about overlooking the city?" She walked to the window and stood in profile.

Boot angled his camera away from the sun, taking in an expansive view of Trenton and the Delaware River. The shutter clicked several times.

"Can you show me the sign?" Dove asked.

"I can find it in my sleep. I'm there every day." He came to the glass and pointed his finger to the south. "It's the old Anderson box factory, just a few blocks from the state complex."

"It's in the middle of town."

"For now. It's scheduled to be wrecked soon."

"Is that true? Thanks for telling me that." She faced Boot. Gray hairs tinged her blond eyebrows. "How do you feel about the Jesus of Trenton? After all you named Him."

"My opinion's not important."

"I know some of the stories, especially from people camped out at the sign, can be unpalatable."

"It's my job to make them interesting." He towed the standard line, hearing Art's words pass through his lips. "The choice belongs to the reader."

"Do I sense skepticism? I shouldn't be surprised."

"I'm enjoying the story."

"But you're not moved by it."

"That gets in the way."

"I see." She gazed at the city, before leveling her sights back on him. "What's your religious upbringing?"

Boot resisted blurting out a wisecrack like, 'your gospel albums.' He waited for the feeling to pass. "I didn't exactly have a religious upbringing."

"Don't you follow the ways of God?"

"You mean the Ten Commandments? Life would be nice if everyone followed them. Of course, my paper might be out of business."

"I bet your parents didn't teach you to say that?"

"That's another complicated area." Boot preferred to keep a tight lid on his past, but he enjoyed thwarting Dove's probes.

"What's complicated about it?"

"If you run into my parents, you might ask them."

"You don't speak with them?"

"I was abandoned as an infant." He watched his response hit home, wondering what she thought of him now. Did it lessen her expectations?

"I'm sorry to hear that."

"I'm not looking for sympathy." He wanted her to see a man standing on his own, free of the hooks and tethers of religion and family. "I answer to myself."

"Is it right to exclude God?"

"I don't exclude God."

"You don't?"

"That would mean I believed." He regretted his choice of words. This type of discussion often led to a gut-wrenching conversion effort. He recalled a Sunday school teacher who rolled up a prayer missal and smacked him in the back of the head.

"You don't believe." She repeated his declaration.

"I don't disbelieve either, mind you."

"Agnostic." The dimple rose in her cheek. "Interesting."

Boot returned to the *Record* by nightfall, and as usual, the rain brought down the computer lines to his office. He crept into the quiet newsroom, searching for the first empty cubicle. He plopped in front of Teresa Ringley's desk and switched on her computer.

He set about uncovering information on Melanie Dove. He dipped into the company archives and culled the Internet. It seemed like a giant fishbowl of unrelated information, and after an hour of clicking and thrashing, he discovered Melanie Dove's real name, Melanie Dovell, but little else he found useful.

Teresa stepped into her cube. She wore a magenta sleeveless dress, and her black hair hung in a bun with an ornate silver clip. Standing, she almost looked Boot in the eye. "Hello."

"Sorry." Boot jumped up. "I can't use my office."

She pushed him down in the chair. "I'm not staying."

"Where are you going?"

"A cocktail party for the Haytana Bill. I forgot my invitation." She pulled a white envelope from her top drawer. "What are you doing?"

"The storm brought down my computer line."

"We don't have those problems over here. Why don't you move into the main building with the rest of us?"

"Not yet."

"Waiting for your triumphant return as the scandal sheet king?"

Boot appreciated her cut-to-the-jugular humor. "Guess who I met today?"

"I give up."

"Melanie Dove."

"Is she still around?"

"Still around? She's only forty-two."

"I was a fan of hers. Now, that dates me." Teresa examined her makeup in a compact mirror. "What did she want?"

"She's come to Trenton to spread the word."

"Ahhh, I remember. The Dove Network."

"She wants to know about the Jesus sightings."

"I hope she does better with this than her last couple of records."

"They weren't any good?"

"I believe she's slipped off the charts, so to speak."

"That's what I want to know. I'm trying to crack her business records."

"That's public information." Teresa raised her slender wrist and glanced at a black watch without numbers. "I have a few minutes. I'll show you."

When Teresa leaned over, a gust of perfume tickled Boot's nose. He watched her pound the keyboard with intense concentration. She jumped from screen to screen, working the Internet like a treadmill. He used the distraction to tackle a difficult subject. "What's going on with the strike?"

"It doesn't look good."

Boot hated to hear that. A strike created a serious pothole in his short-term career path. "Are the talks going badly?"

"Yes."

"Very bad?"

"Storch's cronies walked out of the last meeting. That's something the union reps usually do."

"But there's going to be a resolution, right?"

"I can't say." She kept focused on the screen, shaking her head. "It doesn't look good."

Boot remained stone-faced, clutching the chair in Teresa's office. "What are you going to do if it doesn't pan out?"

"My boyfriend says he'll support me. Maybe, I'll write that book I've been putting off."

"Does it need photos?"

The screen reflected in her onyx eyes. "You have an offer in New York, don't you?"

He'd almost forgotten what he told her and the others. "Right." If it all came crashing down, he decided to disappear. He'd done it before, exiting foster care a year before his eighteenth birthday. If no one cared to find you, you didn't even have to hide.

She slid the computer mouse and clicked. "Here we go."

The screen flooded with fancy graphics and a bright picture of Dove addressing her flock. She stood at a podium in her Seattle cathedral, an acoustic guitar slung over her back. The crowd waved their hands in unison. It reminded Boot of a famous Led Zeppelin concert photo.

Teresa poked her finger at the screen. "It says here, she has branches in the South, Midwest, East, and Northern Pacific Rim."

"That's good coverage."

"Millions of dollars worth."

"Tax free too."

"Hmmm. She still hasn't built her Seattle seminary."

"So what?"

"She broke ground over five years ago."

"Then it should be finished."

"But it's not. You might want to petition Washington State for more information. See how the Dove Network distributes it assets. My guess is it has cash flow problems."

"I can get information like that?"

"Nowadays, you can get just about anything you want." She snatched her purse from her desk. "It depends on the amount of work you want to do."

"Thanks, Teresa."

She stood in the opening to her cubicle. "Has Rico spoken to you?"

"No."

"He was looking for you today. I'll let him know I found you."

"It has something to do with the writers union, doesn't it?"

"Yes. Rico's the local whip."

Boot looked away. He wasn't much of joiner. He didn't know what she or Rico expected from him.

"I'll offer you a tip," she said. "People are drawing battle lines. Don't leave yourself exposed."

CHAPTER 7
Camp Jesus

E ach day, Boot scoured Camp Jesus for new material. He stood on the corner of Jefferson Avenue, watching scores of people in the street. They moved on foot, crutches, and wheelchairs, streaming toward the abandoned Anderson Cardboard & Box Company. Their sheer numbers overflowed the property, clogging the gates and trailing along the fence. Boot wondered why they came. The Jesus image appeared in the newspaper every day of the week.

Boot forged ahead, searching for an answer. He stalked the crowd. Stalking was a good place for him; it meant he was doing his job. He disappeared inside a group of people. His medium complexion and dark brown hair passed for many ethnic groups. People confused him for Spanish or Russian. Others keyed on the slight taper to his hazel eyes, assuming he hid Asian or Arab traces in his blood. In truth, Boot didn't know why he blended so well. He considered this an inherent talent. He often fantasized his mother was a criminal, skipping from country to country undetected, but he knew she might be a toll taker on the Turnpike just the same.

Inside Camp Jesus, Boot felt invisible. The place appeared thick with hope and enterprise. A man opened his front lawn to strangers, offering cold drinks and fresh baked cookies. Teenagers with bulky duffel bags flashed Jesus of Trenton buttons and T-shirts to enthusiastic buyers. A handful of Muslims in beaded hats chanted to the open air, warning visitors against worshipping idols.

Boot focused on the men in purple armbands. They wore dark clothing and black boots. Many had crew cuts and elaborate tattoos. They appeared deep in conversation, but when Boot raised his camera, one of them looked up.

The stranger rotated his face in the viewfinder. He possessed a bushy mustache between a sharp chin and nose. He held his gaze in Boot's direction perhaps. His mirrored shades made it difficult to tell. He never altered his expression, even when Boot swung his camera through the shot.

Boot counted to five and slipped into the crowd. He quickly came upon a purple school bus parked near the factory gates. The title OPEN FAITH FOR JESUS ran down the side in large block letters. It ended with a small graphic: a pair of clenched fists broken free from chains.

Employing the crowd as a buffer, Boot made a large arc around the bus. He spotted two crewcuts with armbands and tattoos and a long-haired guy wearing a ratty army jacket. They huddled by the rear of the bus, passing a joint in a circle. They puffed away, laughing, talking.

Boot snapped three pictures with his telephoto lens. The sunlight fell from behind like a halogen lamp, and the focus drew as sharp as a razor's edge.

As he closed in, he noticed one of the crewcuts was a woman in a leather vest and no shirt. He threw his camera to his side. "Hello."

The longhair saw Boot first. He stubbed out the joint on his heel and stashed the tidbit in his jacket. The name 'Backbone' was inked above his breast pocket in magic marker.

"Hello." Boot stopped beside him.

The man's shoulder length hair looked dirty and scraggly, and his repugnant body odor mixed with the air of burning dope. He sported a loathsome expression, which he leveled on Boot.

Boot took a step back.

"Peace," the woman said.

"What do you want?" the other crewcut asked. "You a narc?"

"Nothing like that."

"'Cause if you are, you can't bust me after you lie." The crewcut wore a gold earring. He folded his arms. He had forearms the size of most men's calves.

"I was just curious about your bus."

"Be cool, Si." The woman sashayed up to Boot. She had a banana nose and a slender neck. Boot found something both androgynous and sexy about her, but in the end, her thin lips counted against his assessment. "You haven't seen the OFJ before?"

"The what?" Boot asked.

"The Open Faith for Jesus."

"Right, that's the name on your bus."

"Are you interested?"

"I am now."

Her right arm revealed a tattoo of a fire-breathing dragon clutching a rose. Its spiked tail curled about the knob of her shoulder. "My name's Kat. That's my boyfriend, Simon."

Simon nodded, concerned. The naked girl tattoo rippled on his forearm.

The longhair stood motionless. If he had a tattoo, Boot imagined that it might portray skulls and snakes.

"I'm Boot." He constructed a lie, already planning how he'd use the pictures for tomorrow's paper: JESUS DOPE FREAKS. "I heard about the Jesus of Trenton and thought I'd check it out."

"So did we," Kat said.

"Are you a religious group?"

"Absolutely."

"What's your position?"

"Libertarian."

"That's unique."

"Anyone's accepted, no exceptions."

"Sounds great."

"We're celebrating Si's birthday." She produced a fresh joint from her vest. "Want a hit?"

"No, thanks."

"Don't you party?"

"You mean pot? I'm cool with that." Boot took the joint and filled his mouth with smoke, waiting to exhale when they weren't looking. He needed to retain his edge. He passed the joint along.

Backbone continued to glare at Boot. It cut right through him, and he swallowed the smoke. The look reminded him of a man he knew on Coney Island. As a teenager, Boot often rode the L train out to the beach to watch the men playing handball. He liked to mill through the crowd with his camera, because in a crowd, everyone has the same relationship, the same feed to what's happening around them. Inevitably, he'd spot the boardwalk man affixed to a bench facing the ocean. The man stared at the water as if not seeing it at all, as if fossilized to that very spot in the city. Boot's earliest portraits came from there, until one time the man caught Boot watching. Suddenly Boot became the subject. The man focused his empty gaze, but it wasn't empty, more dark and angry. He peered deep into Boot, identifying Boot as a phony player among the many authentics in the crowd. Boot—the photographer, the fearless documenter of life—acquiesced and turned away ashamed. He never returned to the boardwalk.

Boot studied Backbone's hardened gaze. It seemed one in the same with the past.

"Just ignore him," Kat said. "Backbone doesn't trust anyone."

Boot searched for an excuse to leave. "Well, happy birthday, Simon."

"Sure." Simon stepped up into the rear of the bus and glanced toward Backbone.

Backbone followed Simon, never taking his eyes off Boot.

"I'll join you in a sec." Kat waited for Simon to shut the door. "Si gets strange on weed."

Boot placed his foot on the curb. "It happens."

"It's a Gemini thing, split personality."

"I didn't realize."

"What's your sign?"

"Gemini," Boot thought aloud, wondering if she heard the doubt in his voice.

"Don't tell me your birthday's today too?"

"No," Boot said, although it might be. When Social Services found him, they'd estimated his birthday to be anytime in June. He might really be a Cancer.

"In any case, happy birthday."

"Thanks."

"Let me find you some literature on us." She flung open the bus door.

Boot heard Simon and Backbone talking, as sunlight filled the rear of the bus. The floor panel in the aisle was open, and the men were dropping things inside. It happened in a flash, but Boot swore that he saw Simon holding a pair of handguns before releasing them. There looked to be a lot more in the floor panel, dozens perhaps.

"Hey!" Simon yelled.

Kat hadn't noticed right away, stretching her arms for a cardboard box on the last seat. She yanked out the carton and quickly shut the door. The last thing Boot saw was Backbone glaring back at him.

Kat studied Boot's face for a clue, but he was a master of the bluff. He smiled like nothing ever happened.

She stabbed the purple pamphlet forward. "Here."

Boot accepted it. "Thanks again."

He wanted out of there. Simon peered from the rear window. Boot smiled and waved. *I'm mister happy-go-lucky. I can't see my hand in front of my face.*

"Peace, man," Kat said.

"Right." Boot turned away, pleased to exit. What the hell was going on? He'd better look out for those guys. He kept his feet moving, not looking over his shoulder. He knew they were watching.

Boot continued probing the scene at Camp Jesus. Perhaps he'd take another peek at the crewcuts later; perhaps tomorrow.

He treaded closer to the abandoned box factory. The surrounding fence glimmered with trinkets and pieces of paper, and he used his long lens to gain a closer view. He saw black rosary beads, three hand-woven crucifixes, a blob of melted candle wax, a pair of tattered running shoes, a crushed pack of cigarettes, and at the foot of a fence post, a spent bottle of vodka. It looked like a dazzling collection of trash caught in a net.

Cutting through the visitation line, Boot approached the fence. People touched the rusted steel as if it were sacred. A few bowed their heads in reverence. They curled up notes and slid them into the chain-link openings. Boot marveled at their behavior.

He scribbled on an empty 35mm carton. He glanced from side to side, careful not to raise suspicion. He shoved his nonsense scrawl into the fence, and with the same motion, withdrew a pink slip of paper. 'Bobby,' it read, with a heart drawn in red ink.

Next, he removed a lottery ticket with the initials E.L. Another offering contained a photograph of a boy holding the controls to a video game console. Over and over, Boot returned to the fence, plucking items from the chain links. They ranged from mundane to bizarre, from heartfelt to cryptic. The last note held an eerie plea, 'Please, don't let me do it again.'

He backed away and mounted the wide angle lens on his Nikon. He framed a seven-foot stretch of fence and pressed the shutter release, satisfied he'd captured the emotion.

As Boot loaded a fresh roll of film, he noticed the crewcut with the bushy mustache and mirrored shades. The stranger approached with a bowlegged gait. He appeared to be slim and average height.

"Touring the shrine?" The crewcut said 'touring' as if it appeared obvious that Boot was not among the faithful.

Boot watched the crewcut stroke his mustache with an index finger. It reminded him of a college professor who struggled to make a point. He wondered if this man had just spoken to the people at the bus.

"My name's Travis LeBlay." He tipped up his sunglasses, fashioning a peek at Boot's camera before dropping his shades on the bridge of his nose. "That's expensive hardware, professional stuff."

Boot pushed past the crewcut. This man couldn't possibly know he had pictures of them smoking pot. "My camera's not for sale."

"I'm not in need of a camera." LeBlay sidled next to him. "I'm in need of a man with a camera."

Boot ignored him. He'd already filmed enough material for a week's worth of Page 6. He moved through the crowd and down Jefferson Avenue, sensing LeBlay on his heels. The crewcut's pursuit worked beneath Boot's skin.

"I don't know what you want," Boot said, "but I've got to leave."

"Sorry, I figured you for someone else."

Boot fixed his sights on the police barricades at the end of the street. New visitors came at him in waves, elbowing past. He sidestepped a pair of boys selling Jesus of Trenton posters. He noticed the picture from his first Page 6 article.

"I figured you might want to hear me out," LeBlay said. "If not you, perhaps someone you know."

Even though Boot's better judgment spoke against it, he seized the bait. He stopped and turned, seeing LeBlay standing several paces behind him. "Why?"

"Call it intuition." LeBlay buried a southern dialect in his voice. "I saw you snapping pictures of the fence back there."

"So?"

"Actually, I first noticed you snapping pictures of my colleagues."

Boot felt a twinge of embarrassment. He clutched his camera a little harder. Was this about the guns? He wished he'd gotten a shot of that. "What do you want?"

"I thought it was unusual." LeBlay closed the gap between them. "You have to be an investigator."

"I'll tell you what I told them. I don't care if they smoke horseshit."

"Then you were photographing them."

"Perhaps."

"What were you asking them?"

"Let's stop playing games. You sound like the investigator here."

"Am I right or wrong? Weren't you photographing them?"

"I photographed a lot of things."

"You don't look like an average tourist." LeBlay swept his hand in the air behind him. "Not one of these. I saw how you picked through the notes at the fence."

"I'm Boot Means with the *Trenton Record*. I cover this section of town."

"Jackpot!" LeBlay said, as if playing dumb all along. He brushed the hair beneath his nose. "This will save me a lot of trouble."

"How?"

"You definitely want to hear what I have to say?"

"Go on."

"Let's take a walk." LeBlay pulled away.

Boot remained in place, watching the crewcut pass through the police barricades. This would be a good time to lose him, but he wondered what LeBlay offered. Many people propositioned him since Jesus came to town, but up until now, he towed a steady line of miraculous claims and acts of faith. It created good fodder for the gossip page but little else. LeBlay might have something unusual, a fresh twist for his column. He decided to follow.

Around the corner, LeBlay let Boot come alongside. "It's safer out here, away from the bus."

"Tell me about the purple bus."

"It belongs to the OFJ."

"What's with the painting on the rear door?"

"The breaking chains?"

"Yes."

"It's a metaphor. Is that the right word?"

"It depends on what you're talking about."

"Some of us have been to prison. The chains say we've broken free of the past."

"Is that true for you?"

LeBlay rubbed his thumb against his fingers. He possessed slender hands, like those of a woman. "I have a record."

This information didn't faze Boot. With his upbringing, he'd seen the inside of a few police stations. "You guys don't make much of an effort to hide your past. You look like a motorcycle gang."

"We get that a lot. Tattoos are a hobby for us."

"Some people collect baseball cards."

"There's a guy in Alberta who does the Hell's Angels. Those are coveted."

"And you?"

"I haven't found a design I like yet."

"I like the haircuts."

"We're not all convicts. It's a way of bringing us together."

"Together to do what?"

"You haven't heard of us?" LeBlay removed his sunglasses. His eyes were beady. The glasses provided a world of improvement. "We help those on the inside and those coming out. The parole system, I should say the government, has failed most of us."

Boot couldn't argue. "Where does the OFJ come in?"

"Paul supplies spiritual guidance. You trust Jesus, and the rest flows from there."

The comment reminded Boot of a twelve step program; everything derived from submitting yourself to God. The politically correct term these days was 'higher power', although the message still rang the same to Boot: give up. He failed to see how strength came from losing control.

Boot rolled LeBlay's information over in his mind. "Who's Paul?"

LeBlay stroked his mustache with his index finger. "Did I mention him?"

"You said he offered spiritual guidance."

"Paul Andujar founded the OFJ."

"He drives the purple bus?"

"There's more than one bus."

"How many people belong?"

"Six hundred, give or take. We're known in many institutions."

"What is it you want to tell me?"

"I see I've strayed off the point."

"I'm wondering what that is."

"Sorry. I want you to know the OFJ is a good organization. It really helps people. So don't get the wrong idea."

"But ..."

LeBlay glanced over his shoulder. Anonymous pedestrians drifted past. "Have you ever believed and been disillusioned?"

"Alright, Mr. LeBlay."

"Travis, please."

Boot stopped walking. "You can contact professionals for this problem. Unfortunately, I'm not it."

"You are." LeBlay latched onto Boot's arm. He developed a worried look, almost weepy. "There's trouble in the OFJ."

"What kind of trouble?" Boot refused to reveal another clue of what he'd seen at the bus. LeBlay must lead him there.

"I have to know I can trust you. I've considered this move for a long time."

"Tell me your issues."

"They're not of a religious nature, Mr. Means. They're challenging."

"Challenging?" Boot stepped back. As challenging as this conversation?

"There's an element within the OFJ, and I don't like it. You have to remember most of these men have spent time inside. They can smell a snitch."

"And you're it."

"Don't say that."

"I'm trying to figure out your role in this. Why don't you speak with Paul ...?"

"Andujar?" LeBlay looked away. "I'm not sure he isn't mixed up in it."

"In what?"

"The trouble."

"All I saw was a little pot smoking. There's people at my newspaper doing the same." Boot offered this embellishment. He knew the cocktail crowd at the newspaper. They hawked the pubs after work, downing martinis until they could barely slot their keys into their car ignitions. They wore suits and ties, but otherwise he calculated little difference.

LeBlay whispered. "Where do you think the funds for drugs come from?"

"I haven't a clue. The OFJ pays well?"

"Try contraband."

"Contraband." Boot waited. *Go ahead. Tell me.*

"Shhhhh, I'm going out on a limb here."

"I need good stuff for the paper. I need proof."

"Be careful. My friends are passionate about their lifestyle."

"Who isn't?"

"No, they're protective of it."

"I need concrete material to write a story."

"I'll see what I can do. Wait for my call."

When LeBlay left, Boot headed back into the crowd. LeBlay's entrée should have sated his appetite for the day, but it only raised his curiosity about the OFJ and the Jesus sign. There had to be something he missed, and in a perverse way, he needed to unravel it to the core.

Boot plunged into the throng, pausing outside the abandoned box factory. The old place burgeoned with a second life as a religious shrine, and the visitation line grew by the minute. He felt the sweltering June heat on his neck and shoulders and the brush of the crowd. The wait to enter the compound seemed intolerable.

A man in a tweed jacket noticed Boot and offered him a place in line. Without hesitation Boot joined in, treading deeper into the heart of Camp Jesus. The line moved with its own impetus, funneling through the factory gates and onto the trampled compound. He let the mass carry him, until the crowd opened up.

He stepped into a small clearing and shot the scene with the scrutiny of his finely ground lens. Several factions attended the Jesus of Trenton. Men and women arrived as couples. Whole families trudged forward as units. Boot saw teenagers singing religious hymns. Another group built a huge labyrinth on the cracked parking lot blacktop, and visitors followed the interlocking maze, deep in thought. All the while, Trenton cops strolled the periphery, steering clear of the masses.

The number of people amazed Boot, several hundred or more. He dropped his camera to his waist. Who would let so many roam the compound unchecked, and why hadn't the city torn the dilapidated structure down yet? He'd queried city hall about it, but it was a tough nut to crack. He became bogged down in dead end referrals and requests for paperwork.

Boot reclaimed his spot in the procession, joining the deliberate momentum heading toward the wall. People hushed around him. The woman in front brought her hands together in prayer. The man with the tweed jacket whispered passages from a pocket-sized New Testament. Boot felt an acute sense of intrusion, as if tapping into a foreign energy. He kept from looking them in the eye.

The line approached the final corner. The OFJ monitored access to the wall. Men in purple armbands counted twenty heads at a time. They allowed each group a few minutes, then ushered them away.

Boot slid his fingers toward his camera and disabled the automatic advance. He spun the lens and f/stop, estimating focus and aperture settings by the distance of subject and the height of the sun. He shot pictures from the hip. People seemed too involved in their own thoughts to notice the click of his shutter release.

When Boot's turn arrived, he marched forward and pressed his heels in the rocky soil at the base of the wall. The woman to his left wept silent tears. The man at his right tucked his Bible beneath his arm and bowed his head. Many in his group mouthed short prayers. Boot took it all in. Incredible.

He questioned his own intentions for coming. Didn't he have enough pictures on file? He suddenly realized that he never looked at the sign in person, really gave it a close examination beyond that first night. He'd met a hooker here. What was her name? Christine. She called him crazy, but she didn't see Jesus in the sign either.

The urge to laugh quivered through his spine, and he fought to stifle it. He considered elbowing the ribs of the man in the tweed jacket. He wanted to see the man wink, let him in on the joke. He wanted to grab the crying woman and slap her face, sober her up when she needed it the most.

With every second, Boot's nervous energy swelled into disgust. The smell of damp mortar and dirt disturbed him. It reminded him of a dark place, a freshly dug grave. He wanted to break loose and run. How long must he stand here?

He raised his chin and followed the coarse bricks thirty feet in the air. The ad for Smythe's Diner hovered above like a bad joke. Its simplicity mocked him. No message for him, not for anyone. He studied the wall for a hint of proof: his rough outline of a face, a mistaken image to appease his sense of reason. He stared until his eyes crossed. And still, he saw nothing.

The man with the Bible tapped Boot's shoulder. The line filed away. People whispered, as a sense of relief washed over the group. Boot stumbled, then caught up with them. He felt altogether inexperienced with ritual. He compared it to a crowd exiting a funeral.

His nerves tingled, vibrating between his shoulder blades. This many people might crush a man. He saw daylight in the sea of bodies ahead and wedged into it. He needed a cold drink and a chance to lay down. He resolved to go straight to his trailer and put the experience behind him.

CHAPTER 8
Bad Dog

On the elevator up to the pressroom, Boot reviewed his encounter with the Open Faith for Jesus. He liked the OFJ as a story. Quirky religious groups provided amusing copy.

He entered a quiet pressroom. A few keyboards tapped from solitary cubicles. Unless a bomb exploded or an earthquake swallowed up a third world city, news people spent Sunday mornings with their families.

Art's office was dark, the sun not yet illuminating that side of the street. Boot discovered Art bent over his desk, snoring. An open bottle of scotch rested on the blotter, next to a half empty glass. A flat white box with three congealed slices of pepperoni pizza laid scattered upon the floor.

From the dark beneath Art's desk, Boot watched a brown and white beagle emerge. The bitch tugged on the leash which anchored her to the leg of the desk. She peered up at Boot and whimpered, twitching her ears in a pathetic fashion.

Boot tossed the OFJ story and photos on the desk, then untied the dog's leash and led her outside.

A *Trentonian* news box stood chained to the utility pole in front of the *Record* building. Boot held the beagle's chain as she squatted at the foot of the metal box. The air felt damp and humid, and the thin fog tasted of car exhaust. He let the beagle finish her business and dragged her back upstairs.

Rico blocked Boot's path in the newsroom. He wore camouflage pants and a matching hat. He struck Boot as someone lost on their way to an arms dealer convention.

"What are you doing with that?" Rico eyed the beagle with contempt.

"She belongs to Art."

"He should put it in a kennel."

"I guess he had work to finish."

"He's in his office?"

"That's where I'm headed."

They glanced at the light emanating from Art's door. A bulky shadow shifted behind the horizontal blinds.

"I've been following your column," Rico said.

Boot played it cool, resisting the urge to stake his territory. The Jesus of Trenton belonged to him.

Rico grinned as if he swallowed a secret. "So you've wrangled yourself a regular spot in the paper."

"No one else wanted it."

"It's a nice hit for you."

"Thanks." Boot savored the moment. He knew the others would come around. He recalled a childhood incident so silly that it made his face flush. His fifth grade teacher attached a gold star to his first essay, and she read it aloud to the class. He'd written about a visit to see the Mets play at Shea Stadium, after standing on the elevated train platform and watching the game from outside.

"You know," Rico said. "If you were represented by the union, it would have been handled differently."

"How?"

"The union isn't all dues and regulations. We'd insist on an upgrade for your column. It could be a feature."

"I can promote myself."

"But with the union behind you ...."

"Right." Boot tugged the dog's leash. Did Rico think he was stupid? "It's Art's decision where to place each column."

"Not entirely."

"I've never spotted a union rep in an editorial meeting."

"We're there in spirit, and you're not represented by anyone."

"You keep reminding me."

Rico extended his hand. "You've earned your stripes. I'd be pleased to support your nomination."

Boot stared at Rico's palm for an inordinate length of time. His pride bore down on a single thought. Shove it. He'd make it on his own.

"Boot!" Art called from the door to his office. His necktie draped about his open collar. He clutched several pages in one hand and a red pen in the other. He glanced down at his beagle, unconcerned to find Boot managing the leash. "Get in here."

"The master beckons," Rico said.

Boot ignored the wisecrack, grateful to abandon the conversation. He shuffled into Art's office and released the beagle. The floppy-eared dog used a chair to reach the window ledge behind Art's desk.

Art paced the floor with his hands behind his back, the pages flapping like a fantail. He seemed preoccupied and furrowed his jaw in his chest as if trying to crush a stone beneath his chin.

"You wanted me?" Boot sat with his back to the inner window.

"I see you met Grace," Art said.

"She looked like she needed a walk."

Art stopped in front of Boot. "Recite Rule Eleven."

"Do not ..." Boot strained to remember the text from *Elements of Style*. "Do not explain too much."

"Meaning ..."

"Don't over explain or tell all. Is that what I did?"

Art dropped the pages in Boot's lap. They screamed with red slashes and scribbles.

"It's not as bad as it looks," Art said.

Boot sifted through the changes in his OFJ story. He wished Art edited his pages on the computer like he did for other writers. Was his probationary period going to last forever? "It's a complete rewrite."

"Don't sweat it. Overall, I like what I see."

"The OFJ? They're a bunch of drugged up Jesus freaks. I have to admit, they're tailor-made for Page 6."

"You're missing the point. It's the first decent lead you've found since I hired you."

"Then I hope you're going to run it in a section other than Page 6."

"Not the way you wrote it."

"I can make changes."

"Who's your story source?"

"Travis LeBlay. He's one of them."

Art looked at Boot for a moment. "What about the contraband? Where's the evidence?"

Boot recalled the guns in the bus. He wasn't certain of it and even less certain of how to develop his suspicions. "I watched them getting stoned behind their purple school bus."

"That's what I thought. If you check your copy, you'll see that I deleted your reference to contraband within the OFJ."

"But I saw them smoking, and there might be more."

"Might be?" Art's neck swelled. "You can suggest things in the scandal sheets, but not in my newspaper. Even on Page 6, you need facts. What you have isn't good enough. You need a reliable source."

Boot swallowed his medicine. He folded his arms and leaned his head against the blinds, waiting for Art to show him the way.

"If you want to be a journalist," Art said, "and I think you've been complaining about that for months, you must learn to refine the good leads. Take what's given you, and work it through."

"I don't get it. What exactly impressed you?"

"I read your story notes." Art snatched a piece of paper off of his desk. "You left this inside the folder."

Boot glanced at his own handwriting, failing to spot anything spectacular.

"First," Art said, "you have a fundamentalist organization doping up at a group function, but more importantly, you have a bell ringer on your hands."

"Travis LeBlay?"

"He's already given you interesting details. Bell ringers give details. They always have an agenda."

"He wants to help the OFJ."

"He probably wants to help himself, but that doesn't mean there's no story here."

"What do you suggest I do next?"

"Find out what you can about LeBlay. He's the man who wants to talk. Get a reference check on him. Find out where he went to prison."

"I'm waiting for his call."

"Don't wait for anything. Research the OFJ also. If contraband is their game, there may be current investigations or recent arrests. See if you can't make LeBlay's claims materialize."

Boot felt stupid for handling LeBlay like he had. He should've never let the crewcut walk away. He gazed into his lap and smoothed his ink-scarred pages. "What about this story?"

"We're going with a scaled down version. You don't want to blow the lid off this before you get started."

"How about the pictures?"

"We can use this one." Art flipped through Boot's proofs, stopping at a photo of Kat and Simon huddled over a joint. "No faces show, but you can be damned sure it will shake them up."

"Alright."

"This is just for openers. Things are getting dicey around here. We could use a good storyline."

"What's 'dicey' mean?"

"I don't need to worry you with financials."

"It couldn't be worse than mine."

"Storch is starting to frown a lot." Art finally found his chair. He reached back and patted Grace's head. "Let's talk about the OFJ."

"I'll do the research as fast as I can."

"I assume they'd be able to recognize you now."

"I didn't give my whole name."

"I want professional contacts from this point on. Get solid documentation, and don't do anything dumb."

"Alright."

Art waved a hand toward Boot. "In your lap is another Page 6 story, but in your notes could be a headline."

After dark, a knock came on Boot's trailer. He opened the door and flicked on the porch light.

LeBlay stood beneath the retractable awning, swatting the mosquitoes from his arms. "You're in the phone book."

"So's my number," Boot replied.

LeBlay handed Boot an envelope. "It was sticking out beneath your doormat."

Boot glanced at the plain white envelope. Its seal appeared to be unglued, perhaps from the humidity. He opened it and found a note from Mrs. Ohm. 'Have you forgotten me?' He wondered how much further he could string her along for the rent.

He glanced at LeBlay. "Did you read this?"

"I found it that way?" He stroked his mustache with an index finger. "Good news?"

"If you're a sadist."

LeBlay tapped his foot. "Are you going to invite me in?"

Boot thrust open the ApacheStar's screen door and motioned his head toward the breakfast nook.

LeBlay found a seat on the spongy cushions. He scanned the trailer's imitation wood interior. "I thought you'd be doing better than this."

"It's the fruits of an honest living."

"Looks about the same as a dishonest living."

"I'll keep that in mind." Boot removed his notebook and tape recorder from his camera bag and placed them on the table. He switched on the recorder.

"I'd rather not use that."

Boot switched off the recorder and set aside blank paper to write. "I need details about the contraband. Who does what?"

"Where do you want me to begin?"

"You said there was a bad element within the OFJ."

"You've already met some of them. They're using the Open Faith as a cover."

"What are they covering up?"

"They transport anything illegal: drugs, cigarettes between states."

"Anything else?"

"Weapons sometimes."

Boot didn't bat an eye. "Does the entire operation involve contraband?"

"More or less."

"Then I might approach them about making a purchase."

"Not smart." LeBlay shook his head. "Besides being a bad move, they neither buy or sell. They only transport."

"For who?"

"Whoever wants to buy or sell."

"Does this group within the OFJ have a name?"

"Like a job title?"

"What do people call them?"

"I've heard the name, defectors, used more than once."

"So I can look up defectors in the Yellow Pages?"

"Certainly. They have an 800 number to call, and they send Christmas cards during the holidays."

"Alright, I get your point."

"It's just a nickname. They're known in the right circles. Remember, it's not everyone in the Open Faith that's involved."

"Then it's word of mouth."

"They have a reputation for being elusive. The Open Faith's purple vans and buses make great cover, and there are certain places that won't check our vehicles."

"Like where?"

"We can get in and out of institutions with ease. We can get through certain customs stations. We cross state lines, all under the guise of the Open Faith's better reputation."

The phone rang. Stacy left a protracted message on the answering machine. She rattled off dates and times to visit prospective catering halls for their wedding. Boot wanted to race across the trailer and turn down the volume. He'd never seen her operate so quickly.

LeBlay's ears perked up. "Girlfriend?"

Boot ignored LeBlay's attempts to become chummy. He considered his next question instead. "Tell me about that long-haired guy. I thought you all wore buzzcuts."

"I see Backbone left an impression on you."

"His smell did."

LeBlay laughed. His teeth looked small and crowded inside his mouth. "He really caught your eye, or should I say nose."

"Tell me about him?"

"He's not OFJ."

"Why's he hanging around?"

"He's popular with some of the men. He sports an outlaw view of the world: hail, hail the open road, and I'll slice you if you get in my way."

"I'm not surprised." That man in particular gave Boots the creeps.

"He's not unlike some of the others."

"OK, so the defectors are all hard asses, like Backbone."

"I remember this rogue in Toronto. He thought he'd do things his way, but the defectors handled him."

"What happened?"

"Let's say he was shipped somewhere else." LeBlay cracked an uneasy smile.

"He ran for the border?"

"No, he won't be crossing the border again. That's what they told me. I don't want to know the details."

"Me neither." Boot tried not to look surprised. Bad stuff, if it was true.

"Actually, Backbone serves other purposes. He's good for certain jobs. He lives on the railroads. It's a lifestyle for him, so he knows the rail network inside and out. Trains are very safe. The feds never check them, and packs move uninhibited."

"Packs?"

"That's the lingo. A pack can be almost anything, but it's always black market."

Boot watched the man seated across from him, recalling Art's orders to dig into LeBlay's past. He wondered how this thin figure handled himself in prison. He knew compact men who projected pure muscle, but LeBlay was not that type.

"How do you know so much about the defectors?" Boot asked.

"They befriended me over a long period of time."

"Befriended you?"

"You wouldn't understand. You've lived a privileged life."

"I wouldn't bank on that."

"You've been inside?"

"No." Boot felt almost ashamed of his reply. Foster care wasn't the same deal as prison. He knew that.

"I didn't think so." LeBlay looked out the tiny window by the table. "I was trying to make a clean start. That's why I joined the Open Faith."

"Did it work?"

"For a while, but I heard rumors about a corrupt pocket. It's basically a good organization. I needed to be sure."

"And you discovered members who weren't so holy."

"Something like that. Actually, the defectors found me."

"Explain that."

"Inside, everyone knows your story, or they find it out. You're always good for one task or another, or you're no good whatsoever."

"What is your talent?"

"I have experience with money. I can handle their transactions."

"They needed you."

"They drew me in. They're not easy to walk away from."

"Why didn't you approach the OFJ leader?" Boot searched his notes from the previous day.

"Paul Andujar?" LeBlay rubbed his temples. "I wanted to."

"Why not?"

"I think he looks the other way."

"You believe he's involved. You said that before."

"I think he needs the money ... for the Open Faith. He does a lot of good with it."

"That's hypocritical."

"We all make rationalizations to get down the road."

"Then Andujar takes a kickback."

"I've never seen him get his hands dirty."

"But you suspect."

LeBlay rubbed his temples again and stared off.

"Are you OK?" Boot asked.

"I didn't expect to be grilled."

Boot let LeBlay settle down, reminding himself not to sound judgmental. To Boot's way of thinking, LeBlay was sunk up to his eyeballs in trouble and looking to bail out. Boot wanted to siphon every last drop of information before LeBlay drowned in his own mess. "I'm sorry. It's part of my job."

"Is there anything to drink in this tin can?"

"I have beer."

"That will do."

Boot retrieved two cans from the refrigerator and popped the tops.

LeBlay drank half the can, before speaking again. He glanced at the stereo. "Who's that singing?"

Boot took a second to recall the CD in the player. The name of the song was Bad Dog. "It's Ted Hawkins."

"You like the blues?"

"What's not to like?"

"I guess I'm asking you what you like about it."

Boot offered the first reply that came to mind. "The simple stories. You can't argue with them."

"That's a funny reason." LeBlay sipped his beer. "There's a place in the French Quarter that plays until three in the morning, but that's delta blues, not like this."

"Are you from New Orleans?"

"I return once in a while. It's a city that stays with you." His small eyes searched Boot's face. "What place created a man like Boot Means?"

"New York City." It seemed like the best answer to Boot, perhaps the most honest. He lived in different boroughs until he was seventeen.

"That town's not home to anyone."

"Only several million people."

"There's too much going on."

"Kind of like your contraband business."

"It's not mine," LeBlay said.

"You sound almost disappointed."

"I wouldn't mind running a legit business one day."

"Is that why you became involved?"

"Many people are involved."

"Which ones did I meet?" Boot asked.

"Simon Talito coordinates the shipments. I think you met him. He's the detail man."

"He's a little paranoid."

"You'd be too if you smoked the amount of pot he does."

"Where does the money from the contraband operation go?"

"Workers get paid, and the rest routes into hidden asset accounts."

"That's your specialty, right?"

"Yes."

"Who controls the accounts?"

"Simon."

"What does he do with it?"

"I don't know. That's for you to figure out."

"You think it leads back to Andujar."

"I have my suspicions."

"Why don't you take this to the police?" Of course, Boot preferred to have LeBlay to himself.

"This way is perfect. You can keep me hidden. With the police, they want signed statements. You have that Freedom of the Press bit behind you."

"It's not always like that."

"No?"

"You sound worried."

"The members of the group are pragmatists. Do you understand?" LeBlay drained his beer. "They solve problems without much circumstance. Even Paul Andujar has killed in the past. You can look it up, if you don't believe me."

Boot started thinking of those guns again. "Have they threatened you?"

"I'm cautious, and you should be too."

"Why?"

"You're going to help them get caught."

Boot let that idea sit for a while. If any part of LeBlay's tale proved true, the wrath of the government would fall on the OFJ like the side of a building. The potential for destruction loomed large, but the career possibilities seemed endless. He wondered how Eric Pulvermann felt as he approached his first big story. Did he shake with fear? Did his gut twist with excitement?

"There's something you ought to see next week," LeBlay said. "It involves everything I've been telling you."

"When? Where?"

"I'll give you as many details as I can gather. They don't tell me everything. I like it that way."

Boot nodded his head.

"Keep out of sight and bring your camera," LeBlay said. "Pay attention to the faces you don't recognize."

"Why is that?"

"Save those questions. You'll know what to do when the time comes."

"Can I reach you?"

"No."

"But if I ..."

LeBlay closed his eyes. He seemed to close his ears too. "No."

Boot let the subject slip. The rain started, and the first thick drops pelted the windows. The storm grew until the ApacheStar echoed with the noise. Boot glanced outside. The river danced, like a sheet of corrugated metal.

"You must have other questions," LeBlay said.

Boot's mental checklist stood near completion. "You said you were good with money?"

"I have experience."

"Why did you go to jail?"

"Wrote a few bad checks."

"Bad checks?"

"Forged checks, if you must know."

"Someone else's bad checks then."

"There's your first good rationalization," LeBlay laughed. "I knew you had it in you."

"Where did you do time?"

"You're checking up on me. I don't mind. Satisfy your curiosity."

"Like I said, I want to know where you went to jail."

"Cold River State."

"Sounds like a nice place."

"It was a regular picnic."

CHAPTER 9
Cold River Blues

After a breakfast of leftover ribs and beans, Boot packed his gear for a trip to upstate New York. He needed to make sense of LeBlay as a person before moving ahead with the OFJ story. He stepped outside his trailer, spotting Stacy's red Corvette speeding down the gravel road. It kicked up a cloud of dust in its wheels, like an army tank charging through the trailer park.

She parked behind Boot's rusty Pinto and jumped out. Her hair was yanked into a ponytail, post workout style, and her mouth bent to one side as if she bit her tongue. "Where have you been?!"

"Busy."

"Have you considered answering your phone once in a while?" She walked up to him as he threw his bag in the back seat of his car. "I asked a question."

"I meant to call you."

"Where are you going?"

"To prison."

"Where?!"

"I have an appointment at Cold River Penitentiary."

"I never heard of it."

"It's hours from here."

"I'll drive." She grabbed his bag. "We have plans to discuss."

Boot tended not to argue. He let her drop his bag in her trunk.

Stacy took the wheel first. She drove with supreme tunnel vision and a lead foot. Twice along the Garden State Parkway, Boot informed her that she switched lanes too often, but she received it as a compliment. A procession of indignant commuters beeped their horns and flipped their middle fingers, not that Stacy ever used her car mirrors to notice. Boot thought about asking to drive, until he realized she was shortening the trip. He double-checked his seat belt and hoped for an open stretch of pavement.

The car barreled ahead. Boot tried to direct the conversation. He recounted vivid details of Camp Jesus. He read sections of the OFJ brochure out loud. He even recited a few of his news articles, and in a last ditch effort to keep things light, he discussed the weather, pointing out cloud formations through the Corvette's sunroof.

But inevitably, the conversation turned, and two long miles outside of Kingston, NY, Stacy popped the question. "I was planning on a fall wedding. Do you prefer September 18th or October 9th?"

"That's not this year?"

She scowled, before cutting off a family of five in a blue minivan. "No, it's next year."

"Oh," Boot said, relieved. He calculated the time—14, 15 months to go.

"Which day?" she asked.

"Whichever." In the side mirror, he saw the minivan flash its high beams in broad daylight.

"Don't act so excited. I get the feeling you couldn't care less."

He left that question alone. "Why do we have to decide today?"

"You just don't throw a wedding together. It's not one of your news stories. There's a church to book and a catering hall."

"I thought you had it under control."

"And there's hundreds of invitations."

"I hadn't thought of it."

"It sounds like you dread it."

"It's a lot of people, Stacy."

"Joining a family isn't the worst thing in the world."

"What did you say?"

"Forget it."

He watched her eyes pick a target on the horizon. Why couldn't she and him just marry, plain and simple without the organized hysteria. "How much time do you need?"

"Please." She turned the wheel to block the minivan as it came around to pass. "So which day?"

"I don't know. How about October 9th?"

"Why that one?"

"Why?"

"Because it's better for you? Or because it's the furthest away?"

"Because it's one of the dates you gave me?"

"Is that it?"

"Are you trying to drive me nuts?"

"Do you even know what day it is?"

Boot hated this. Why was everything about their relationship a special event? And why did he have to remember them? "It was our first date. Right?"

"Which one?"

"September 18th."

"Good guess. And the second day?"

"I give up."

"You don't remember anything. It's the day we first did it."

"Did what?"

She rolled her eyes.

"Oh, I get it." He started to laugh. "We'll have a sweet time explaining that to your father. Maybe we should print it on the invitations and save ourselves the trouble."

"Boot, if you don't want either day, just tell me."

"October's fine."

"October it is."

Boot felt a sense of finality wash over the decision. He bartered away an unknown part of his freedom for an uncertain reward. Most betting men wouldn't place odds on a risk like that.

Glancing to his right, he watched the blue minivan edge alongside. The father raised his fist and mouthed something anatomically absurd, especially at seventy-five miles per hour. For punctuation, his youngest son pulled down his pants and pressed his bare ass against the window.

"Disgusting." Stacy pushed the pedal to the floor and made the minivan vanish from sight.

By late afternoon, they raced through the lush Adirondack Mountains. According to Boot's map, the Cold River lay ahead, as well as the prison with the same name. He noticed four guard turrets rise above the foothills in the valley. They looked regal in an English manor kind of way, as long as he ignored the double length of razor wire fence that circled the property.

Stacy stopped the car at the first gate. "Where do we go from here?"

"You're staying outside," he said, "while I go in."

"Hell no. I'm not waiting for you in the wilderness."

"This is not the wilderness."

"All I see are trees and mountains."

"Go do some shopping. I'll finish in a couple of hours."

"We haven't passed a mall since Albany, and that was four hours ago." She scanned her makeup in the rearview mirror.

"Just keep your mouth shut." Boot sighed. "You're my assistant, alright?"

"Yes, boss."

They registered with the entry guard and parked near the complex. Stacy popped out of the Corvette door. She wore shorts and a sheer sleeveless blouse. She pulled her ponytail loose and tousled her hair, drawing immediate attention from the inmates on the lawn.

One by one, men in orange jumpsuits stopped working. They tracked her progress across the parking lot, whistling and cheering her every step.

A stocky man with a garden rake grabbed his crotch. "Hey Baby! Come to visit me?"

The attending guard marched over and quieted them down.

Boot watched Stacy study her reflection in the reinforced glass beside the main entrance. When she whipped out a hair brush, he felt like hiding in the car. How do you tell your girlfriend to make herself less attractive? "Tone it town, Stacy."

She paused mid stroke, tilting her head to the side. "Huh?"

"Cut it out."

"Cut what out?"

The security chief guided Boot and Stacy through a series of sliding gates inside the prison. They passed the infirmary, where two prisoners were chained to metal rings in the floor beside their cots. One man had a neck brace and a shunt draining fluid from his ear. He looked battered and bruised but alert enough to notice Stacy gawking.

"Fuck you, bitch," the prisoner mouthed through the glass.

Boot looked the other way, trying to collect his thoughts for the interview.

The innermost gate slammed behind them, and the magnetic locks buzzed and clicked into place. Boot jumped at the clamoring sound. Not long ago, he pictured himself in a joint like Cold River. Before college, before he was legally free of foster care, he spent a year on the road, gathering tuition money. He hustled knockoff designer clothing to crooked retail outlets. His supplier offered no illusions about the phony shirts and pants. 'Get busted,' he always said, 'and we never met.'

Boot glanced at Stacy. She'd never understand his past. She never went hungry. She never slept in a bus station. This fantasy life troubled him. How could he keep her dream suspended in air? For now, she made it easy, pretending not to know his history, ignoring his lack of grace and style, but for how long? And for how long would her family tolerate his dreams? Boot sensed the cold iron and stone that surrounded him and shuddered. He made himself dizzy, attempting to divine the future.

"Step through there." The security chief pointed toward an open doorway at the end of the hall.

The warden greeted them in his office. Ed Manning stationed himself behind an ornate wooden desk. Bookplate etchings by Howard Pyle hung on the walls, and the windows donned heavy royal blue curtains with gold fringes. His office reminded Boot of the dean's setup at state college, a genteel haven within an otherwise bland setting.

"How do you do?"

Boot handled the introductions and sat on the teak mission bench against the wall. He wondered who footed the bill for this decor.

"Travis LeBlay," Boot said.

"When you called," Manning said, "I had to remind myself who he was. It's been two years since he was paroled."

"Is that good?"

"If I don't remember them, it is."

"Was LeBlay a good inmate?"

"He struck us as being on the mend."

"That's good, I assume."

"It's good enough. This is a medium security prison. Inmates aren't considered an immediate threat to society, but they can be punchy. We have con men and the like, mostly non-violent offenders. And then there are those with wings."

"Wings?"

"Men finishing longer terms." Manning seemed annoyed with Boot's ignorance of prison jargon. He began defining relative terms like a cop explaining the speed limit. "They've earned that status. I've worked in maximum facilities. Good is a different animal there. Here, good means you've learned. For most, it means you've stayed out of trouble."

"I understand LeBlay was in for check forgery."

Manning examined the open file on his desk. "That is correct."

Boot knew a thing or two about stretching funds past the acceptable limit. He expected a threatening call from his credit card company before the week ended. "Were there any defining circumstances in LeBlay's case?"

"It appeared rather ordinary. He served good time."

"Good time?"

"He participated in the rehabilitation programs. I like to see that."

"Could you be more specific?"

"He attended a class in real estate sales and one in farm management."

Boot amused himself with images of LeBlay tossing slop into a pig trough. Burying profits for the defectors seemed a far cry from that. "Anything else?"

"Personal Management. It's a self-actualization course, esteem building."

"Does it work?"

"Ask his parole officer."

Boot scribbled down the parole officer's name and the name of the NY City DA who prosecuted LeBlay. He noticed Stacy staring at her shoes and twirling her hair with her finger. She was already bored.

"Did LeBlay have a lot of visitors?" Boot asked.

"I wouldn't say that."

"More or less than average?"

Manning reached for the box at the edge of his desk. He lit up a cigar without offering or asking. "I see where you're going with this."

"I'm trying to get a feel for his associations."

"That won't be fruitful."

"Why is that?"

"He had no visitors." Manning protruded his lower lip and released a plume of smoke. "He has no family either."

With that statement, Boot understood LeBlay. He hadn't counted on LeBlay and him being anything alike. Moreover, he pinpointed the exact reason why the prison gates disturbed him. Cold River existed for people like LeBlay and him. Some were just better at avoiding it.

"What do you know about the OFJ?" Boot asked.

"We've entertained them for five years altogether."

"What do they do at Cold River?"

"They roll out Bibles on Sunday and cheer up the men."

"Do you approve?"

"Do I approve?" Manning scratched his chin with his cigar hand. "Off the record, I prefer the practical programs. If you teach an inmate to read and balance a checkbook, you and I are far better off."

"LeBlay works for the OFJ."

"I'm not surprised. He seemed to be headed that way. It was part of the reason why he earned early release."

"Do you expect to see LeBlay back here again?"

Manning chewed his cigar. "I always expect to see them again."

That night, Boot laid awake in his trailer. The Delaware lapped the shore, marking time with its relentless rhythm. Stacy curled into his shoulder. Her skin felt damp and sticky from their lovemaking, and a sweet perfume filled the air. Boot valued this quiet time above most.

He felt the itch to work. He should be doing more to fulfill Art's expectations: combing through his notes, canvassing Camp Jesus for better insight, or sinking his latest negatives into developing solution. But if he rose in the middle of the night and left Stacy alone, he'd play into her hand, affirming her most ardent complaints.

The sound of the phone ringing came as a relief. He slipped Stacy's cheek off his arm. It was a practiced maneuver, accomplished with a gentle sweep of his palm along the side of her head.

He picked up the receiver. "Hello?"

"Mr. Means?" The man's voice was unfamiliar and gruff, a tired late night connection. It wrought through the wires, faceless and without expression. "I want to speak with Mr. Booth Means."

"Speaking."

"Lay the guilt on them, God. Make their intrigues their own downfall."

"Is that supposed to mean something?"

"It's from the fifth Psalm. Are you familiar with the Bible, Booth Means?"

"I am." Boot disliked that the caller employed his full name. Hardly anyone knew it, much less used it to address him.

"What keeps you awake at night, Mr. Means? Is your trailer too warm? Is that little house lonely at night? Do you bounce off the walls in there?"

Boot thought of a smart-assed reply but let it go. "Did you phone me at two in the morning to quote the Bible?"

"Do you have any fear?"

"Should I?"

"You write very interesting articles."

"I'm glad you like them."

"Does the *Trenton Record* report on what fills its stories? Betrayal? Backstabbing?"

"Get to your point."

"Where do you think you're headed?"

"You're with the crewcuts, right?" Boot didn't expect his news photos to be popular with them. "I'm going to hang up now."

"Excuse me." The caller never raised his voice. "You haven't covered yourself very well."

"Should I?"

The line disconnected, and the sound of the dial tone resonated in Boot's ear. He held the receiver in the air. If the caller intended to rattle him, he'd done the job. He recalled LeBlay's words about the defectors: 'passionate, violent.'

He glanced at Stacy, sensing his pulse rise. His focus moved past her sprawling limbs on the mattress and through the tiny window. At the trailer park entrance, not far from Mrs. Ohm's house, a pair of headlights illuminated the access road. The stones in the dirty gravel reflected silver in the high beams.

His eyes filled with the light, and he shuddered. The responsibility of Stacy felt unmanageable. Her father was important and wealthy. If anything happened to his daughter, he'd have the resources to track Boot cross-country, and who would blame him? Boot didn't have a single asset to protect his most precious cargo.

The car backed up, and the headlights rolled through the trailer's windows. They illuminated the clippings and photographs that decorated Boot's walls, a flash photo of his home life stripped bare. He listened to the sound of gravel crunching beneath the car's tires, until it faded into the night.

CHAPTER 10
Instant Margarita

At 10:00 A.M., Boot's beeper startled him awake. Art wanted to see him. Pronto!

Boot sprung into action. He left Stacy asleep in bed and threw on yesterday's clothes. He snuck behind the trailer and tweaked the Pinto's carburetor. His car rolled slowly past the trailer park entrance, avoiding Mrs. Ohm and her open palm, but once beyond the gates, Boot pushed the pedal to the floor. When he reached the *Record* building, he jogged through the newsroom, bearing down on Art's office, like the first marathon runner to pass the finish line.

Art stood with his arms crossed. "What the hell were you doing?"

"Working."

"I left three messages on your voice mail."

"Sorry, I was working the phones." Boot turned and noticed a short, chubby man seated behind Art's desk. Damn if he didn't look exactly like Sheldon Storch.

"Get anything?" Sheldon Storch was bald and unattractive but well-groomed to glean the most from his appearance. For this reason, he appeared noble. "Find another hot lead?"

"No, sir." Boot's spine went rigid. "Just following up on the OFJ."

"And?"

"It's business as usual."

"I want the unusual."

"Yes, sir."

"When I was a kid in Hoboken, I kicked coal off the train cars for money."

Boot wondered if this was Storch's way of telling him to steal what he needed. "I didn't know that."

"I never came home empty-handed."

"I understand."

Art scratched the mole on his nose. He glanced at a young woman leaning against the wall behind Boot. "This is Candace Hohl."

Candace leapt forward and planted herself in front of Boot. She wore bluejeans and a yellow T-shirt with a picture of Geronimo. She had titian hair, cut into a bob, and chocolate brown eyes, but Boot noticed her mouth first. She possessed lips like the scrolled head of a violin, curved and detailed to a point.

"Hi!" Candace said.

"She graduated from Brooklyn College," Art said.

"I've scanned your Camp Jesus photos," she said. "Love the OFJ shots."

"She's a camera jockey like yourself," Art said. "She'll be your assistant."

Boot took a second to regain his poise. "Right."

"We're getting swamped with calls," Art said. "Candace can do the pre-interviews, as well as some of the legwork."

"She'll be a lot of help," Boot said.

Candace moved from the center of the room. "How did it go yesterday?"

Boot glanced at Art, then Storch. They waited for an answer.

"I filled her in," Art said. "She's going to be your right arm."

Boot hoped Art hadn't doled out byline credit too.

"It's your story," Art said. "Yours alone."

"Good."

"Well, how did it go?"

"The warden depicted LeBlay as a model prisoner. I have the names of his parole officer and the prosecutor."

"Talk to them, especially the prosecutor. At a minimum, I need two references on LeBlay."

"He has no family."

"They'd be colored interviews anyway. It might be time to ask their leader a few questions. What was his name?"

"Paul Andujar."

"If he runs the club, then he ought to know what they're up to."

"I'm not sure the timing's right."

"Why not?"

"I've been getting calls."

"What sort of calls?"

"Threats."

Art laughed. "Death threats?"

"Not exactly, but he seemed pretty angry."

"Has he called you at home yet?"

"Two o'clock in the morning."

"That's par for the course. I'd say someone in the OFJ is steamed about your latest Page 6'er."

"Yes."

"I recall a Washington politician who sent me a case of rotten eggs every time I shot down one of his policies."

"That really happened?"

"Hell, there was a reporter in Cincinnati who got a dead rat in a pizza box, and let me see, I think they threw paint on his house."

"You're kidding me."

"Get used to it. People don't appreciate the truth, and when you tell the truth, they blame you for it. That's when you know you're on the right track."

"Geez."

"Just keep your eyes and ears open. Let me know when it gets too hot for you."

Boot felt relieved. He filled his chest as if the threats constituted a compliment. "I have a lot of work ahead of me."

"Then quit wearing a hole in my carpet."

Storch stood. He tugged his starched shirt cuffs, one after the other. "We're counting on you."

"Yes, sir."

"I want 110 percent."

"I'll try." This sounded familiar to Boot. Storch recorded his 110 percent philosophy on cassettes and passed it out to everyone in the company. Boot often joked about it with Teresa.

"How do you feel about your job at the paper?" Storch asked.

Boot fired back a reply. "I love it."

"The Miss Record contest was my idea. I've used it elsewhere. I asked Art to personally oversee it."

"I know, sir." If Boot owned the *Record*, features like Miss Record would be the first to go.

"Circulation jumped four points with that column."

"I had no idea."

"I expected better. I don't think we got behind it enough."

"I see."

"There'll be a few adjustments, like Miss Record at the Beach. I want you to oversee that one. It's too late to put it in someone else's hands. Is that a problem?"

"No, sir."

"Good." Storch smiled, the creases in his face drawing back like a folding door. "I need maximum effort from my best employees."

"Yes, sir."

When Boot and Candace left Art's office, they headed up the central corridor of the newsroom. Boot noticed more than a couple of glances coming his way. He wondered if he was being paranoid.

Rico confronted Boot at the elevators. He looked tired and itchy.

"I'd like to finish our conversation from Sunday."

Boot pushed the elevator button. "Can we do this later?"

"No."

Candace grabbed the elevator door as it opened. She seemed perceptive enough to leave them alone, although Boot wanted her to stick around as a buffer.

"I'll meet you in your office," she said.

Boot noticed her fingernails were discolored and cracked. Photographic developing chemicals had a tendency to do that. "It's in the next building. Above the ..."

"I was there this morning."

Boot watched her slip away. He took a breath and faced Rico. "About the union ..."

"That's exactly what I want to talk about."

"I'm considering your offer."

"I don't think you realize there's going to be a strike."

"I've heard the talk."

"More layoffs are on the books. Anyone could be affected, including you. This paper could be sold for scrap."

"I'm not banking on that."

"I saw you in there with Storch." Rico said 'Storch' as if classifying a disease. "Regardless of what he says, you're going to be on the other side of management."

"I understand." It sounded like scare tactics to Boot. If the paper was going under, if more jobs were on the chopping block, the wheels were already set in motion. He didn't think the union held the power to prevent it.

"Why not join the fight? We can mediate a better position for all of us."

"When did a strike become mediation?"

"Management says that."

Boot pushed the elevator button twice more. "I'm not on any side."

"You should be on our side, the side of your peers."

"My peers?"

"You sound ungrateful."

"Your timing's a little off." Boot watched the opposite elevator retract. He tried to step through, but Jimmy D stepped out, pushing him back into the lobby.

"Hey, golden boy." Jimmy D clutched a bagel and coffee from Krammer's. He looked irascible, like when his favorite sports team mired in a losing streak.

He stood beside Rico. The pair formed a nasty duo in front of Boot.

"I was just explaining the facts of life to Boot," Rico said.

"Our facts of life or Boot's?" Jimmy D asked.

"Now what?" Boot replied.

"I heard about your new assistant."

Boot was impressed by the speed at which word traveled around the newsroom. "She's going to be very busy."

"What did you do, sleep with the boss?"

Boot stared at the open space between them. His mind shuffled through the dozens of tasks ahead, and Jimmy D's insults hardly punched through his thoughts.

"Gotta' go." Boot stepped inside the elevator, waiting for the doors to eclipse Rico and Jimmy D from sight.

"We're not through yet," Rico said.

"I'm not interested." Boot watched the doors slam shut.

"You're on your own."

Boot laughed at that.

By evening, Boot and Candace fell into a snappy routine. He set up the lights in the Downtowner Hotel lobby and dusted the lens for his camera. She kept the Miss Record candidates in line and handled the interviews. She even sprayed and combed a few hairstyles for the women as they posed.

The photo shoot finished in half the usual time. Boot stashed his camera and broke down the tripod. He watched Candace looping the power cords for the standing lamps. He liked that she moved without being told what to do. She wanted to make a good impression.

Candace piled the last lamp against the arm of a rattan loveseat. "What happens next?"

"We develop the proofs," Boot said, "and select next week's lucky finalists."

"No, I mean tonight."

"Tonight? We go home."

"I thought photographers were supposed to stay up all night drinking."

"Only in the movies."

"You're going to have one drink. It's my first day on the job. Or do you have a date?"

Boot needed to discuss wedding plans with Stacy, but there was no fun in that. "I have no plans."

"I'll buy you a quick one. You can tell me about the OFG."

"The OFJ."

"I don't even know what it stands for."

"I'll teach you." Boot led her across the lobby to the bar.

Inside Club Maui, formerly known as the Downtowner Lounge, the tiki lanterns on the mock lanai burned like glorified mosquito torches. Boot and Candace found a table in the corner. The Thursday night lineup was in full swing. A droll Don Ho imitation crooned from the stage, and in between routines by a flame swallower, a white girl with a painted tan feigned a hula dance.

Candace ordered a multi-colored drink in a fluted glass. A paper orchid draped off the rim. "So what's the *Record* really like?"

"In a serious down cycle." Boot poured his beer into a mug. The smell of burning pineapple wafted through the air from scented candles. "Don't count on staying too long."

"My father says it's one step above tabloid."

"Some days."

"He says it's a rag actually."

"He must be proud of you."

"He's ecstatic about my job. He's afraid I'm going to live at home forever."

"Where's home?"

"Lawrenceville. I've got to get out of there."

"You love it that much?"

"My return from college was a real eye opener. I think Mom sprinkles holy water on my clothes when I'm not around."

"Is it working?"

"She's old fashioned. She's practically turned the living room into a chapel."

"My prayers go out to you." He saw her eyes were large and round, and she spent a great deal of time plucking her eyebrows. Her skin was fair and even in complexion, except for a pair of freckles to the left of her nose.

Candace sucked on her straw. "So really, what's the paper like? What did you do when you first arrived?"

"Gofer work: run the copy, drive the reporters, get more donuts. Once in a while, I tagged along with a reporter to take photographs. Miss Record was my first steady assignment."

"But you have the Jesus of Trenton and the OFJ piece."

"Getting into print is not as easy as you think. Art oversees every new feature."

"He seems tough."

"He can be brutal. Let me give you a piece of advice: buy *The Elements of Style*."

"That writing book, why?"

"You'll find out soon enough."

Candace drained her glass, then licked the foam from her mouth. "I didn't expect it to be like this. I guess I never really studied the newspaper. There's a lot of photographic work like Miss Record."

"Welcome to journalism. It's never what you expect."

"I guess I can add some flair."

"Flair?"

"Like Richard Avedon."

"You mean portraiture. You're going to get fancy on me."

"You say that like it's a problem." She sounded almost indignant. "Avedon's more than style."

"I'm not always sure what his context is."

"Does a picture need context?"

"For the news it does."

"He has an excellent sense of the absurd."

"I'll give him that."

"Oh boy. I have a head case here." She jiggled her empty glass. "Who do you like?"

"I prefer hardcore journalism."

"I can see that. Like who?"

Boot sipped his beer, deciding whether to mention his idol. "Eric Pulvermann."

"Didn't he win an award?"

"The Pulitzer."

"And he was almost killed for it."

"He stepped on a land mine in the Gaza Strip and lost part of his leg."

"Crazy work."

"I'd like to be crazy like that."

As Candace searched for a waitress, Boot wondered about the bar tab. Yesterday, his credit card bounced back in upstate New York, and he needed to ask Stacy for cash.

Candace's sights stopped in the center of the lounge. The bartender unfolded a reclining seat resembling a barber's chair. Candace's mouth curled in the corners. "What's he doing?"

Boot watched him manage bottles of tequila. "Instant margaritas, I think."

"Ooooh, I want one of those. How about you?"

"I'm sure it's an authentic Polynesian delight."

"Don't be a stick in the mud. Haven't you ever?"

"No, you go ahead."

"Come on. It's on me." She grabbed his hand and yanked him from the table.

Annoyed by her audacity, Boot prepared to lace into her, but she giggled like a misbehaving child. Her tone disarmed him.

They stopped in front of the bartender's setup. Candace pointed at Boot. "This old man goes first." She pressed her palms into Boot's chest until he sat down.

The bartender wore a flowered shirt. He flung a plastic apron around Boot's neck.

Boot looked up at him. "Do you enjoy this?"

The bartender's hands choked the necks of the bottles. "I used to be on the tool and dye team at GM."

Boot knew that General Motors was basically shutting down in Trenton, like most of the factories. "Waiting for a callback?"

"Yeah, when this booze turns to gold."

Candace released an impatient sigh. "Interview's over. Stop talking and open up!"

The bartender raised the bottles above Boot's head, and before Boot counted to ten, his throat filled with cuervo and an acidic lime juice concoction. He flung his head forward and swallowed in order to breathe.

Candace cheered and several people applauded.

"Not bad for the first time," Candace laughed.

The alcohol rushed Boot's system. "Remind me to never drink with you again."

"Tomorrow, you'll be begging me to take you out."

Boot looked up to fire a quick retort, when his eyes locked onto Julia Sherowich standing before him.

Julia wore a smart business suit with high heels. Her wild red hair was pinned up to the back of her head. "You look like you're really enjoying yourself."

Boot wiped the sticky fluid from his mouth, seeing the furtive squint in Candace's expression. His journalist's savvy kicked in again. He did not want Candace near his contact to Melanie Dove. "Wander in for a drink?"

"The man at the hotel desk said I'd find you here." Julia waved a manila envelope in the air. "Melanie asked me to deliver this."

Boot accepted the thick packet. "What is it?"

"It's a press kit and pass for Sunday. Melanie would like you to observe her weekly broadcast."

Suddenly, he didn't care what Candace overheard, especially if he was getting an in-depth interview with Dove. "What's the pass for?"

"It will take you backstage, and there's tickets for the service. She insists that you attend."

"Will Miss Dove meet with me?"

"She plans to."

"Tell her I'll be there."

CHAPTER 11
A Man with Festering Sores

Early Sunday morning, Boot crossed town to reach Trenton Central High. Cars lined the street, and the foot traffic appeared brisk and determined. Dove's TV stage occupied the north end of the football field, and a line for tickets formed outside the iron fence that surrounded the school property. Boot cut to the front of the line and flashed his press credentials at the gate.

"Hey there, snapshot." A woman yelled from the football bleachers. "What'd ya think?"

Boot saw a black woman in jeans and a loose-fitting sweatshirt. Christine sat alone, when most others gathered in the folding chairs that faced the stage. Boot almost ignored her, but he recognized the funny pink streaks in her hair and the scar along her cheek.

"You got the stupidest look on your face," she said, "like you're lost."

"I'm working." Boot walked by the stands, sizing up the crowd. He wanted to get near Melanie Dove and catch her at work behind the scenes.

"Don't you take a day off?"

"Not today."

"I remember. You're a big newspaper reporter."

"I never said that." He paused on the thirty yard line of the football field.

"Well, don't let me stop you." She leaned on the bench behind her and tilted her face to the sun. "I was only going to say one thing anyways."

"What was that?"

She grabbed a handful of her sweatshirt, flashing the Jesus of Trenton picture which was silk-screened across the front. "Looks like Jesus came to Trenton after all."

Her candor sank his sarcasm, and he stood there fighting for something clever to say. "Right, I suppose."

Boot noticed several OFJ members streaming through the gates. They made him nervous. Were they defectors? Were they tailing him? Just yesterday, he read a police report about a man with a crew cut and tattoos beating up someone in the Chambersburg section, but it was hard to say for certain. An odd blend of people roamed everywhere in Trenton these days. With Jesus in town, the city looked a little too much like Woodstock.

The loudspeakers near the stage switched on with a hard thump and whine of white noise. The turf jumped beneath Boot's feet. He heard guitars strum and brass horns squeal, as the band tuned their instruments for the show. Boot decided to lose himself in the crowd near the stage.

He headed toward the scaffolding, where a few dozen fans pressed for a glimpse of Melanie Dove. He readied his Nikon and stalked the crowd, framing the zealous fans with his camera. A pair of teenagers clung to the stage, covered in Dove buttons and paraphernalia. A homely man raised a sign above his head: MELANIE ROCKS HEAVEN AND EARTH.

In between sound checks, Dove approached the edge of the stage, flanked by a pair of bodyguards. She wore a navy blue warm-up outfit and a Dove Network baseball cap. Boot photographed her touching hands and signing autographs.

Julia Sherowich came upon Boot near the stage. She'd donned a white sun dress with a slit up the thigh. "You were supposed to come straight to the tent."

Boot finished his roll of film and hit the automatic rewind. "When can I speak to Miss Dove?"

"In good time." Julia turned to examine Boot's perspective. She squinted her eyes to guess what Boot photographed. "Absorbing the surroundings?"

"Well put."

"I'll help you with that."

They walked behind the stage, toward a large white tent. Boot surveyed the elaborate set-up that made the Dove Network possible. A convoy of tractor trailers and travel coaches parked outside, and a satellite dish and antenna towered atop one of the trucks. Three electricians examined the heavy cables that ran from the tent, while a handful of production assistants readied the choir for their entrance.

"We wanted to broadcast from Jefferson Avenue," Julia said, "but Karl didn't want to disturb the squatters at the shrine."

"Karl?" Boot asked.

"Mr. Voss, the mayor."

"I've heard of him." Boot saw the serious look on her face, deciding to lay off the dry humor.

Inside the tent, Boot viewed the interior of the telecast operations center. Men hovered over control boards, and a woman stared into a computer screen, double-checking graphic overlays. They seemed tense but steady, like engineers counting down a missile launch.

"Forty minutes to air!" someone shouted.

"We do three or four live remotes a year," Julia said. "We'd like to do more, but it's expensive and time consuming."

Boot saw the Jesus of Trenton pop up on an overhead monitor. The control room aimed a live camera on Camp Jesus and another on the boarded up homes along Greenwood Avenue. People liked to show Greenwood on television. The decaying mansions and crack houses created the type of eyesore politicians loved in ad campaigns.

Along the main console, Boot watched three separate views of the crowd appear. A black man in a red button-down shirt studied the screens, tapping his finger on the flat glass. He whispered into a head-set microphone. "Let's get her, her, and him seated and fixed. And I like this couple in the third row."

"This is Russell Jones," Julia said. "He's our broadcast director."

"Pleased to meet you," Boot said.

"I'm the leader of the asylum." Jones looked at Julia, scratching the nappy hair beneath his headset. "We need more bodies in the back row."

"I gave out extra tickets," she said. "I expected standing room only."

"I need another hundred or two."

"Which is it? One or Two?"

"More like two."

"Don't say another word." She glanced at Boot. "Eastern cities are such a pain. No one shows up on time. Will you wait here until I return?"

"Sure," Boot replied. "Can I take a few pictures?"

Jones shrugged. "I don't see a problem, just keep out of the way."

"Be back in five," she said.

When Julia left, Boot framed candid shots of the operations tent. Jones became engrossed in his work, pushing buttons and dispatching orders into the mike. The rest of the crew fed off his energy. They buzzed around him, fulfilling requests.

Jones reared his head from the console. "Thirty minutes to air!"

The woman at the computer grunted. She grabbed her coffee, jig-gled the styrofoam cup, and dropped it on the ground.

Boot slipped out of the tent and walked behind the stage, hoping to glean more of the inside story. The electricians argued over how to run a cable from the tower to the speakers. A female intern circled a folding table, organizing donuts and cups of refreshments into perfect rows. A sweaty kid in bicycle shorts raced by with a stack of programs heavy enough to crush a small child.

Continuing around the stage, Boot discovered people standing in a semi-circle. He recognized some of their faces from the monitors in the control room. They were the people that Russell Jones plucked from the crowd.

An elderly woman with thick eyebrows pulled the group closer. A Dove Network ID badge dangled from a chain around her neck. "Is everyone clear?"

They nodded. A few glanced at the index cards in their hands.

"Not everyone will get to pose their questions," the woman said, "but Melanie thanks each of you personally for your devotion."

The group followed along, like kids in a classroom.

"Remember," she continued, "speak slowly and clearly, and don't forget to smile."

Boot knelt on one knee to shoot the scene. The upward tilt of the camera lent the elderly woman a commanding authority.

Julia caught him from behind. "It's not what it looks like."

"What's it look like?" Boot noticed she barely kept her annoyance in check. He raised his camera to take more pictures, but the group started breaking up, so he turned his lens on her.

Julia pushed it away. "They had questions of their own."

He wiped her fingerprints off his lens with a soft cloth. "I bet they came with their own index cards too."

"It keeps them focused and eliminates confusion."

"Sure." Boot preferred that she drop the subject.

"Some get nervous on camera."

"I get your point."

She frowned. "Follow me. Mel has a few minutes."

They entered the coach nearest the stage. A pungent odor of fresh cut flowers filled the interior cabin. Boot spotted Melanie Dove through the partially opened doorway in the back. Her blond hair was teased and moussed to perfection, as a young lady stroked powder across her brow.

"Good Morning," Boot shouted before Dove saw him coming. Now was his chance for a one on one. He was determined not to let her slip through his fingers, like he'd done at the Downtowner.

Dove's lone dimple formed in her cheek. "Ahh, the journalist who uncovered the Jesus of Trenton." She rose and disappeared from view.

A thin man cut through the doorway, stopping Boot halfway across the trailer. "God Bless." He had a rough New England accent and dressed in a black suit with subtle yellow piping.

"This is Reverend Zachary Flesch," Dove called from inside her dressing room.

Boot recognized Flesch from Dove's broadcasts. Since meeting Dove, Boot videotaped a few of her shows. Flesch shared the stage with Dove. He played a righteous sidekick, offsetting her unorthodox air.

Flesch looked much skinnier in person. "It's a pleasure meeting you."

"Zack and I were discussing the miracles of the shrine," Dove said.

Boot watched her face run past the crack in the door. "I'd like to discuss other topics with you as well."

"Aren't the miracles paramount?"

"To be honest, not for my column. I'd like more in-depth material."

"So there's no depth in miracles?" Dove asked. "You're a skeptic, I think."

"In my line of work, that's a compliment."

"The Jesus of Trenton would not amount to one iota without your skepticism."

Flesch smiled.

Boot wished he saw Dove's face.

"Did Julia show you around?" Dove asked.

Julia cut in quickly. "When I didn't lose track of him."

Dove peered around the door, glancing at Boot's camera. "I believe you're determined to uncover terrible things."

"What do you mean?" Boot asked.

She sounded stone cold sober. "You'd prefer to get the dirt on me, on all of us."

Boot decided to make a joke of her remark. "I'll be hearing confessions all day."

"You might be the best person to do that." Dove sounded frank, at least as far as Boot gathered from the hallway.

"We can begin right now," Boot said.

"Unfortunately, I'm on stage in a few minutes. We'll speak afterwards."

"I'd like that, Miss Dove."

"Melanie, please."

"Alright, Melanie." Boot saw Julia nod toward him, as if he'd been accepted inside a privileged circle. He immediately felt uncomfortable.

"An usher will show you to your seat."

"I look forward to speaking with you later," Boot said, unsatisfied with the encounter. He headed for the door alone.

He stepped outside, glancing back at Dove's coach. Silhouettes moved in the rear window. It looked like Julia massaging Dove's neck. Dove threw back her head and rolled it to the side.

The theme music began precisely on the hour, and the folksy twang of The March of Angels broadcast over the Dove Network. Boot sat in the last seat of the front row, able to view a TV monitor to his right. Events on the air lagged seconds behind their actual sequence on stage, offering unchallenged possibilities in the delay. Boot imagined Russell Jones seated in the dark control room. The edgy broadcast director hovered over the satellite kill switch, studying the camera angles, marking every word of dialogue. There was no such thing as live television.

Dove entered the stage during the first stanza. She wore a slick pantsuit with leather lapels. Her guitar poked above her shoulder like a machine gun at the ready. She grabbed the neck and tugged it across her chest, taking center stage to belt out the final notes of the opening number. The music sounded more like the national anthem than a Grammy-winning gospel tune, and near the climax, the song acquiesced to a flurry of cheers and applause.

Boot studied the monitor. The overhead camera revealed the stage in all of its glory. It looked like the sky, powder blue with a blazing sun at the center. Dove stood in the sun position, as the camera descended level to capture her smiling face.

"Good Morning," Dove said. "May the Lord enter your lives this day."

The screen cut to a live remote shot from Camp Jesus. People milled along Jefferson Avenue, unaware of being viewed by thousands. The camera pinpointed the box factory and the alleged image of Jesus, but somewhere in the control room, Russell Jones uttered a command, and the shot from Camp Jesus shrunk into a small box in the upper corner of the TV screen.

Dove looked over the crowd, as if addressing one and all at the same time. "Today, a pilgrimage is underway. Christians are gathering in Trenton, New Jersey. They've come to witness a miracle. They do not question what they see. They do not betray their beliefs. They have maintained faith and have been rewarded."

On the teleprompter, a Bible passage scrolled through the reflective glass. Boot listened to Dove read about Saint Thomas who doubted the resurrection of Christ. Dove moved her hands with the words, raising the pitch in her voice, and without marking the transition, she shifted into a sermon on faith, as if reading from the Bible.

She edged closer to the audience, gathering rhythm in her voice. She almost sang the words. Her sentences ebbed and flowed like the bars of a blues tune. Her hands waved as if conducting a symphony of speech. The crowd swooned with her cresting voice. Eyes locked onto her movements; breathing seemed to synchronize with her own. Boot recalled the best work of John Lee Hooker and Muddy Waters, the way they bridged a story, made you feel the emotion. He sensed a chill up his spine.

"Today you all will be rewarded," Dove concluded, singing the words outright.

She found a chair adjacent to Reverend Flesch. Two lines formed before the microphones at the head of each aisle. Russell Jones' hand-picked candidates reviewed their index cards.

With shining faces and unbelievable sincerity, men and women passed before the camera. Their questions bounced off more subjects than a bad advice column. Dove provided the easy responses, while Flesch—all hard truths and Sunday school one-liners—flirted with controversy. Boot fought to keep from dozing. He believed most people gleaned better advice from a fortune cookie.

The final question involved a school prayer referendum in Colorado. Flesch walked the conservative party line, rebuking liberal members of Congress by name. He worked himself into a fury. His hands sliced through the air in crude resemblance to Dove.

Dove stood and touched Flesch's suit jacket, stopping him short. She waited for the crowd to quiet.

"They're doing it again," she said, letting her statement echo through the loudspeaker until the people standing near the street had time to think it over. "The enemies of God are mounting another attack."

"Yes," Flesch said.

"This issue is not about whether school prayer should be allowed. The issue is whether Christians should have a voice."

"That's it," Flesch agreed.

"Why does our government, of the people, by the people, and for the people, think Christian people should not have a voice? Where are their hearts? Where are their souls?"

The audience burst into applause.

"I believe the good people of Colorado will turn out in force. They will choose the way of God. They will rise up and make the righteous heard. My prayers are with them. My prayers are always with them." Dove returned to the sun position of the stage. "And on this 4th of July weekend, I hope that God-loving people everywhere make caring and reverent decisions in their lives."

She strummed the opening chords to 'God Bless America.' The band picked up the beat in sections, as if her song choice was impromptu and they were left unprepared. But the audience members knew their part, coming into their own by the second stanza. A huge American flag unfurled behind the stage.

Boot tried not to roll his eyes.

"I know you understand," Dove said at the conclusion. "We need more than prayers and letters to see God's mission through."

Boot wriggled in his seat, feeling the urge to cover his wallet. The electronic tin cup was about to appear, but he was so broke that picking his pocket would only be practice.

"The Dove Network provides ministers to assist those in need of God's love and grace," Dove said. "There are many projects. We hope to complete the seminary at the Dove Center in Seattle. We have a prison outreach program, among many vital programs in our mission."

Flesch joined her on camera. "Tell the people how they can help."

The television screen listed Dove's pitch for funds. "For joining the Dove Network," Dove said, "you get the newsletter, which tells you about our special missions of hope. You get our prayers, and of course, you get the CD sampler of the upcoming releases on Dove Records."

When the broadcast broke for a brief commercial message, Boot seized the opportunity to visit the bathroom. He ducked below the TV cameras and bolted for the portable sanitary stations behind the stage.

Julia Sherowich intercepted him on his return. "What are you doing?"

"Taking a break," Boot said.

"Aren't you watching the service?"

Damn, Boot thought, she's annoying. "I'm heading back."

"Good."

He waited and snapped a few pictures, but Julia scowled from the base of the scaffolding, ready to whip back around the stage and unload on him. He hurried back to his chair before she popped a blood vessel.

A handful of crewcuts lingered in the standing section at the rear. Boot didn't make eye contact, convincing himself that they wouldn't start trouble here. What was their game? When was LeBlay going to deliver?

The audience held dead silent. Dove and Flesch were seated again, calling off blessings in an eerie tone. Boot returned his focus to the stage. He'd never seen anything like it.

"There's a man with a mass in his right lung," Flesch said. "He has no cure, but God hears him."

"A woman suffers from spousal abuse," Dove said, achieving her sing-song rhythm by leaps and bounds. "God has heard your suffering, and a path to freedom is being prepared."

"There's a woman with a blockage in her lower intestine," Flesch said. "She will be relieved."

"A young boy is losing his hair," Dove said. "It's a sign of great illness, great illness. His parents are frustrated. You shall worry no longer."

"There's a man with festering sores on his feet," Flesch said. "The doctors do not understand what's wrong. You've been abroad to uncover your sickness yet without satisfaction. A time of trial has been set for you, but you will have faith."

The audience fixed to the interplay between Dove and Flesch. Boot shook his head. They were sold—lock, stock, and barrel. It was nothing more than smoke and mirrors, the magic that encompassed most religions. Why didn't they see past it? No one was going to be healed. Why hadn't the human race left this crap behind with witch doctors and men who drilled holes in skulls to cure headaches?

Dove assumed the sun position again, as Camp Jesus returned in the upper corner of the TV screen. A red graphic overlay outlined Jesus' face within the billboard for Smythe's Diner. To Boot, the image appeared forced at best, no better than what he did in the darkroom.

"Observe a miracle in Trenton," Dove said. "This sign, this simple billboard exemplifies Christ and, in many ways, faith itself. You can stray, you can put it down, but it is always there, then one day you see." She signaled for people offstage to enter. "Let's hear the testimony from witnesses of God."

Boot watched a parade of people pass through center stage. A hodgepodge of loners, posers, and misguided loonies spilled their guts, like a live review of Page 6, but under Dove's spell, they related a similar tale. Hell, she even had them dress up for the occasion.

Dove spun in Boot's direction, lowering her arm toward the front row of the audience. Boot barely noticed. He'd heard all the stories before and started to doze again.

"My friends," Dove said, "this is the man who thought enough to bring Jesus to the public."

Boot waited for someone to enter the stage from the right. He saw a TV camera swing toward him, feeling the white hot blare of the television lights.

"He's one of Trenton's most important journalists," she continued, "Mr. Boot Means."

As the crowd applauded, Boot wanted to crawl beneath his folding chair, painfully aware of his reflection on the TV monitor.

"I think," Dove said, "if we coax him, we can get him up here."

He reeled in his chair. Was she actually asking him to go up? His face flushed red, as if he bled from the pores in his skin.

"Please, Mr. Means."

He stood and waved, trying to appease her with a quick acknowledgment, but Julia tugged his arm and guided him toward the stage.

His steps felt clumsy, and his stomach dipped. He hit the top of the stairs, sensing the applause like a strong gust pushing against him. Julia pulled him, and he plodded forward by remote control. He reached Dove at center stage, a lemon yellow sun burning beneath his feet.

"You brought your camera today," Dove said. "Always vigilant, I see."

"It's my job." Boot was conscious of his words echoing through the loudspeaker.

"Don't you think it's unusual that the city has not torn down the sign yet?"

"I thought you might have an answer for that."

Dove placed a hand over her heart. "With my word, I had no part in the Jesus of Trenton's preservation."

"Then the city is as timely as ever."

The audience giggled.

Dove addressed the main camera. "I have to apologize for my esteemed guest. He's critical when it comes to acts of faith. He's exemplary of many professionals today, especially one who has seen so much heartbreak."

The crowd whispered among themselves, a few nodding heads. Boot tensed up. Where was Dove going with this?

"Mr. Means," Dove said, "I have a question for you. Doesn't the testimony you've heard today bring evidence of Jesus?"

The crowd cheered, as Boot considered an answer. He scanned the faces in the front rows, realizing no reply was necessary.

"Let me offer a piece of Mr. Means' background," Dove said. "He was raised as an orphan, having no real instruction on faith, but Jesus came to him anyway."

Boot felt his collar grow hot again. He wanted to charge the exit. He looked back and spotted Julia standing offstage. She gave him the thumbs up.

Dove clutched his sleeve, fastening a hard grip around his upper arm. She closed her eyes. "Mr. Means, the Lord believes in you. He sees your reverent acts and your potential, regardless of your upbringing. He is preparing the gift of faith for you."

The audience jumped to its feet and clapped hands. Flesch approached and patted Boot on the back. Boot cringed. The only thing Dove didn't do was strip him naked and baptize him in a tub of water. He scanned the stage, just to see if there wasn't one waiting.

A nerve twinged wildly between his shoulder blades, like a snapped rubber band. He tried not to look at Dove or Flesch. He wanted to sock them in the jaw. "Shit," he muttered. "Shit, shit, shit." He hoped no one at the newsroom watched Sunday morning TV.

CHAPTER 12

A Little Dark Place Below the Street

Boot grew tired of waiting on LeBlay. He drove to the Polish section in the city's northern ward. The Open Faith for Jesus stationed temporary headquarters in a disused church. Three purple vans lined the sidewalk, and a handful of crewcuts worked outside, trimming the hedges and cutting the lawn like an army of biker clones.

The flag stone path leading to the arched double doors was scraped clean and glistened in the sun. Boot walked quickly, sensing the unfamiliar faces tracking his approach. He pretended not to notice. He double-checked the film in his camera and smoothed the creases in his suit pants. This was strictly a professional visit. *Make like you know nothing yet.*

In the vestibule, a pair of crewcuts blocked his progress. The taller man had words tattooed on one arm: "Vengeance is Mine." It struck Boot like a clever warning label.

"I'm looking for Paul Andujar," Boot said.

"Who wants to see him?" the tall crewcut said.

The other crewcut simply stared, snapping the thick purple armband that strapped his biceps.

Boot stated his name and nothing more.

The tall crewcut disappeared, leaving the other to glare in silence. He snapped his armband. Boot busied himself with his camera. The time waiting in the vestibule felt like an eternity.

When the tall crewcut returned, Boot followed him into the basement. He ducked beneath the low stucco ceiling in the stairwell. Bare light bulbs dangled in the air, and memos curled from the musty walls. He noticed scattered soda cans and food containers, and someone had cleared a section of the floor to roll out a sleeping bag.

Boot buckled down on his courage, keeping note of the exit. This wasn't a good idea. The basement resembled a catacomb. Had he told anyone where he was going?

Paul Andujar sat in the last partition, behind a folding table. As the men entered the room, Boot watched him stab an index card into a black leather Bible and fold it shut.

"Good morning." Boot pushed up his smile.

Andujar peered up from the desk. His bulbous eyes were dark brown, almost black in the badly lit space. He wore a loose beige tunic top. The tips of his black work shoes dangled above the floor.

Boot extended his hand to shake. *Keep it firm and quick.* He swallowed his jitters, his necktie pinching his throat. He felt like a moth wriggling out of a cocoon.

"Please sit." Andujar's voice stalled, achieving rhythm in spurts. "So you've finally decided to show your face."

Boot wiped the notion of an apology from his mind, then located a folding chair in front of the table.

"I wonder if you wouldn't mind." He glanced at the camera in his lap.

Andujar shook his head.

Boot knew about Andujar's shyness with cameras. He'd found a web site that listed hard to get portraits, and Andujar fell within the top fifty. Boot wondered what it was worth. He scanned the room, hoping for a personal photograph within arm's reach, perhaps a framed photo on the desk. He was not above stealing what he needed. All the good journalists swiped a picture now and then.

"Did you lose something?" Andujar asked.

"We could use a current picture."

"Tired of using my mug shot?"

Boot's eyes adjusted to the room. His subject appeared even smaller in person. Andujar possessed a wide flat nose and kinky hair cropped short to his scalp. His tiny features appeared incomplete, as if there came a point when they simply stopped maturing. There was little wonder why he refused cameras.

Without raising his Nikon, Boot spun the aperture to its widest setting, getting the most from the fragments of light in the room.

"Are you aware of trouble in the OFJ?" he asked.

"I know you've been poking around."

"Excuse me, poking around?"

"Looking for trouble."

"Why are you in Trenton?"

"The prison system here demonstrates a great need. We consider all inmates part of the family." Andjuar didn't sound all that different than Dove.

"Do they know that?"

"They become aware."

"Why must they be family?"

"I have a responsibility to remain loyal to them."

Boot tried to fit this explanation into a semblance of logic. He decided to press on with his questions instead. "There are rumors of undesirable activities within your family."

Andujar looked at his Bible. He pressed his palms flat on the table, as if preparing to launch into a handstand. "Melanie Dove sent you."

"I work for the *Trenton Record.*"

"You must be honest."

"I've spoken with Miss Dove, if that's what you mean. She's part of a project I'm working on."

"I hope you're giving her the same scrutiny."

"I've interviewed her too."

"Has Melanie ever mentioned my name?"

"I don't think so."

"She never told you that I once belonged to her organization?"

"I found that out on my own. That is, I read your profile."

"Then you know I started the Open Faith from my bootstraps."

"Yes."

"And you know that it has grown larger and more potent than the Dove Prison Ministry."

"I read that." Boot also read that Andujar was a promising young intern in Florida but served fifteen years for manslaughter. In a drugged up rage, he mowed down a rival intern with his car.

"It's just the beginning," Andujar said. "It's just the start of good things for our family."

"So where does corruption fit into the plan?"

"You don't have a clue?" Andujar's smile opened up, like a gaping wound slashed across his face, a compliment to his godforsaken appearance. "I expected more from you."

Boot recalled Pulvermann's Law #3: Present the questions succinctly, and get out. "Are OFJ members screened before employment?"

"We are volunteers."

"Are their backgrounds researched? Is a basic screening process in place?"

"We are about giving second chances."

"When do the chances run out?"

"When do yours?"

Boot forgot about his tape recorder, but didn't bother to switch it on. Good quotes stuck in his mind like poignant blues lyrics. He slowly inhaled, angling the camera lens upward, edging a finger toward the shutter release. "Let me speak hypothetically. Suppose there were men using the OFJ as a cover for illegal activities. Could you comment on that?"

Andujar drummed his stubby digits on the table. "I heard you were a television celebrity."

The Dove broadcast was five days ago, but it still fazed Boot enough to disrupt his concentration. "Do you watch Dove's show?"

"Now and then."

"It wasn't what I expected."

"Melanie loves surprises."

"Does my visit surprise you?"

"No, your slander about us does."

"I based my piece on firsthand accounts."

"Firsthand accounts of private matters."

"There are no private matters."

"So I see."

"There's only the information you know about and the information that people haven't reported yet. Everything's for sale. Everything comes out in the end."

"Does this apply to you?"

"It applies to everyone."

"It appears you have your own set of rules. Good luck with them."

"It's the way of the world. It's not my doing."

"So you'd like me to believe, but you make the decisions on what to report. Why didn't you come to me sooner?"

"I apologize for the delay."

"I'll answer the question for you. Your newspaper couldn't use a logical explanation, not up front. I've read your column, if that's what you call it."

"I'm offering you an opportunity to explain."

"How can I explain, if you don't understand my position and what I've built here?"

Boot felt ashamed to say that he did not fully understand the OFJ.

He found their ways colorful, not to mention worrisome, but he failed to see a need or function for a group like them. "I'm here to learn."

Andujar forced another long pause. The cramped church basement magnified sound. Andujar tapped the surface of his desk like a drum. His desktop clock hummed, an echo of the printing presses at full tilt. Boot heard himself breathing.

"I'm going to have to ask you to leave," Andujar said.

Boot felt the hand of the tall crewcut clutch his shoulder. It clamped hard enough to make him wince. He backed off the camera's trigger without getting the shot.

Around the block from the church, Boot's Pinto stalled at a traffic light on Olden Avenue. He banged the clutch in neutral and twisted the key, grinding out the starter. Black smoke seeped beneath the rear bumper.

Boot heard someone tap the passenger side window.

Travis LeBlay opened the door and plopped in the seat. "Drive."

"Where did you come from?"

"I cut through the alley." A fat blue vein bulged in his forehead. "Drive!"

"What's it look like I'm trying to do?"

"It looks like you're aiming to get me killed."

Boot let the ignition rest. "You mean my visit with Andujar?"

"Is that you're idea of keeping out of sight?"

"I'm growing old waiting for your next tip."

"I was just about to contact you."

"How would I know that?"

LeBlay pressed both hands against the Pinto's cracked and peeling dashboard. "Drive, will you?"

Boot twisted the key until the sputtering engine came to life. He slapped the Pinto in gear and merged into traffic.

LeBlay flicked the specks of dashboard vinyl off his palms. "Your car's falling apart."

"You should take a peek at the engine."

"Sounds like it's dying?"

"Slow and ugly." Boot felt the transmission buck and grind. "Maybe not so slow. I think my mechanic's got a few more dollars to bilk from me."

"You could use a raise."

"Tell that to my boss."

LeBlay brushed his mustache. "We're a couple of heirs to the throne, aren't we?"

Boot laughed, directing the Pinto into the Trenton Farmer's Market. He jammed the emergency brake into place and glanced through the windshield. Women with bags of groceries wandered through the parking lot, shying away from the black cloud seeping from his tailpipe.

LeBlay kneaded his fingers together. "Why didn't you let me know what you were going to do?"

It sounded oddly like Andujar's questions. "I didn't have a choice."

"But you popped in on Paul unannounced?"

"First of all, he won't grant interviews, so I came on my own, and second, you never left me a way of contacting you. You insisted on being hard to find."

LeBlay twisted his lip. "Yes, I did." He pulled off his sunglasses and polished them on his shirt sleeve.

"So do you want to work something out for the future?"

"How?"

"Give me a phone number or an address where I can reach you."

"I can't do that. I can't have you surprising me."

"Then you have to live with the results."

"OK." LeBlay pointed his finger. "The next time you want to do something crazy, leave me a note."

"Where?"

"Camp Jesus. You're there a lot."

"Should I put it in a bottle and float it down the Raritan Canal?"

"Stick it in the fence. Tie it up with a purple ribbon."

"You'll never find it among the other crap."

"Put it next to the second fence post from the left of the gate. I'll call you as soon as I get it."

"That might work."

"And for God's sake, don't bother Paul again. He's been running crazy since you started writing about us. People in the group are asking questions."

Boot struggled to pin down LeBlay's attitude. Just when he believed he had a handle on the skinny crewcut, he came at him from a new direction. "I thought you wanted them shook up."

"Not with your gossip stories."

"Then give me the goods. I'm dying here."

LeBlay opened the car door and plunked his boots on the blacktop. "Tomorrow night, after midnight, there's a shipment of handguns coming up from the south."

"Are you kidding me?"

"It's something we've done before. They're coming through the rail yard and then off to New York by van."

"You're serious, aren't you."

"I wouldn't joke."

"I hope not."

LeBlay got out of the car and poked his face back inside. His pointed chin stabbed forward. "This is the real thing. Don't stick your neck out. I'm starting to like you."

Boot watched him shut the door and walk away. LeBlay's bow-legged strut turned behind a sausage delivery truck. Boot tried to track him, but LeBlay disappeared into the crowd of milling shoppers.

CHAPTER 13
The Logic of Department Stores

In the afternoon, Boot entered his office loft to kick back and plan his stakeout in the rail yards. He discovered Candace sweeping the floors. His scattered paperwork and photo proofs stood neatly stacked and organized on one of the folding tables.

Candace wore tight bluejeans and a yellow cotton T-shirt with a wide neck. She worked the broom beneath Boot's desk. "Where ya been partner?"

"Researching the OFJ piece." Boot noticed the straps of her bra riding up on her shoulder.

"You look snazzy."

"Thanks." Boot loosened the tie beneath his collar.

"I was waiting for you to get in before I left."

"Headed somewhere?"

"Home."

"Are you sick?"

"It's just a concession." She appeared confused by Boot's question. "It's hard to understand how this is going to wind up."

"What are you talking about?"

She stopped sweeping and held the broom above the floor with two hands. "You haven't heard?"

"Heard what?"

"There's no one here. Didn't you see the parking lot?"

"It's after lunch. I parked down the block."

"It's a strike. Management cut the national and world news departments this morning, or something like that, and the writers walked out."

"All of them?" Boot felt the rug being yanked beneath his feet. "All the writers walked out?"

"The entire union, and as soon as my resume finishes printing, I'm out of here too."

"But you're not in the union yet."

"My father advised me to make a token gesture, so I'm gone, at least for a couple of days. I'm calling in sick."

"I get it."

"Oh, I almost forgot. Some guy named Charles Goodner called twice. He left his number."

"What did he want?"

"He didn't say exactly. He saw you on TV with Melanie Dove."

"Geez, I've got a fan club now."

"He said he needed to speak with you. It sounded urgent."

"Probably another religious freak with a miracle."

"Yeah, probably." She passed him a yellow post-it note. "Here's his number. It's a Texas area code."

Boot swiped it from her hand and stuffed it in his pocket. He knew that the crewcuts were big in Texas. "I'll let him call back."

"He said he would."

"I bet."

The newsroom held an unsettling quiet. Boot saw no one, except a handful of editors sequestered behind the conference room's glass walls. They hovered over the long table. A myriad of paperwork and pictures spread out before them, and even more sheets hung from the corkboard staging wall.

Boot discovered Art in his office. He sat behind his desk, riveted to a trio of television sets. The screens flickered with images from CNN, ANC, and C-SPAN. Boot wondered why Art bothered. The *Record's* current headline involved a mouse doing the backstroke through a bowl of minestrone soup: PIZZARIA FROM HELL.

Art looked away from the screen to study a container of antacid tablets. "How many of these can you take?"

"I don't know," Boot said. "What's the label say?"

Art popped three tablets in his mouth.

"So everyone went home," Boot said. "Candace is going too."

"I can't blame her. She probably doesn't know were to put her eggs. How come you're still here?"

"Working."

"Isn't that contrary to a strike?"

"Who's on strike?"

"Why am I not surprised to hear you say that?"

"I kind of blew off the union."

"That leaves you in a strange place."

"I guess."

"Boot, why don't you go home? You have your whole career ahead of you. If word gets out, you'll be blackballed. Writers aren't pretty when they're angry."

"I'll survive. Hey, shouldn't you be in the war room with the others?"

"They have a handle on it. Besides, they need some elbowroom. If you haven't noticed, I can breathe down people's necks."

They stared at each other. Art appeared sapped of energy, unable to mount a cantankerous exchange. The story of his life was written across his face. He raced against time, as one newspaper after another collapsed behind him. Boot could visualize Art losing ground. He saw how life fast-forwarded you ahead in time and dumped you in the place you started.

"So you're going to fly solo," Art said.

"I decided a few days ago, before all of this."

"What did you decide?"

"I decided Rico bugs the hell out of me."

"Me too, but he's a good field reporter. You can learn a trick or two from him. The rest, you can pitch in the scrap heap."

"I'll keep that in mind when I'm out there solo."

Art reached into his drawer and popped another antacid tablet. "You're a persistent son of a bitch, Boot Means. That's why I like you."

"I didn't think you liked anyone."

Art laughed.

"I mean," Boot said, "isn't that against the rules?"

"Fuck the rules. There are no rules today."

"What are the editors doing next door?"

"Planning the most important week in the *Record*'s history."

"So we're still putting out a paper."

"If we don't, we haven't got a chance. I wasn't kidding about this paper being on the edge."

"How bad is it?"

Art started pacing. "We have a good run for tomorrow and maybe the next day. Don't ask me to go further. Beyond that, it's dicey. We're discussing contingency plans."

"Contingency plans?"

"What we'll do if the paper folds."

"You can't be serious."

"The *Trentonian* has made an offer."

Boot felt the urgency to succeed stronger than ever. He guessed how many days he had left. "Will I be working for the *Trentonian*?"

"I'll be honest. You haven't had time to build up a decent resume."

"You're saying that I won't make the cut."

"In the end, it'll be a selection by seniority. I'd start looking elsewhere."

Boot listened to Art spell out the future in plain language. The road ahead was a cliff that raced forward at rapid speed. "There must be something we can do."

"Storch wants to bring in replacements, but that will take a few days."

"What about serialized columns?"

"They only cover so much."

"You can use me."

"If you're willing to stay, there's a lot you can do. For one, you need to do the Miss Record special tomorrow."

"That shore thing? I meant real work."

"That shore thing has been advertised for weeks. They'll be more chimps in bikinis than you can handle. You'd be surprised to know how important that is."

"Please don't make me do that."

"We need excuses for people to pull the *Record* from the racks, even if half of them are teenage boys with screaming hormones."

"I know but ..."

"Don't lose your jockey shorts, there'll be plenty of assignments if we keep this paper afloat. Of course that's a big if. Most of the staff will be circling the pavement out front."

Boot saw his position changing. His goal moved in a foot race with the paper's collapse. It carried an odd side effect. His story might salvage the *Record*. He longed to be the one to pull it back from the brink. "I have a tip from LeBlay. I'm staking out the rail yards tomorrow night. He's promised contraband."

Art stopped pacing. "It has to be solid."

"I'll get photos."

"That's good, but I need for you to finish your legwork. Have you spoken to Andujar?"

"This morning. He denies everything, and he's none too happy about me snooping around the OFJ."

"Have you completed the reference check on LeBlay?"

"I have a phone interview with the prosecuting attorney, Dexter

Washington—some ex-DA in New York." Boot glanced at his watch; it was almost time.

"Get as much information as you can, and follow his leads."

"Then you'll go with the OFJ story?"

"Let me see what you find in the rail yard."

"I'm sorry, Stacy." Boot sat in Teresa's cubicle, using the phone. His lone voice in the newsroom sounded eerie. "Please, I just can't make it."

Stacy murmured over the line. She whined like a toy doll caught on the same note. "I've canceled appointments with the caterer twice already. He's going to think we're not serious. We have to see the room before we book it."

"I have to finish my story. With everything going on at the paper, this is important."

"Is this what it's going to be like? At this rate, we'll never be married."

"Really, the paper's in crisis mode."

"Forget that job. I'm in crisis mode."

"You don't mean that." He could hear her tousling her hair about her ears. He recognized it as a nervous habit whenever she grew angry. Her split ends were flying in the air, static-charged.

"Sure, Boot. You call me when you have a definite day and a time when we can meet." She slammed down the phone.

He pictured her in a cozy pink bedroom on the third floor of her father's mansion, throttling the phone in her well-manicured fingers. The crash of the handset seemed to thunder down the Delaware Valley and into the heart of the city.

Boot waited for the dial tone and punched in the number for a New York City law office. Since LeBlay passed through Cold River State, his prosecuting attorney graduated from the DA's office and into a private practice at the Empire State Building.

The receptionist came on the line. "Maglione and Washington."

"Is Dexter Washington in?"

"Who's calling, please?"

"This is Boot Means with the *Trenton Record*. He has a five o'clock ..."

"Yes, Mr. Means. Mr. Washington has been tied up in court."

"He's canceled three times already."

"He's very, very disappointed."

Boot burned, and Dexter Washington's overly polite secretary failed to cool his fire.

"I can wait," Boot said. "When will he be back?"

"He would be grateful if you phoned tomorrow to reschedule."

"Can't I reschedule now?"

"At this juncture, his short term plans are uncertain."

"Is he in town?"

"Mr. Means, you can be certain that your interview is a priority for him. Please call in the morning."

"But I have to ..."

"Thank you very much."

Boot put down the receiver and left the building, still fuming. The streets were desolate after the state offices closed, and he wandered down the block, wanting to scream out loud.

A crewcut circled Boot's Pinto. Boot stopped, then ducked behind a trash dumpster to watch. Since the OFJ threats, he couldn't be too paranoid.

The stranger wore blue tinted glasses but didn't dress like the OFJ. He donned tan chinos and a red polo shirt. He copied the Pinto's license plate number and left.

Boot crept into the street. Geez, were the crewcuts dressing like normal people now? That notion spooked him. He counted on being able to pick them out of a crowd.

The street appeared free to roam again, but he felt leery of going straight home for a change of clothes. He jammed his hands in his pocket and found the note from Candace Hohl.

He unfurled the crumpled yellow paper. He read Charles Goodner's phone number in Texas, whoever he was. Candace had scribbled her number on the paper as well.

The Hohl's lived in a refurbished Victorian home in Lawrenceville. Boot pulled up to the emerald green lawn and left the Pinto sputtering ghastly post-ignition fumes by the curb.

Candace answered the door in shorts and a sweatshirt with Jerry Garcia's face printed in the center. "Are you being followed?"

Boot looked over the flower beds and hedges and the quaint white rose trellis leading into the side garden. "I don't think so."

"Man, you're like Woodward and Bernstein."

"Which one?"

"Both, I guess."

"I need to talk to you."

"Come on in, partner."

She led him through the foyer and paused outside a sitting room with votive candles and a statue of the Madonna. Crucifixes constructed of dried palm branches poked from the edges of oil paintings of the Vatican. The air smelled of bayberry.

"This is the chapel," she said dryly.

Along the stairs to the second floor, photographs of military men in full dress uniform scaled the steps. Boot noticed a diploma from Pan Am flight school. "What's this?"

"My dad's a pilot."

"Where does he fly?"

"Commercial American routes, mostly east coast. He did the Australian gig when I was in high school."

Boot stepped into Candace's room. In the corner, a small turret protruded from the house. He walked across the hardwood floor and stood within the three-quarter circle of windows. It overlooked the neighborhood. The suburbs, he thought, a world he never knew, the setting for movie plots and one-liners.

"This is nice," Boot said.

"I guess."

"I always wanted a spot like this, a place to curl up in and watch the world."

A narrow bench followed the arc of the turret. Boot sat on the quilted cushions and scanned her bedroom walls. Old posters of Woodstock and 70s art rock groups clung to the plaster. She was not even born before most of it.

Candace leaned against the edge of her bed. "How's the strike going?"

"According to Art, the paper's ready to fold."

"There goes my first job."

"Don't joke about it. There goes everyone's jobs."

"I guess I'll hit the beach. I don't really care."

"I suppose you don't." Boot's eyes roved around the room again. As long as daddy flew home the bacon, Candace didn't care. If Boot knew what was best for him, he might follow up on Stacy's requests. The future looked to hold a lot of free time for him with no cash in his pockets.

"You could always get work," Candace said.

"The Sears Photo Center is accepting applications."

"It's not so bad."

"It might pay the rent. My current job barely does."

Candace looked at him as if he spoke another language.

Boot shifted gears. He might spend all night explaining his sordid finances. The OFJ story was his best shot at success, and he knew it. "I need a favor tomorrow."

"That depends."

"Can you cover me at the shore?"

"Miss Record at the Beach?"

"That's right."

"Didn't Storch ask you to handle that personally?"

Boot gambled on LeBlay's tip about the rail yards. "I have better fish to fry."

"You have a job interview?"

"I have a great lead on the OFJ." Boot considered telling her more but thought better of it.

"No fooling?"

"It might put the story over the top."

"Wow."

"If I go to the shore, I won't make it back to Trenton in time. Can you cover me?"

"I'd planned to do the political thing," she said.

"The shoot's out of town. No one will know."

"You think?"

"Just get the proofs. I'll say I did it if you want."

"If I'm going, I might take credit."

"Either way. Don't blow it."

"I can get credit then?"

"Sure."

"I'll do it."

"Great." Boot stretched out his legs and crossed his ankles, satisfied he'd covered his bases. He felt on the edge of something big.

"You want to tell me about your lead?"

"Not yet." He looked to change the subject, spotting an old barn-stormer's cap on the post of her bed. It was made of leather with glass goggles. "What's it like having a dad for a pilot?"

"Rent-a-Dad: three days on, three off."

"What does your mother think of that?"

"She hates flying. It scares the life out of her."

Boot loved to hear about other people's parents. It fleshed out his imagination about his own. In one scenario, his father was a college professor, strolling between classes without the slightest knowledge of Boot's existence. "Your dad's a pilot, and your mother hates flying?"

"And it seems to be getting worse. Whenever he goes up, that's when the real praying starts. She has a crowd that comes over. It's like an in-house novena."

He pictured his own mother—the fleeing criminal. She had no time for prayer or friends. He was a lot like her. "What do you do when your mother's group comes over?"

"That's a good question." She walked to the closet and pulled a large shoe box from the shelf. She plopped it on the bed and tossed the lid aside, coming out with a bottle of tequila and plastic cups. "Want one? I don't have anything to mix it with. I've got some cherry brandy in there too."

"Whatever."

"Exactly." She poured tequila into clear tumblers and slid next to Boot on the turret bench. "Now this place is cozy."

Boot toasted her cup.

She drank the amber booze like a shot. "Want another?"

"I haven't finished this one yet."

"Bottoms up!" She poured herself another.

He watched her curvy lips on the brim of the cup. "What about your mom? Does she approve of drinking in your room?"

"I hope you don't mind getting sprinkled with holy water?"

"You're kidding, right?"

"I'll lock the door if you'd like."

"I don't care."

"That's the spirit." She grabbed the neck of the tequila bottle and brought it to pour. "Come on, down it."

Boot emptied his tumbler and let it fill again. He studied Candace up close. The flesh on her wrists and thighs looked very soft, slightly pudgy but appealing. He wondered why the spoiled girls always wanted to make friends with him.

She turned her chocolate brown eyes on him. "How was it for you?"

"What do you mean?"

"Growing up as an orphan."

"You know about that?"

"Teresa told me."

"I thought no one knew."

"I'm sure most people don't."

"I didn't think I told anyone." He felt slightly betrayed before remembering that news people tended to talk. Still, he'd heard things about other people that he never repeated. "I suppose I told Teresa."

"Then all the women know. Why do you think they make such good reporters?"

"Why?"

"They network. Men don't share anything."

"There's a good generalization." He drained his cup.

"It's true." She refilled his tumbler. "So answer me. How was it growing up?"

He considered the pathetic answers: the shuffling between foster homes, the empty holidays, the incredible spans of loneliness that became so familiar they felt normal.

"I'm lucky," he said. "In another country, I might have been left on the roadside to die. Look at me today."

"I heard they found you in a department store. Is that really true?"

"Macy's. At least it wasn't a bus station toilet."

"So your parents were middle class."

"How do you get that?"

"Think about it. If they left you in Woolworth's, you'd be dirt poor; if they left you in Saks, you'd be filthy rich."

"I never thought of it like that."

"See, you're middle class like me, like everyone else."

"I wouldn't call you middle class."

"I am, except for my mom. She's in the Middle Ages."

He put his drink to his nose, sniffing the sweet ferment of tequila. "So I'm from ordinary stock."

Candace stared off into space. "Right now, somewhere in the world, your parents are pushing a shopping cart through the Acme, shuffling through coupons for dish soap and paper towels."

"Yes, but probably not together."

"Probably not."

CHAPTER 14
Riding the Local

Boot entered the Trenton train station after dark. The neon tubes in the ceiling bathed the garbage and bums in sickly amber light. The main terminal displayed that flimsy and unfinished look that was notorious in the Soviet Union. When he first came to town, he was nineteen and broke, moving from train car to train car to avoid paying the fare from Manhattan. He hopped off at Trenton, disappointed by the sorry sight of the station and the stunted city skyline. He thought he'd made a mistake and left the train too soon.

Descending onto the open platforms, Boot waited for the cops to finish their rounds and walk upstairs. Eventually, he stood alone on the edge of the rail yard. He slid off the platform and sprinted north along the tracks.

He expected the crewcuts to enter from the Lincoln Avenue bridge on the opposite side, if they hadn't already. He kept to the deep shadow of the retaining wall, avoiding the watchful eye of the yardmaster. But trespassing in the rail yard was his least concern. The defectors held a nasty grudge against him and threatened to follow-through.

A bulky diesel rolled into the station. It slowed past the platforms, towing a line of freight cars of various size. Boot marveled at the length of the train. It curved beyond the station, like a mechanical serpent with no end in sight.

The horn sounded, and the brakes squealed, metal scraping against metal. The cars compressed at the hitch. Boom, boom, boom, like doors slamming shut. Even at a crawl, the noise enticed Boot. He recalled the subway tracks as a kid and the relentless clap of cars rushing past. He used to lay bottle caps on the rails, letting the wheels squash the caps into long flat ovals. He always wondered what those wheels might do to a finger or hand. He entertained these thoughts as a test of strength. If he envisioned the pain, made it horrible enough to imagine, he might deaden reality.

When the train halted, two men jumped from an open car. Boot grabbed his camera, positioning his lens to glean the most from the weak light. He followed the men, until they vanished beneath the Lincoln bridge.

Several minutes passed, before Boot saw more action. Familiar faces emerged from the bridge: Simon Talito and a handful of defectors whom Boot recognized from Camp Jesus. They walked to the open freight car and began unloading boxes.

Boot aimed his camera and shot up the scene. A cop strolled toward the train and watched the men working. Boot struggled to make out the type of uniform—transit or regular police. He took more photographs, hoping to sort it out later.

He moved in, pressing lightly into the gravel and dirt. A rush of adrenaline surged through his body. He was in the hot zone, stalking as well as Eric Pulvermann. Boot slunk to the corner of the bridge, finding a pile of creosote-soaked railroad ties. He scaled it to get a higher vantage point.

The bridge reeked of diesel smoke, and the scent of burning grease permeated the air. Boot heard voices echo beneath the arched stone overpass, and he pinned himself against the foundation to listen. Men loaded boxes into vans. He heard doors sliding and closing. Two purple OFJ vans entered the yard from the north. They cut their headlights and drove beneath the bridge.

Boot readied his camera like a weapon. Hell, there must be more than one official on the take. He wanted to speak with LeBlay. A hundred questions popped into his head.

A crewcut emerged from the bridge. Boot held a clear line of sight on the position. He spun the telephoto lens. He hardly needed the long lens from this proximity.

Simon carried a box. He knelt down before the cop. His big forearms dug inside the cardboard carton, and balls of crumpled up newspaper spilled onto the ground. He plucked out a handgun, and the cop grabbed the black metallic piece and flipped it over.

Boot pressed the shutter release, hearing the camera click and advance. Bingo! That was the money shot. He imagined it splashed across the *Record's* front page. He couldn't have captured it any better if he'd asked them to pose. He squeezed the Nikon's trigger again, rotating the f/stop to bracket different exposures, and by the time the cop left, Boot had a dozen or more frames of the payoff.

Gravel shifted in the background. Boot saw a shadowy figure coming from the platforms. He turned his lens on the approach. His stomach dropped. Some faces he'd never forget. Of the many people Boot loathed to meet in the dark, the stone-faced Backbone topped the list.

Boot checked his bearings: a thirty foot retaining wall at his back, a length of barbed wire fence across the yard, and the uncertain darkness beneath the bridge. His best exit was the platforms, and Backbone blocked it.

Backbone strode nearer, the tails of his army coat flapping against his legs. He moved like a tank, grim and steady. Boot clipped the case over his Nikon, sensing his knees quiver. Every one of LeBlay's warnings raced through Boot's mind.

Boot ran, cutting a desperate line for the freight train. Simon dropped his load and joined the chase. Boot dared not look back and miss a step. Backbone churned up the stones behind him.

When Boot reached the train, he dove over the hitch. He bent to protect his camera and tumbled on his head. He wound up seated in the dirt and rocks, eyeing a line of defectors pouring out from beneath the bridge. They were yelling, threatening. Boot wanted to crawl under the train and hide.

Backbone passed through the cars, angry and cursing. Boot got up and rushed to the ladder at the other end. Something about getting on top of the train seemed right. If he hopped along the cars and reached the platforms, he might spot help and get in the clear.

He scaled the rungs, placing his palms upon the slanted roof of the car, digging his fingernails into the old roof boards to hoist himself up. He threw one leg on top, when Backbone latched onto the other.

"You little fucker!" Backbone yelled, fastening his grip around Boot's ankle.

Boot thrashed his leg from side to side.

"Payback time." Backbone twisted his ankle in two directions, wringing it like a wet towel.

Boot's sock tore. His knee twisted in pain. He groped for a better hold on the train. He felt Backbone's fingernails skinning his ankle.

Three crewcuts mounted the line of cars. Boot felt an involuntary quiver. *No time to be afraid.* He almost said the words aloud.

As Backbone reached one hand into his army jacket, Boot saw his chance. He rammed the longhair in the shoulder with his free leg, causing Backbone to lose his footing.

Their weight shifted, pulling Boot down the roof. He braced himself against the handrail. The iron bar bit into his shoulder.

Backbone dangled above the ground, spitting and grunting obscenities. He clawed the side of the car, like a dog set loose on a frozen lake.

Boot hung on, pinned against the train, barely holding their weight aloft. He turned his hips, catching a glimpse of the crewcuts hopping the cars and closing the gap.

"Fucking fucker!" Backbone slipped down his ankle, taking hold of the cuff of his shoe.

Boot curled his toes, trying to release his shoe, but it was laced tightly around his ankle. He'd have to lose the foot along with it.

"This is dumb," he called down, trying to make light amid the madness. "Let go!"

"No way, fuckhead."

The steel-plated flash of a switchblade cut through the moonlight. It planted in Boot's heel, thrusting deep into the rubber. He braced for extreme pain.

Backbone regained his position on the ladder. He squeezed Boot's ankle, tugging downward, fighting to work the knife free.

"Look at you now," Backbone growled, bearing his stained and twisted teeth. "I know who you are."

The crewcuts approached, two cars away. Their feet pounded the rooftops, growing louder by the second. Boot tasted his own fear, the strange half-life of his blood turning to poison. He wished he possessed the strength of ten men.

"Where should we start," Backbone said, slobbering, stinking. He tugged at the blade. Frustrated, he smacked the handle, driving it to the hilt. The blade popped through the other side of Boot's heel, completely missing his foot like a magician's trick. They paused at the odd sight of it.

Boot cocked his other shoe as far as it would go. This was it. He stared into Backbone's dreadful glare, punching his heel between the eyes.

Backbone stood straight up, twisting his lip. "You little ...."

Boot drove his heel home again, blasting the longhair's nose and mouth. He wanted to smash that nasty face to pieces. He needed to purge his own fear with the blows. He latched onto Backbone's wrists, kicking him repeatedly, until he felt him release and drop from sight.

The crewcuts were almost on Boot. Simon led the way, sprinting over the space between the last train car. Boot didn't have time to catch his breath. He hopped to the next car, but the blade in his shoe caused him to stumble.

He knelt on the train roof, mustering the strength to fight. The evening local train barreled into the station. The air swirled around him, knocking him off balance. He pushed himself up and hobbled toward the platform. The local train engaged its brakes. The familiar screech of metal rang in his ears.

Running, limping, he glanced back as Simon lunged for his shirt. Boot swatted the chunky hand away. The crewcuts were close enough to hear him gasp for air, close enough to smell his panic. Any second they'd have him. He tried to wash it from his mind, focusing on a single chance: the line of silver passenger trains pulling alongside.

With his last burst of energy, Boot jumped onto the back of the local, throwing his arms across the huge silver whale. He slid over the gentle dome of the roof, nearly hitting the electrical transformer and ending his life in a white hot flash of a thousand amps. He curled into a ball and continued to slide. He didn't even try to stop himself from going over the opposite edge. He seemed to fall in slow motion. *If I die, I die.*

He found himself sprawled across the platform, staring up at a confounded train conductor. The local hummed and groaned by his head. His heart beat like a drum in his chest. He sat up and looked at the train. The crewcuts withdrew into the night, afraid to bring more attention.

Boot checked his shoe. The heel was missing, as well as Backbone's shiny blade. He clutched his Nikon, hoping it'd survived the fall.

The conductor blinked his eyes, as if someone played a dreadful prank. He scanned the platform, searching for the hidden camera. "Where did you come from?"

Boot stood up, wobbling on his bad shoe. He probably looked like a drunk. All he needed was a bottle in a paper bag.

The conductor studied his every move, but Boot dusted his pants, confident he was safe. No broken bones. The exhilaration of beating the crewcuts would carry him clear of the station. "Sorry, I trip all the time."

"You weren't here a second ago."

"Of course I was."

"No, you weren't."

Boot limped past him. "What do you think? I jumped off the train?"

CHAPTER 15
A Step Closer

Boot reached the trailer park, bruised and hyper. He feared that the defectors might follow him home. He tossed lit matches in the trash dumpster, waiting for the first sign of flame. He knew better than to warn the cops about his troubles. If he summoned the fire department, the cops had to come.

Fingers of black smoked curled between the trailers like dead tree limbs. Boot bolted his trailer door and covered the windows with black felt.

He submersed beneath the red glow of the safelight for two hours. Explicit images took shape, like stills of a black and white movie. He had the OFJ right where he wanted them: guilty and at his disposal.

When someone knocked at the door, Boot held perfectly quiet. He bent toward the window, peeking through a slit in the black curtains. Firemen checked the charred dumpster. A Trenton cop leaned against a blue and white squad car.

Boot's landlady occupied the tiny front stoop. Mrs. Ohm balled her hand into a fist. "I know you're in there."

Boot dropped to the floor, throwing his back against the flimsy aluminum doorjamb. He wondered if she saw him set the trash dumpster aflame.

The blunt force of her fist vibrated the door behind his head. "I know you're in there."

Boot didn't speak. After a long hot summer and two bounced rent checks, his status as favorite tenant quickly diminished.

"Where's my check?" Mrs. Ohm demanded, pounding the door. "You owe me June, July, and pretty soon August."

She tested the knob, jiggling it as if she could rip it free with the flick of her wrist. Boot folded his arms and dug his heels into the floor.

"This isn't going to work," she insisted. "I have other options. You don't have to stay."

Boot listened to the heavy breathing on his front stoop. Her fingers and toes were swollen with arthritis, and it meant a lot that she bothered to walk down the hill from her house. Typically, she filled his answering machines with wandering messages about friendship and doing the proper thing. If he could only take his career to the next level, she'd get paid.

"I know you can hear me, Boot."

He wanted to apologize, but without the money, any attempt seemed hollow. He wasn't a liar, and he wasn't a con man. He hunkered down against the door, waiting for her to leave.

"This is not like you, Boot, to take advantage. You know my husband would've hired someone to clear you out. You know I can still do that. There are laws. Don't make me do that."

She pounded a few more times, then left.

Boot watched her struggle up the hill. He exhaled, feeling the tension in his neck and shoulders. He'd run out of time.

He picked up the phone and dialed New York. He needed to speak with the DA this morning. He wanted to complete one decent story, before the *Record* folded up shop and Mrs. Ohm made him homeless.

The receptionist at the law offices of Maglione and Washington projected her most apologetic voice through the receiver. "Mr.

Washington sees no opening in this week's calendar."

Boot gripped the receiver like a hammer. He wanted to slam it over her head. "When can I speak with him?"

"Call back on Thursday, please, to reschedule."

"Thursday?"

"Mr. Washington is ..."

"I know," Boot interrupted. "He's very, very sorry." He hung up the phone.

He scanned the dry line that strung across his narrow kitchen. His pictures of the OFJ looked so hot they might jump into print on their own, but a simple reference check stood in the way. He could already hear Art's voice: Did you speak to the DA? It sickened him to watch this story drop dead because of a stupid technicality.

Boot gathered up his proofs. His hands were shaking. He decided to give it his best shot. Maybe the photos would be enough to persuade Art.

At the *Record* complex, a picket line circled the front curb. Boot attempted to walk around it, but the Trenton police had set up barricades in the street, allowing the union protesters a wide berth to maneuver.

A man with a megaphone wore a sandwich board: ANOTHER FIRED EMPLOYEE, ANOTHER PENNY FOR STORCH. He was none other than Rico Torrez.

Rico turned his horn on Boot. "Boot Means, scab!"

Boot refused to look in his direction.

"Having fun at the expense of others?" Rico yelled. "Be sure to tell Storch these men have mouths to feed."

Boot ducked beneath the comments and pushed inside the building. What did Rico know about mouths to feed? Did Rico ever miss a meal? Boot lost track of the meals he'd skipped last week, and the future didn't look paved with steak and eggs either.

Outside, Rico barked into the horn. "A curse on your family, scab!"

Boot jumped in the elevator. *Shut up, creep.*

He reached Art's office a bit shaken. The television showed live footage of the strike on the Philadelphia midday news. A handsome black news anchor, the one married to the swimsuit model from Brazil, talked up the plight of the American journalist, as if he had anything to worry about with his paycheck.

"You weren't fooling about the union." Boot flopped in a chair. "Rico just gave me an earful."

The TV switched to an ad for baby diapers, and Art looked away from the screen. "There's no turning back."

"Is there any chance of resolving this thing?"

"Don't ask. The first replacements are showing up on Monday."

"Geez."

Art put his hands behind his head and cracked his neck. "How did the shore photo shoot go yesterday?"

"Fine." Boot hoped Candace's Miss Record photographs were good enough. He banked on her college education providing more than a load of useless photo theory.

"Do we have the chimps in order?"

"I'll deliver the proofs this afternoon."

Art cracked a smile, always laced with sarcasm. "I saw your submission on the network." He called the office computer system 'the network', because he was from the generation that forever struggled with the technology.

"You already read my story on the OFJ? I only downloaded it from home this morning."

"I read it."

"What did you think?"

"It's a nice piece of work. I'm surprised by how well you write."

"Then lay your eyes on these." Boot tossed a manila folder on Art's desk. It slid in front of him in perfect position.

Art flipped through the proofs of the OFJ in the rail yards. "Very nice. Crisp. Who's this?"

Boot came behind Art's chair to see. "It's a cop."

"I can see that. It's transit police. What's his name?"

"I'm not sure. He wasn't exactly giving interviews at the time."

"Did you interview the DA yet?"

Boot ignored the question, pointing to the next photo. "Did you see this one? That's one of the defectors unloading the guns from the train? They've got a system going."

"So you mention in your article."

"I thought it would be nice if the *Record* bagged the exclusive."

Art looked up at Boot. "Did you speak with the DA?"

"Sure." Boot could not believe what he'd said. He simply cast out his reply like a piece of bait to test the waters.

"What did he tell you?"

"You know."

"I don't know. What did he say about LeBlay?"

Boot saw the solution to all his problems. The possibility of Art reaching Dexter Washington was slim, even if Art wanted to double-check the interview. What did Art really want after all? Confidence. Hadn't Boot provided that already? The OFJ story seemed like a microcosm of his career, his life for that matter. He always fell one step short of being in the right place at the right time.

Art folded his hands. "So what did he say?"

"LeBlay's a reformed man." The lie rolled off Boot's tongue as easily as taking a photograph. He hadn't planned to do it. He planned on bartering a story line with a preponderance of evidence. Isn't that how it's done? Besides, he believed he knew enough about LeBlay. Things about that man reminded Boot of himself. "He's the product of a tough upbringing and wants to make things right. Don't forget what the warden said."

Art nodded his head. "What about the police charges?"

"Check fraud. He was trying to make ends meet."

"The illegal way."

"He did his time."

Art nodded again. "You think you have the story sewn up, don't you?"

"I think it's ready."

"I can tell."

"I'd like a spot off of Page 6."

"I told you there'd be opportunities." He scooped Boot's pictures into the file. "I'll walk this into the war room right now."

Boot didn't need to hear more. In fact, he wanted to vanish from the room before he said something dumb to change Art's mind. Boot bit his lip, listening to Art's final words. He held completely still, trying to preserve a perfect moment. The chief editor at the *Record* poised to suggest the paper's next headline.

PART 2

CHAPTER 16
Maximum Effort

After wasting the night drinking and celebrating with Candace, Boot wandered into his loft, bloodshot and foggy. The presses roared beneath his feet, shaking the windows, giving his headache a reason to linger beyond the morning. He grabbed his throbbing skull with both hands. It felt like an empty can with a ball bearing rattling inside.

A loud thud shook the building. Boot walked to the window overlooking the pressroom. A ragtag group of strikebreakers accidentally toppled one of the huge paper rolls, sending the crew chief into a tirade. Boot shut the frosted glass windows, wondering how they managed to print the news.

The phone rang several times, before he mustered the drive to answer it. "What do you want?"

"Is that any way to answer your phone?" Candace's voice bubbled over the line.

"You're lucky I answered it, after the way I feel."

"Didn't you get your beauty sleep?"

"I have you to blame."

"You weren't so ungrateful last night. Next time, go celebrate by yourself."

"Ignore me. My head's in another time zone." Boot recalled the loud dance club where Candace ordered rounds of tequila like glasses of water. The thought of it made his stomach turn.

"I'm calling to extend my congratulations," she said. "I saw the paper."

"Which paper was that?" He knew damn well which paper she saw. He'd read the article three times already. His first feature was plastered across the *Record's* front page.

"SPECIAL DELIVERY," she said, repeating the headline. "Even my Dad liked the story."

"Your father? The newspaper critic?"

"Yeah, him."

"I'm honored." Boot glanced at the copy on his desk. His photos were printed in five point color, and page three carried his in-depth feature on the OFJ cult. He brushed his palm over the newsprint. He'd never grow tired of the feel and smell of the page.

"I love the part about the defectors," Candace said. "How did you get that?"

"I have an inside source." He pictured LeBlay, reminding himself to leave a note at Camp Jesus. He needed to keep his hot streak alive, before the paper folded.

"It was a great job of reporting."

"The union reps don't see it like that."

"Having trouble?"

"My answering machine's flooded at home. You'd think I single-handedly caused the strike."

"Yikes!"

"Rico Torrez got me on the line at 6:00 A.M. and started bitching about brotherhood and respecting your peers. Blah, blah, blah."

"What did you say?"

"I suggested he go back to work."

"I bet that went over well."

"I never said I'd join them."

"But they expected it."

"Rico's got a lot of nerve."

"This trouble will blow over. You'll see."

"Not any time soon."

"People get jealous. They're crazy because they missed out on your story."

"I don't know."

"Poor baby." Her voice seemed as rich as butter.

"And of couse there's Charles Goodner from Texas." Boot mimicked Goodner's low Texas accent. "He left another message last night."

"Did you ever call him back?"

"No, and I won't if he doesn't state his business."

"You sure?"

"He acts like he knows me, and lately, that spells trouble. I bet he's OFJ, dying to chew me out."

"You think?"

"Forget it. I've got better news. Want to know what else happened?" Boot found himself ready to brag about something he'd planned to keep secret.

"I give up."

"Art's secretary walked over a message from the main building."

"It must be important?"

"You'll never guess who sent it." He let the question linger. "Sheldon Storch."

"Really? What did he say?"

"Maximum effort."

"What?"

"That's all, just maximum effort."

"Weird."

"I must have topped 110 percent on the Storch scale."

"Now you're losing me."

"You haven't listened to your Sheldon Storch audio tape, have you?"

"Yeah, I've got it queued up after the Grateful Dead."

"Bad girl."

"That's me."

"I won't tell anyone."

"So what does 110 percent mean? What's maximum effort?"

"I'll explain it another time."

"How about tonight over drinks?"

Boot rubbed his temples, unable to fathom a schedule beyond the morning. "Tonight?"

"What do you think?"

"I'm trying not to think. It hurts too much."

"Let's see a movie then. You can nurse your hangover in the dark."

He tried to guess where she was headed. He enjoyed her company, and she seemed to enjoy his. They burned through entire evenings with clever conversation, but determining a woman's motivation wasn't one of his top skills. "You want to go out, tonight?"

"Aren't you free?"

"Maybe."

"I see." Her cheeriness fizzled like a dud firecracker. Perhaps he'd taken too long to respond.

"Is everything all right?"

"Yeah, I'm cool. Call me later if you want."

He heard her disconnect the phone. Hell, if she didn't remind him of Stacy just then.

An hour later, Boot pulled himself together and made his morning trek to Camp Jesus. He drove to Jefferson Avenue, spotting a parking space near the cross street. An odd sight caught his attention. A crewcut lurked half in the shadow of a bank building, winding up his arm like a baseball pitcher.

Boot watched the crewcut from the corner of his eye. The stocky man stretched across the sidewalk, cutting his hand down through the air, as if tossing an invisible ball.

At the last second, Boot saw a brick hurling toward him. It burst through the Pinto's windshield, imploding the safety glass and bearing down on his right eye.

He glanced away, pulling the car off course. Tiny squares of glass pitted his cheek and neck, then the brick caught the top of his ear, skimming off his head.

Stunned, Boot reached for his ear, just as a utility pole raced at his careening Pinto. He fumbled for the brake, fighting to turn away, straining against the steering column, but the hood met the pole, crunching hard and fast. His forehead punched the wheel, snapping back like a whip.

The car groaned to a halt, straddling the curb. The smell of oil and antifreeze filled the air. His head did loops. He struggled to keep alert in broad daylight.

Boot stared through the hole in the windshield. He felt as foggy as the blue cloud of steam hissing from the Pinto's front end. A headlight popped and shattered in the road. The windshield bowed inward, forming a thousand intersecting lines and cracks, a huge geometry puzzle he'd never solve.

"Is he OK?" someone yelled from the street.

"Is he dead?" asked another.

Boot reached for the ignition. The starter ground unevenly. The engine sputtered and coughed. He ignored it, leaning into the key, hoping to beat the odds and drive off.

People surrounded his car, peering through the windows like the peep holes at a demolition site.

Boot grabbed his head. Blood clouded one eye. His breath felt thick and nervous. He feared losing grip, the vulnerability rising up, strangling him. He pulled his camera to his hip and braced for the worst.

When the curtain in the emergency room yanked to the side, Boot saw Art Fontek looking down on him. Art wore an olive suit and a fat red tie stained with drops of coffee.

"I spoke to the cops," he said. "You can kiss off that car of yours."

"I thought so." Boot sat up on an examination table in Helene Fuld Hospital. Seventeen stitches closed his forehead and the gash behind his right ear. His head ached worse than in the morning. He'd trade this feeling for a hangover any time.

"I spoke to the nurse too. I told them I was your next of kin. I assumed you wouldn't mind."

Boot scanned his hospital gown, brushing the cut hairs onto the floor. The nurses had shaved patches of his scalp to reach his cuts and stop the bleeding. "I must be a sight."

"I've seen worse."

"That's not very uplifting. You started in this business by writing obituaries."

Across the emergency room laid a man who'd severed three fingers with a power saw. A crimson line of blood squirted across the nurse's goggles, before the doctor clamped the vein shut. Boot felt relieved that they diverted their attention away from him.

Art leaned over Boot's head, inspecting the stitches. "You believe the OFJ did this?"

"He looked like one of them: short hair, dark clothes, wanted to crack my head like an egg."

"They worked you over. This episode will go into my memoirs."

"Glad to be of service."

"The doctors say it's not too bad."

"Doesn't feel like it."

"A mild concussion at the worst. You'll be back in the game soon."

Boot just stared at Art. He wanted to back off the OFJ story, at least for a short while. With the union on strike, there must be other pressing leads, one without such an angry contingency. Boot shivered. What a way to make a living. He regretted not getting Andujar's photo and selling it to the highest bidder. He'd be minus a stack of bills to pay, and his credit card company would cease calling.

"Like I said," Art continued. "They gave me a rundown on your condition. You're going to live."

"As soon as I get out of here."

"That's the winning attitude."

"Now if I can get the OFJ off my back."

"There's an upside to this, if you want to hear it."

"I'd love to."

"The *Record* sold out today."

Boot thought Art meant that the *Record* was sold to the *Trentonian*. He sat there, waiting to learn how long he had to find another job.

Art beamed. "You can't find a copy of the *Record* anywhere. The shelves were stripped. Classified has already roped fifty new orders for tomorrow's edition. We're very excited. Twice, Storch dropped your name in conversation."

"I guess this means we're continuing with the OFJ investigation."

"Affirmative. Storch wants a different OFJ lead every day. He doesn't care if it's about what color underpants they wear."

"Black probably."

Art smiled. "Hold onto that sense of humor, and you'll go far."

"Maybe we've gone far enough."

"On the contrary. It may not seem like it today, but you're right where you want to be. You wouldn't believe who phoned and asked to take over your story."

"The New York Times?" Boot quipped, wondering if Art was capable of shifting his story to another, more experienced writer.

"It's nothing like that."

"Don't tell me someone from the *Record* wants to steal my piece?"

"You've got it."

"He's willing to cross the picket line?"

"Yes."

"Who?"

"Don't fret over the competition. It's your story. Put today's business behind you, and in the future, be careful."

"I thought I was."

"Be extra careful. I want to get this right, and I want you standing at the end of it."

"That's my plan."

"As long as the OFJ's running loose, this story will be great for the paper, and if you can unearth more goodies on them, who knows where it will lead."

"LeBlay is the key."

"Keep him working for you."

"I'm trying." Boot surprised himself with his own ambivalence. Perhaps he was just tired and sore. He kept it from showing. He was certain Eric Pulvermann hit speed bumps along the way to success but never lost his sense of direction.

The man across the room screamed at the sight of his abbreviated hand. Two nurses pushed him back down on the gurney.

Art glanced over and mumbled. "Sorry son of a bitch."

"I hope they can reattach his fingers," Boot whispered.

"I overheard they couldn't find one."

"Geez."

"See, it could always be worse."

"That's encouraging."

"Get dressed," Art said. "I'll be in the waiting room. I'll give you a lift."

"Thanks."

Art turned to leave, then switched back to face Boot. "Another thing. It's about time that I met with LeBlay."

Boot pretended like he hadn't heard.

"Set up something within the next couple of days. Do it however he feels comfortable."

"Who?"

"LeBlay."

"You want to see him?"

"That's what I said."

"He wants to remain anonymous."

"I'm not going to upset that situation."

"I really don't ..."

"Get the meeting arranged," Art said. "This is not a request."

CHAPTER 17
Raw Exposures

Inside the ballroom of the Foxx Manhattan, Boot stood at the side, absorbing the party atmosphere. The champagne fountain was a large crucifix made of white lilies, and sharply dressed people wandered off the dance floor to fill their glasses in the arcing springs. Boot recognized Tibbs from Newsweek, Rosenthal from BlackStar, and Hart from the Times. The Eastern Christian Alliance's Annual Press Dinner attracted the big names, although Boot came close to missing the event altogether. When the guest invitation arrived from Melanie Dove, he nearly ripped it to shreds.

Boot fell in line for the bar. It was two days after his car wreck, and he looked to fortify his stamina with a stiff drink. He caught a glimpse of himself in the ornate wall mirror. His new buzzcut covered the mess that the hospital had made of his hair.

The broad-shouldered man ahead of Boot turned from the bar, pivoting on his right leg. The contents of his martini glass sloshed over the fluted edge, dribbling on Boot's rental tuxedo.

"Sorry about that." The man mopped the dampness from Boot's lapel with a cocktail napkin.

"Don't worry about it." Boot couldn't believe his eyes. "Mr. Pulvermann?"

Eric Pulvermann stood a mite shorter than Boot. He had a square chin and silver hair draping over his shoulders. "Do I know you?"

"I'm Boot Means. I mean, you've never heard of me, but I've certainly heard of you, that is. I know you." Boot listened to himself babble in front of his idol. Every word leaving his mouth sounded stupid.

"I'll take you one better." Eric shifted on his false foot, digging the heel into the parquet floor. "I've heard of you."

"You must be mistaken."

"Noel Van Dycke was just talking about you."

"That's impossible." Boot felt increasingly stunned. His words caught in his throat.

Eric slapped Boot's shoulder, laughing out loud. He raised the kind of ruckus that demanded an audience. It made people turn and listen. "Don't look so surprised. You know who Noel Van Dycke is, don't you?"

"*Focus Trend* magazine."

"He's the top dog."

"Right."

Eric dabbed Boot's lapel again. "I've made a mess of your penguin suit. Let me buy you a drink."

"Sure."

Holding his glass above the crowd, Eric called for the bartender's attention. He poked two fingers in the air, and the bartender loaded the shaker and filled a pair of martini glasses on the counter.

Boot handled his drink and raised the strong concoction to his lips. "Cheers."

Eric toasted his glass, the edges pinging a treble note. "The secret of a perfect martini is very little vermouth."

"I'll keep that in mind."

"Don't forget the olive. A twist is for amateurs."

"Right."

Eric eyed the stitches along Boot's scalp. "Did you get into a fight?"

"Someone didn't like my brand of journalism."

"Tell him to submit an editorial next time."

"I'll be sure to mention that."

Eric pulled a pocket 35mm camera from his suit jacket. He aimed the lens at the dance floor, snapping pictures of a tall woman in a sexy mauve dress.

"Isn't that that actress?" Boot asked.

"Heidi Wynne. Fresh from Minnesota detox."

"I didn't know."

"Take a look at her." Eric laughed aloud. "I bet she's loaded before the night ends."

"I didn't know you did paparazzi stuff."

"This is for my personal collection." Eric aimed his camera in another direction. Melanie Dove and Julia Sherowich cozied up with Charlton Heston by the champagne fountain, as Dr. Schuller worked his way through the crowd to join them. They all wore impeccably reserved clothing, as if stepping off the pages of the Brooks Brothers catalog.

Eric lowered his camera. "You think they have anything in common?"

"Who's that?"

"Dove and Chuck?"

"Those two?" Boot turned his head, avoiding Dove's glance. He didn't want a conversation with her just yet. "I don't think so."

"Me neither." Eric shrugged and took a picture of a chubby senator who looked like Newt Gingrich.

Boot thought the senator looked shorter and fatter in real life. He watched the famous Washington lawmaker bend the ear of Tibbs from *Newsweek*.

He sipped his drink, careful not to wince as it burned a path down his throat. His head still hurt from the accident. "So this isn't a working night for you?"

"No." Eric's eyes roved about the room, looking for the next shot.

"I never expected to meet you here, at a party like this."

"This isn't my gig, not this setting. I leave the cocktail parties for *People Magazine*."

"So why are you here, if you don't mind me asking?"

"The drinks are free and the women are terrific." Eric laughed again. "They fuck like heaven's on fire. It must be all that pent up sexual desire."

Boot didn't know how to respond. He smiled and put the martini glass to his mouth.

Eric tucked his camera away and downed his drink, signaling to the bartender for another round. "I guess you want me to introduce you to Noel."

Boot hadn't the nerve to ask.

"Noel Van Dycke," Eric said.

"I know who you mean."

Boot was surprised by Eric's swiftness afoot. He struggled to follow him without spilling his drink. They moved past the appetizers, where Eric snapped up two wedges of caviar on toast and a hunk of brie cheese. He popped them in his mouth, mumbling something incomprehensible.

Noel Van Dycke sat at a table with the current editor of the *Dallas Morning News* and their respective spouses. Boot recognized the men from the trade papers. They drank glasses of Scotch, and the women sipped white wine spritzers. Dirty plates and crumbled cocktail napkins were sprawled across the red tablecloth in front of them.

"Speak of the devil," Eric said. "I found your man at the bar, and I thought I'd save you the trouble. Let me introduce Boot Mean."

"Means," Boot said.

"Means," Pulvermann repeated. "You ought to think about changing it."

Van Dycke had thick curly hair and dark glasses. He rose and extended his hand to Boot. "Pleased to meet you."

"Same here." Boot shook Van Dycke's hand, overwhelmed by the men around him. Stacy was right. When he'd told her about the invitation, she said, 'Well Boot, you've finally hit the big time. It's where you've always wanted to be.' It irked him to think that she knew him so well. That was why he didn't bring her along.

Van Dycke rolled his eyes. "I see Eric's introduced you to the perfect martini."

"It's not bad." Boot rested his glass on the table.

"Sometimes I think that's all he cares about, with the exception of his work."

"I'm going to take that as a compliment," Eric said.

"I meant it as one."

"On that note, I have business to attend." Eric bolted straight into the middle of the dance floor.

Van Dycke watched him trail away. "Eric answers only to himself."

"I can see that," Boot said.

"Shall we go for a walk."

"After you."

Van Dycke placed his hand on Boot's back and guided him toward the French doors along the back of the ballroom. Boot saw Eric chatting with Heidi Wynne on the dance floor. He thought Van Dycke did too, although neither man commented.

When they reached the balcony, Van Dycke shut the door. The slim space was enclosed in glass, which overlooked Fifth Avenue. Boot stood by the handrail, watching the traffic silently march below. The sound of the ballroom jazz ensemble seeped from the next room. He felt too nervous to speak. What did a man like Van Dycke want with him? *Focus Trend* catered to the best in the business.

"I won't keep you long," Van Dycke said. "Your name came to my attention about two weeks ago, and since then, I've been keeping an eye on Trenton."

"You must be bored," Boot joked, then immediately wished he hadn't said that.

Van Dycke gave a knowing smile. "I like what you're doing down there."

"I'm excited to hear that."

"Your hard work shows."

"I've been living at the office." He was sleeping there too, since the OFJ wanted to skin his hide. He returned home only for quick visits to change his clothes and check his messages.

"Melanie Dove tells me you're aggressive."

"You know Miss Dove?"

"I was a stringer like yourself when we met. I was on assignment for *Rolling Stone*, I think, but that was many years ago. She has a good eye for photography, and she likes yours."

"Thank you."

"*Focus Trend* is putting together a composite piece on the state of religion. We're gunning for next Christmas."

"That's a tight schedule."

"I'd like to include the photographs of one or two young talents, and you fit the bill."

"I'm flattered."

"Just give me the name of your agent."

Boot came right out with it. "I don't have one."

"That's not a problem."

Boot felt relieved. He loathed to appear unprofessional, especially in front Van Dycke. "I'm still putting together a body of work."

"It'll be refreshing to skip the agent business. We'll let my secretary coordinate a contract and some working cash for you."

It seemed unfathomable to Boot that he was being considered to appear in *Focus Trend*. Was the martini fogging his brain? Had his concussion made him delusional? Was Van Dycke really talking about a contract? A payday like this would save him from bankruptcy, not to mention the magazine launching his name onto the national front. He stifled an involuntary shudder.

"Of course, I'll have to see sample proofs first," Van Dycke said.

"You'll have to hustle."

"Yes."

"But I wouldn't worry about it," Van Dycke continued. "If your proofs are anything like your newspaper work, they'll be winners. Melanie tells me you've been inside the OFJ."

"They're an interesting group."

"I'd like to hear more about it." Van Dycke handed Boot his business card. "Call me Monday, and we'll rough out an outline. I want to hear your ideas."

Boot stared at the raised lettering, rubbing his thumb over Van Dycke's title.

Van Dycke's brow turned down slightly. "Unless you're not interested."

"I'm interested. I'm definitely interested."

Boot left the party early and found his way to a midtown steak house. The restaurant was famous for one mobster gunning down another in the street out front. Boot checked his coat and stepped into the barroom, feeling war weary himself. He still buzzed from cocktails and recent career explosions at the Foxx Manhattan.

The bar looked out onto the sidewalk through tinted glass. Boot spotted a svelte black man in a double-breasted suit by the chrome bars of the waitress station. Dexter Washington dug a hand into a bowl of mixed nuts, while fisting a pint of golden lager in the other.

"You're ten minutes late," Washington said.

Boot felt cocky from the evening. "That means you still have several hours of wasted time to make up for."

Washington smirked. He had a gap between his top front teeth, big enough to hold a book of matches. "I've got a dinner date in less than an hour. You have me until then. That's the best I can do."

"I'll take it." Boot grabbed the adjacent stool. "Travis LeBlay. What do you know about him?"

"Did he kill someone yet?"

Boot didn't like his tone. "I need to do a reference check on him."

"Don't tell me he wants a job."

"I'm using him as an informant."

"That's funny."

"What's funny about it? He's been good so far."

"Are you certain of that?"

"Why not?"

"If you say so." Washington glanced at the TV in the corner of the bar. A blue ticker tape scrolled across the screen with Friday's closing stock prices. He scowled as a negative stock figure zipped past.

"I thought he went in for check fraud," Boot said, restarting the conversation.

Washington looked at Boot. "What's that?"

"Travis LeBlay. I thought he went in for check fraud. I know it's not the life of a priest, but you make him out to be a serial killer."

"Man, he's got you on a string."

"How's that?"

Washington clutched his forefinger. "Number one: it wasn't simple check fraud. He's a goddamned chameleon. He took over people's names and financial assets, before you ever heard about those kind of crimes. Man, they don't have laws yet for half the crap he pulled. I wouldn't send him to the corner with change for a can of Coke."

"So why was he arrested for check fraud?"

"Check fraud was the plea bargain. He knew I couldn't get him on the rest."

"What was the rest?"

"He's an entrepreneur of con games, very slick. He prays on women mostly. He does the Mr. Wonderful routine. Next thing you know, he's plugged into every dollar they ever made. It's hard to bust men like that when assets get signed over to them."

"OK, what else do you know?"

Washington grabbed the next finger. "Number two: it's in his blood, and he can't help it."

"Explain that."

"His mother was a con artist."

"I knew she was dead, but that's all."

"You won't find her history on the books, but believe me when I tell you, Hedda was as bad as they get. She ran sweetheart swindles for years, and when sonny boy Travis grew up, he covered her back end. Everything he knows he learned from her."

"What happened to her?"

"Hedda liked to drink and smoke too much, and that got her before the cops did."

"Sweetheart swindles." Boot'd read about that. He pictured his own mother in that line of work. He could be the product of an affair gone awry.

"You know, romance old men, take all their money. She conned this guy in Florida out of 100 G's. I don't know what she did with it, because she was back in action about a year later in Arkansas."

"So that's his mother. I didn't know that."

"A guy like LeBlay, he makes sure you don't know. He's an actor. If he was truly clean, you'd know everything about him. He would've told you himself."

"Hold on now. I'm not so sure of that. You don't put those things on your resume, even if you are reformed."

"I'm not going to tell you how to do your job." Washington scooped up another handful of nuts, eyeing the TV and the weekly Dow Jones summary. His diamond Rolex watch clinked the edge of the bowl.

The throbbing in Boot's head started to increase. A huge hole was opening up in his OFJ story, as unsightly as the gap in Washington's teeth. Boot needed to close it quickly. "You don't really like LeBlay."

"What's to like? He's a scumbag."

"That's harsh."

"Let me ask you this. What's he doing now?"

"He works inside the Open Faith for Jesus. It's a religious organization."

Boot expected this response to astonish Washington, but the lawyer laughed instead.

"That's a good one." Washington sipped his beer.

"I mailed you the news clippings."

"I remember now. I saw them."

Suddenly, Boot found himself defending LeBlay. Who was Dexter Washington but an overpriced mouthpiece. He probably looked at everyone without a platinum credit card as a potential criminal.

"He's blowing the whistle on the defectors," Boot said. "He's trying to make the OFJ clean again."

"That's a little too admirable for Travis."

"I admit he's somewhat involved in the corruption."

"I wouldn't be surprised if he was running it." Washington glanced at his watch. "I'm not giving you a hard time. You look like you're trying to make something happen here."

"I'm fleshing out a story."

"But keep asking yourself one question. What's in it for LeBlay? That's the point I'd be researching."

"I suppose there was money in it for him."

"That's a good reason, but why talk to you? Are you paying him?"

"No. He's talking because he wants to clean up the OFJ."

"I'm thinking there's a grift here."

"How?"

"Call me an old fashioned bastard, but guys like LeBlay don't ever change. Look at the angles. It's the thrill of the con that lights LeBlay's fire. Why is he talking? What's in it for him? That's what I would be asking myself."

CHAPTER 18
Wrong Number

Early Monday morning, Boot sat with Art in Smythe's Diner, waiting on LeBlay's arrival. The place looked as dismal as ever. Strains of sunlight dribbled through the dusty blinds facing the state complex, and a handful of men stared blankly over stale coffee and cold pieces of toast. Smythe's billboard on Jefferson Avenue was the most unlikely place to purport the face of God.

Boot kept quiet, holding an eye on the door. His conversation with Dexter Washington festered in his brain, poisoning every thought. LeBlay was the linchpin to his success. If the shifty crewcut proved fraudulent, then Boot's photo proofs for *Focus Trend* were baseless. In fact, the entire OFJ story appeared phony. He wished LeBlay held an explanation for it all.

Art dug into Smythe's Breakfast Belly Buster: a plate of pancakes, fried eggs, bacon, and homefries. A piece of dried egg stuck to the corner of his mouth. "You told him 8:00 A.M., correct?"

"LeBlay chose the time."

"Is he usually tardy?"

"Maybe he got held up somewhere." Boot recalled their last phone conversation. He felt LeBlay had agreed to this meeting too quickly, although he didn't worry until this moment.

"It's been forty minutes," Art said.

"I know."

"This is a real person?" Art asked, half kidding.

"He'll be here." Boot glanced at the door.

Art devoured a syrupy wedge of pancake. "Maybe your pals in the OFJ reached him first."

"Don't joke about that. They're still calling me with threats," Boot said, although they'd stopped, since his last article. This bugged him even more.

Art put down his fork. "Speaking of phone calls. Yesterday, I had an interesting conversation with the head of the Watershed Corp."

"What's that?"

"A manufacturing group in Indiana. Their CEO phoned. He wanted to learn more about the OFJ."

"Why?"

"His brother belongs to the OFJ program. It turns out Watershed donates a hefty annual check to the OFJ, and now they want to stop."

"Because of my story?"

"Yes."

"How did he find out?"

"Your story has legs. I told you we sold out on Friday, and so did your follow up on Sunday. I put your last piece on the news wire. I'm sure the nationals are mulling it over."

"I never expected it to cause such a stir."

"You've got a lot to learn, my boy. Everyone loves a real crime story."

"I suppose."

"Believe me. They cry and scream about the effect on children, but people love to watch a man robbing the Seven-Eleven on video tape. They love to see a decapitated head rolling through the streets. Why do you think TV is killing us?"

Boot struggled to hold onto his purer idea of journalism. Maybe it was all some sick form of entertainment, and nobody really cared about the news. Maybe people only wanted to stare into the boob tube and avoid the minutia of their lives. It certainly wasn't worth risking his life.

"You know," Art said. "I never said this to you, but I think you're going to be a helluva reporter."

Boot took the comment to heart. Despite Art's rough and tumble demeanor, Boot respected his opinion.

Art pushed aside his plate and checked his watch. "I can't wait here any longer."

"He'll come."

"If he does, call me and I'll return."

"Give him another ten minutes."

"I've wasted enough time." He rose from the table and left Boot alone.

An hour later, LeBlay still hadn't shown his weasel face in Smythe's Diner. Boot's stomach gurgled, and his head throbbed. The little details that once seemed so stupid, like reference checks and follow up calls, loomed larger than ever. What could he do now?

He walked to the pay phone and shut the door. He dropped seven quarters into the slot and dialed LeBlay's former parole officer in upstate New York. Better late than never.

Officer Prince possessed a cheery voice, the type one might encounter at a fast food drive-thru window. When she picked up the line, she laughed from a conversation which trailed off in the background. "Can I help you?"

Boot introduced himself with a fake name and title. "I'm doing a reference check on Travis LeBlay. He's applied for a job with my organization."

"Which organization is that?"

"Boot Technologies. It's a private consulting firm."

"I've never heard of you."

"Mr. LeBlay has applied for a research position, and he's given us your name."

"A research position? That's interesting!"

Boot ground his teeth. He imagined her saying, 'Would you like fries and a soda with that?' He tried to work her natural enthusiasm to his advantage. "Oh yes, we use a wealth of information."

"Don't you have computers for that?"

"Not for everything. Much of it is still done by hand, and we need diligent, hard working employees to perform the task."

"Travis is very energetic."

"Could you answer a few questions?"

"I'll do what I can? Did you say that Travis gave you my name?"

"He said, 'Officer Prince helped me through a rough period.'"

"No fooling. What's your question?"

"We're already familiar with his criminal record, and we've spoken with other people regarding his background."

"I see."

"Let me say that my company doesn't hold that against him."

"Great!"

"We're looking for a more personal benchmark of his character. Could you help us?"

"Travis gave me the impression that, if he was pointed in the right direction, he could do almost anything."

"Really."

"He was a fast learner, a very quick study. Does that help you?"

"Very much." Boot felt relieved in light of his dreadful discussion with Dexter Washington. "I understand Travis joined a religious group, the Open Faith for Jesus."

"He was great about that. He sampled a few."

"What do you mean, he sampled a few?"

"At least a couple. I think he tried, what's her name, Melanie Dove for a while."

Boot believed she was mistaken. "The Dove Network?"

"Melanie Dove wrote him a glowing letter when he came up for parole. I remember it. It was very nice, even though he'd switched over to the Open Faith by then."

Boot shrunk in the phone booth seat. The deeper he dug into LeBlay's past, the worse it looked. Now, Dove's name had surfaced, and nothing about her rubbed Boot the right way. "Why did LeBlay leave the Dove Network?"

"I don't recall. It seemed abrupt."

"There had to be a reason." Boot clutched his forehead. What was LeBlay's relationship with Dove? Boot hesitated to ask. "Did LeBlay say anything about the Dove Network?"

"I thought he liked it. I was surprised when he made the switch.

"Why did he switch?"

"I can't say. He didn't seem the type for the Open Faith. They're very hardcore."

"Yes."

"But if you're looking to hire him, it appears the Open Faith kept him honest."

Boot watched the pieces of LeBlay's past form an unsavory picture. He cursed himself for not seeing it sooner. LeBlay and Dove knew each other, and that was just the start.

"I always like to hear good news." Officer Prince released a happy sigh. She grated on Boot's nerves.

Boot cleared his throat to cloak his sarcasm. "Is there anything else you'd like to add?"

"He was one of the most outgoing people I'd met in years."

"I'm sure."

"Many parolees have chips on their shoulders, but not Travis. He was so pleasant. He could sell eyeglasses to blind men."

Boot cut the line. He was just about to push out of the phone booth, when two OFJ men entered Smythe's. He dropped into the seat again and shaded his face, keeping an eye on the crewcuts. There was no way to tell if they were defectors. Tattoos scrolled up one man's arm—a bad sign. Boot picked up the phone and pretended to speak. The dial tone squealed in his ears.

A man in a suit wandered up to the phone booth. Boot kept talking, waving the man off. What could he do to defend himself from the crewcuts? He pulled the penknife from his camera bag and unfolded the pathetic little blade. Would they jump him here in public?

The man checked his watch and knocked on the door.

"Just a minute," Boot mumbled behind the glass. He heard the sound of his voice. He was jittery.

The man knocked again. "Hello?"

Boot made a fist and tapped the glass. *Geez, you're going to get me killed.*

"Is this gonna take all day?" the man asked.

Boot eyed the crewcuts across the diner. They were studying Smythe's plastic-coated menus. He stood and retracted the folding door.

"Move it." Boot wedged past the man, knocking him off balance. His heart was racing. He managed his way to the street without looking over his shoulder.

CHAPTER 19
Impossible Lunch

Boot was clear of the crewcuts, at least for the moment. His fears jelled into anger. All of his life, he channeled it like that. He marched across Trenton. The image of Melanie Dove burned in his mind. It was late July in the armpit of New Jersey, and he stomped the stinking hot pavement, focusing on the grimy roof of the Downtowner Hotel and its penthouse suite. He barely noticed he was coming upon the *Record* complex in the center of town.

Outside the *Record's* main building, Boot saw a picket line block the parking lot entrance. Scores of writers and pressmen waved plaques and fists in the air, as a line of cars clogged the street. Boot recalled that the replacement writers were due to arrive.

Boot steered around them, keeping one eye peeled. They pressed the entrance, and riot police wedged into the bristling mob. The cops were leading the cars forward, as union protesters tossed garbage in the air. Styrofoam cups and balled up paper bags flew over the cop's shiny blue helmets and bounced off the approaching windshields, but the cars kept coming.

The strikers cursed and screamed, pounding their hands on the car hoods. The first replacements hit the parking lot, cowering, sprinting for the main building. They yanked their collars high to cover their faces.

Boot saw Rico Torrez mount a plastic milk crate and rise above the crowd. He pressed a megaphone to his lips, before catching a glimpse of Boot on the sidewalk.

The bitter union rep turned his horn on Boot. "Going to join them, scab?"

Boot started to walk away.

Rico aimed his finger at Boot. His voice scratched through the horn, like an old 45 recording. "Boot Means puts himself ahead of the union. Selfish bastard."

Boot kept moving, growing as hot as the sun beating down upon his shoulders.

"Job stealer!" Rico barked. "Thief!"

That was enough. Boot couldn't contain himself. He stopped and stared Rico down, conjuring his fiercest expression. The mob hissed. Boot clenched his fists. If the son of a bitch stood alone, he'd jam those words back down Rico's throat.

"Come on through, scab!" Rico yelled. "Steal another paycheck from a real journalist!"

A handful of strikers peeled away from the pack. Boot planted his feet on the sidewalk. He saw Stan approach with two men from the pressroom. Stan was a nice guy with fat cheeks and a friendly smile, but at the moment, he looked ready to split open Boot's head with a length of wood.

Boot stepped back. He wasn't about to stand and take a beating, but he wasn't going to pull his eyes off of them either.

Stan slapped the wood in his palm, spitting on the curb.

From behind, two large hands yanked Boot off the sidewalk. He teetered in the street, surprised that he'd been surrounded so quickly. He whipped around, raising his arms to engage trouble.

A single man offered an intense stare. He seemed as annoyed as the strikers. "I'm Detective Drake." He shook Boot's shoulders. "What are you doing?"

"What's it look like?"

"Get in." Drake shoved Boot into the back of a navy blue sedan and slammed the door.

From the back seat, Boot watched Drake mount the sidewalk. He was a black man with intimidating size. He flashed his badge and the gun near his hip.

The strikers stopped short of the sedan, clutching their jagged sticks.

"We have some options," Drake said, loud enough that it resonated through the car's sealed windows. "You can go back to your little party and behave, or we can go to the station and figure out what to do with the lumber in your hands."

The strikers dropped their sticks and retreated.

Drake straightened his suit jacket and came around the sedan. He sat in the passenger's seat and turned to look at Boot. "Are you trying to get killed?"

"Again," the driver added. He angled the rearview mirror to study Boot's face.

Boot saw a pair of Asian eyes in the rectangular glass.

"This is Detective Chau from Organized Crimes," Drake said. "I'm Timothy Drake from Special Crimes."

"I know who you are," Boot said. "I took your picture at the PBA awards dinner last year."

Drake didn't recall, but he knew Boot's name. "Then we're practically friends, Mr. Means."

The sedan pulled away from the curb, cruising by the mob. A few strikers offered the middle finger salute, but Drake ignored it.

"Thanks for pulling me out of there," Boot said.

"All in a day's work."

The car turned onto Brunswick Avenue, before Boot spoke again.

"You can drop me here."

The sedan continued rolling.

"This is a lousy spot," Drake said.

"That's alright," Boot said.

"There's nothing to eat here."

"This will be fine."

The sedan turned another corner, its tires screeching.

"You're not hungry?" Drake asked.

"No."

Drake glanced at Chau. "How can a man go to Frankie's and resist eating? This man must be Super Reporter."

Chau studied the road and laughed.

"I get your point," Boot said. "You want me to go to lunch with you."

"That's what friends do. They have lunch and talk. Everybody leaves happy."

They drove to Frankie's Tavern in the city's eastern ward. A dozen police cars parked along a side street. Boot followed Drake and Chau through the barroom entrance. Cigarette smoke spewed as thick as car exhaust, and Boot squinted through the haze, noting the lopsided assembly. The place teemed with cops. Uniformed officers and plain clothes detectives gathered around tables by the bar, even more packed the rear dining room. Boot saw them laughing and talking over large baskets of fries and foaming mugs of root beer. The meal of choice was a hamburger the size of Drake's meaty fists.

Boot noticed Drake whisper to the waitress, and a minute later, he found himself in the restaurant extension alone with the two detectives.

The waitress drew the room divider to a slit, dampening the noise, yet from time to time, the frenetic sound of two-way radios leapt above the din of the jukebox and conversation.

"I suppose this is what they call a cop bar," Boot said, attempting to break the ice.

Drake looked up from his menu with a deadpan expression. "What do you mean?"

Chau delayed his laugh, long enough to signal that nothing Boot said was going to be funny.

Drake smiled. "Does this place make you uncomfortable?"

Boot found the courage to flaunt his own sarcasm. "With all the firepower in here, I've never felt safer."

Chau laughed again, equally difficult to read. His face was smooth and without folds or wrinkles, and his eyes—the same white slits that studied Boot in the rearview mirror—offered no solace. They blinked shut every few seconds, melding into the overall plainness of his face.

They quickly ordered, and the waitress disappeared. Boot waited for Drake to guide the discussion. His experience with detectives involved incidents surrounding one foster care situation or another. The police typically assumed he'd done something wrong and wanted evidence to the contrary. He'd learned to develop solid excuses at the snap of a finger, regardless of his guilt.

"I've been reading the paper," Drake began.

"What did you read?" Boot asked.

"The Trenton Record."

"I'd take you for a Trenton Times man."

"Why's that?"

"Dry facts. None of the fluff."

"I like Page 6. How's that fit into your assessment?"

"You know I photographed those girls."

"I didn't know that. You're the man behind Miss Record."

"It's not my career highlight. It was before the Jesus of Trenton."

"We're big fans of that," Chau said.

"And the headlines too," Drake said. "Your paper doesn't scrimp on the front page. Big letters."

"Color photos," Chau added.

"I especially liked Sunday's headlines," Drake said. "The OFJ story."

"I figured you'd notice that one," Boot said.

"What was it again?" Drake spread his hands apart in the air, as if wrapping them around an enlargement of the headlines. "DOPE, GUNS, AND MONEY. Very clever. Did you think of that?"

"That's an editorial decision."

Drake shook his head. "Trenton's sure been busy."

"Yes."

"And your headlines are making it busier."

"How's that?"

"You've been finding things we've missed."

"Things?"

"Jesus. Guns. I suppose the list goes on."

"That about tops it."

"You might want to consider your position in all of this."

"My position? It's right below the headlines before the story begins. That's the spot where my name goes."

"So you're just a reporter."

"The last time I checked my job description, that's what it said."

"I can respect that. Do you know what my job is?"

"I can imagine."

"My captain thinks my job is to keep the feds happy. You can guess how they feel. ATF agents are asking questions, especially about firearms in the Trenton rail yard."

"A lot of people find that interesting."

"I know you did."

"It's a no-brainer, as they say."

"Then why does my head hurt?"

"I don't know, but I think you're going to tell me."

"Let me explain my job. It's simple. I make pieces fit together. Every time I look at a crime, it's like a puzzle. When I hear about illegal guns, I see pieces scattered on a table. I see the OFJ at first, but then I see you. After a while, I see a whole bunch of you." Drake placed his elbows on the table and propped his chin on his hands. "You're like the glue that ties it together. Can you help me make sense of that?"

"What do you want to ask me? I'm sitting right here."

"That's true, but in general, you're hard to find."

"Very hard to find," Chau said.

Drake glanced at Chau. "Detective Chau thinks you're trying to avoid us, but you wouldn't do that, would you?"

"I don't know where you're getting that idea."

"Friday, you never returned home."

"I've been sleeping in my office."

"I can't blame you. I read your police report—the one where you claimed the OFJ tossed a brick at you."

"You don't believe me?"

"You wouldn't drive your car into a telephone pole for no reason."

"Not even my old Pinto."

"If you'd like, we'll send a squad car by once in a while to check out your place."

"You don't have to do that."

"We might anyway."

Boot struggled to separate the concern from the authority in Drake's tone of voice, although he harbored little desire for either. "Do you think that squad car might be able to give me a lift now and then?"

Drake laughed. Chau blinked. The moment played out like a bad job interview.

"But you weren't in your office on Saturday," Drake continued.

"No."

"Or home either."

"I was researching my column. It requires a lot of legwork."

"On Sunday," Drake said, "when we tried to find you, we learned that you went to New York."

"So now you have an itinerary of my weekend."

The waitress returned with a tray of food. She quickly distributed the plates and glasses and disappeared through the slit in the room divider.

Drake removed his wedding ring and placed it beside his plate. He tucked the tip of his tie inside his belt. He shook out his napkin and draped it across his lap. The entire time, he studied Boot's face, without betraying his thoughts. "You're a busy man."

"When you lay it all out like that." Boot watched Chau stab his fork into his salad. Chau's jaw slid to the side as he chewed, like a dog gnawing a piece of leather.

"I've done some digging of my own," Drake said.

"I bet you have," Boot responded.

"Let's start with the rail yard. What makes you so clever?"

"I was in the right place at the right time."

"And you just knew to be in the rail yard, just when they were smuggling guns across state lines."

"Look, none of this is new information. It's in my article. It isn't like I helped them."

"Don't kid us. Even knowing about a crime in advance can be considered aiding and abetting."

"I didn't plan it."

"What made you so curious about the rail yard at that particular moment in time?"

"I had a hunch that something might happen, but I didn't know what."

"Are you psychic?"

Chau scoffed.

Boot released a slow breath. "I had a tip, alright?"

"Don't get worked up. It's bad for your digestion." Drake bit into his rare hamburger, and drops of greasy blood splattered onto the plate. He ate a portion of his meal before speaking again. "My captain keeps saying, 'Have you talked with Means? You've gotta get hold of Means.' He's like a broken record."

"I know what that's like. You're not the only one with a boss."

"Mine wants to understand how you know so much. So now I want to understand."

"I told you. I get tips."

"From who?"

"I'm not at liberty to say."

"You don't want to do this the hard way."

"I don't even want to know what the hard way is."

"I didn't think so."

Boot put his hands on his camera. He assumed Drake knew about his past. He was one of the invisible people, no family, few friends. If Drake knocked him around in a jail cell, who'd complain? "I can only imagine what you have in mind for me."

"You make me sound awful."

"That's not my intention."

"What is your intention?"

"I want to finish lunch and carry out my business."

"But you haven't even touched your burger yet."

Boot lifted his hamburger and took a bite. He wished that they got to the point soon. He reached for a trio of cheese fries and shoved them in his mouth.

Chau dug into his pocket and removed clippings from the *Trenton Record*. He cleared a section next to Boot's plate and laid out photos of the OFJ in the rail yard. He spread them out, one after the other. "Do you recognize these?"

Boot despised the protracted way in which they revealed their inquiry. He knew some detectives worked this way, but he never had the displeasure of being on the receiving end. He dropped his hands in his lap and swallowed his food. "You know I took those photos."

"We raided OFJ headquarters last night and found nothing."

"I thought you read my column. The guns were bound for New York."

"Where in New York?"

"If I knew, you'd have read about it in the paper."

"It would be nice to know in advance."

"You keep saying."

"Who are the men in this photograph? The picture's grainy."

"It was shot with a long lens."

"Who are they?"

"That's what you want to know? Why didn't you ask me sooner?" Boot found himself looking at Drake again. "I'd rather not play games anymore. Let's get right down to it. Ask me what you really want."

Drake wiped his hands on his napkin. "Fine. We'll do it your way. We want the names and location of the men in this photo."

"Is that it?"

"Let's begin there."

Boot folded his arms and leaned back in the chair. In all of his lousy dealings with cops, he never felt so much in control. He studied Drake's stolid expression. He considered being spiteful, but there was something much larger at stake. "I want in on the bust."

"You do?"

"I don't give a crap about the men in this photo. The crewcuts are responsible for the stitches in my head. I want to be there when you arrest them. I want exclusive photos."

"Who are they?"

Boot pointed at the clippings. "That one with the cop is Simon Talito. There's another with long hair who goes by the name Backbone."

Chau scribbled down the name.

Boot glanced at Chau's note pad. "That's one 'l' in Talito."

Chau nodded.

"Where is he?" Drake asked.

"Am I getting the exclusive?"

"I'll do my best."

"That's all I ask."

"The feds are crawling up our asses, making us look like fools."

"I'm sorry about that."

"Your picture of an officer receiving a carton of handguns didn't help."

"It's not personal. That's what I saw."

"Who was that officer in the rail yard?"

"I've never seen him before."

"Then answer my first question. Where can we find the men in these pictures?"

Boot thought of a place LeBlay mentioned once. "Supposedly Simon has a cousin in Chambersburg. It's a hangout for a number of defectors."

"Defectors," Chau scoffed. "That's a cute name. I always liked that."

"You seem to know a lot about the defectors," Drake said.

"I get good tips."

"From who? What's his name?"

"Who said it was a man?" Boot tried not to grin but found it impossible to resist. He pictured himself leaving the table soon, and Drake and Chau couldn't stop him. He certainly didn't want to stick around for the lunch bill.

Drake leaned back and folded his arms. A strange resignation washed over his face. "I thought you wanted to play it straight."

"I'm not telling you about my source. So don't ask again."

"Don't worry. I won't be asking next time."

"I don't even want to know what that means."

"We'll be doing it the hard way, but not like you think."

"I can't wait."

"You might not have to." Drake slapped a grand jury summons in front of Boot. "I told you you've been hard to find. We had to special delivery this one."

"What's this for?"

Drake smiled. "You're going to help us fill in the blanks."

CHAPTER 20
The Far Reaches of the Dove Network

Boot finally reached the Downtowner by late afternoon. He called from the lobby and convinced Dove to let him come up.

The elevator doors parted in the anteroom of the penthouse suite. Boot found Julia Sherowich waiting. She wore a short leather skirt and a kelly green satin shirt that made her hair appear fiery red.

She rose from the chair beside the artificial palm plant. "Good afternoon."

"Right." Boot saw three boxes stacked by the inner door marked 'Seattle, WA.' Six more waited behind him by the elevator.

He followed her inside the plush suite. He noticed the recording equipment was missing, and the folding tables were stacked against the wall. "Going somewhere?"

"Home." Dove entered from the sliding door to the terrace. She wore a black suit with a rhinestone crucifix pinned above the breast pocket.

"Then you're finished with Trenton."

"Only beginning. I've made a splash here, wouldn't you say?"

"I'll never forget your television broadcast. That's for sure."

"It's more than that. I've put down roots in your city." Dove had a satisfied look about her. "The prison ministry is up and running at Trenton State."

"I heard about that."

"Still keeping tabs on me?"

"I heard the OFJ was banned from the premises too." He studied her face for a reaction—any indication of guilt. "I guess you saw an opening to fill."

"The OFJ situation is unfortunate, but you know more about that than I."

"Yes."

"I wanted to extend my condolences to them in person."

"You better hurry. I heard Andujar's top two men are resigning."

"In any event, I don't have time. I'm flying out this evening."

"Then I've caught you just in time."

Her stare remained intact. Her ice blue eyes looked transparent, as if Boot saw what passed through her mind, yet it was far from true. She was as easy to read as a stone.

Boot presented a bouquet of flowers. He'd purchased them in the lobby, passing another bad check in the process. "Thank you for the other night."

"You're welcome." Dove sniffed the outer buds.

"It's the least I could do."

"I'll handle these." Julia took the flowers and fluffed open the green wrap.

Boot shuffled his feet.

"Is there something else I can do for you?" Dove asked.

Boot remembered their first meeting, when just seeing her made his stomach flip. Now, his nerves trembled again but for an opposite set of reasons. "Can we talk?"

"I have a moment." Dove glanced at Julia, and Julia wrinkled the corner of her mouth, before disappearing into the bedroom.

Dove stepped near a pair of Victorian armchairs and took a seat. "Make yourself comfortable."

"Thanks." He sat close, facing her. He felt a sense of urgency, as if her limo might arrive any second to shuttle her to the airport. He wondered how to wedge the truth from her without prying. Nothing in Pulvermann's handbook prepared him for this.

Dove poured herself a glass of water from the crystal pitcher beside the chair. "What would you like to talk about?"

"I'm having a problem."

"Yes?"

"A grave problem."

She put down the glass and leaned forward. Her straight blond hair scraped her shoulders as it fell to the front. "Don't be afraid to speak with me."

Boot noticed slight wrinkles about her eyes and mouth. He thought her makeup hid them well. "I fear the solution more than the problem."

"That's nothing to fear."

"It might be, coming from you."

She closed her hands around Boot's. "Open your heart."

He felt her warm fingers across his knuckles. Was he wrong about her? Or was she completely audacious, forever on stage? "A few days ago, I wasn't seeing things clearly. I must have been distracted."

"Go on."

"I used to believe that I understood what I was doing, but I'm no longer sure."

"You're in doubt."

"Yes."

"We all have moments of worry, right before breakthroughs occur. You must endure and find your faith."

"That's not my problem. The problem is that today I see more clearly than ever before."

"I don't understand."

Boot tried to reflect the look in her eyes, cold, impenetrable. "How do you feel about Paul Andujar?"

Dove released Boot's hands and sat back in the chair. "Is this an interview?"

"What do you mean?"

"Is this on the record?"

"It's a personal matter."

"Then I'll help you the best that I can."

"As I helped you?"

She looked through him. "I don't know what you're asking?"

He already sensed the answer to his largest question. He just wanted to hear her say it out loud. "How do you feel about Paul Andujar?"

When she smiled, the dimple puckered in her cheek. "This is your problem?"

"I think so."

"Let me alleviate your fears."

"I know he used to work for you."

"A long time ago. He was very devoted."

"He's taken a good bit of your prison ministry away, hasn't he? I didn't realize what the numbers actually meant until recently."

"What do they mean?"

"Less people. Less money."

"Do you need to pursue this?"

"I have to. It's not for my paper. It's for me. I have to know." He watched her smile become a hardened thing like politicians and movie stars did for the cameras. "I know Andujar ran your prison ministry for four years."

"He worked for me."

"You must've felt betrayed. When he left, he took so much of it with him."

"Those things happen."

"But he hasn't really stopped. As far as I can tell, the OFJ keeps eating away at your prison ministry."

"That's a relative thing."

"Is it? Perhaps you feel a little pleased that you've gotten one back in Trenton, but overall, you must feel betrayed by him."

"That's an excellent word. Betrayed. You keep mentioning it. You might want to ponder it for a while."

"I'll tell you what it means to me. People expect certain things, and when they don't get it, they're disappointed."

"How's your article for *Focus Trend*?"

He knew about Van Dycke's relationship with Dove. If this was a veiled threat, he decided to see where it led. "*Focus Trend* is interested in the OFJ, but you already know about that."

"*Trend's* a cutting edge publication, and the OFJ scandal makes a good story. You wouldn't want to ruin an excellent opportunity for yourself."

"Or have it ruined for me."

"Why would that happen?"

"Let's just say that my story has holes."

"Nothing you can't patch up. I have faith in you."

"My key informant seems suspicious. He might have ulterior motives."

Dove folded her hands like she did on her broadcast when people lined up in the aisles to ask questions. "While you were examining everyone's motives, did you stop and take a look at your own?"

"I want to get at the truth."

"I remember the first time I saw you. You reminded me of an eager beaver, an ambitious beaver. You had an agenda."

"Tell me about Travis LeBlay."

"You mention that name like I should know him."

"He used to belong to the Dove Network."

"When was that exactly?" She cocked her head.

"Two, three years ago."

"A lot of people pass through Dove. You can imagine I have trouble remembering them."

"How deeply are you involved in the OFJ's problems?"

"Excuse me?"

"Could I find you at the top of it? Could I discover that you caused it?"

"That's a large accusation."

"Why would Travis LeBlay want to talk to me?"

"You're asking me?"

"I'm having difficulty finding him."

"It's easy to see why you're frustrated. You seem lost. I'm sorry, but I can't help you."

When Dove rose from the chair, Boot latched onto her arm. "You used me. You at least owe me an explanation."

She yanked free. "You're over the line, Means."

"I'm over the line?!" He saw Julia stepping through the side door. "You must think I'm pretty stupid."

"I don't." Dove waved Julia back into the bedroom.

"What is it then?"

She closed her eyes for a moment, taking a single breath. She searched Boot's face, donning an expression he'd never seen on her before. It looked genuine, and it scared him.

Her voice sounded calm. "I almost didn't meet with you today, and now I wish I hadn't."

"I think I understand why."

"You don't. It wasn't my desire to anger you, and your pain disappoints me."

"It was unavoidable."

"You're missing the big picture." She tapped her index finger into his chest. It seemed to delve deep inside of him, exposing his private thoughts to the light. "You made this decision. You wanted to be famous, and now you have the opportunity."

"Not like this." It made him ill to think that she might be right.

"You wanted to be successful. I saw it in your eyes. You practically begged me for help."

"This is all wrong."

"Listen." She pressed her finger against her lips. "Success isn't easy or free. Everyone helps everyone else. No one gets there alone."

"If I had a shred of evidence to connect you to LeBlay, I'd print it."

She dropped her hand. "Don't be stupid."

"I'd do it in a heartbeat."

"That would be libelous."

"I'd take that chance."

"But your paper wouldn't. It doesn't want a lawsuit. And then where would you turn? Especially when everyone finds out the truth: Boot Means can't even write a solid article."

"It isn't that simple."

"It'll look that way, even if you find Travis LeBlay."

"Then you do remember him. Where is he?"

She shrugged. "You should get down on your knees and pray he stays missing."

"You make me sick."

"You're taking this much too hard." She flashed her million dollar smile. "Keep the big picture in mind, kid. You have a future."

"At what cost?"

"I was like you once. Do you want to spend the rest of your life at the bottom? You're forgetting that you have talent. I saw that in you. Van Dycke sees it. Do you want to shoot tacky photos for a nothing tabloid? Does that sum up your aspirations?"

"It's honest work."

"So is picking up garbage off the street. I don't believe you'd want to lose your article for *Focus Trend*. The other night, you looked very comfortable in a tuxedo."

"I can get there on my own."

She shook her head. "You haven't been listening to me, have you?"

"Trouble is I have been listening."

Boot pulled away from her. He stomped to the elevators and got inside, turning back to view her through the doors.

Julia came to Dove's side and clutched Dove's elbow and wrist. She leaned her head against Dove's shoulder.

"You're going to be a martyr," Dove called, without displaying the least bit of fear or remorse. "I can see it in your eyes."

"At least, it will be my decision." Boot pressed the button for the lobby, letting the women disappear from sight.

CHAPTER 21
A Snapshot for the Files

Boot walked through the city, until the sky turned gray and it began to rain. He reached his trailer near the river, feeling wet, heartsick, and bitter. The truth of Dove's lies weighed heavily upon his conscience, and the stench of it clung to his skin, like a bottle of cheap cologne dumped over his head.

Down the gravel road of the trailer park, Boot saw Candace scribbling a note by his front door. He didn't see any sign of trouble—no crewcuts, no more cops—but he thought about turning back into the city.

Candace spotted him and waved her arms in the air. "Hey, Boot."

Boot plodded up to the porch. "What are you doing here?"

"Living the life of leisure." She wore white cotton jeans and a short yellow tie-dye tank top that revealed a gold ring in her navel.

"Unemployment's been treating you well. Maybe I'll try it."

She raised her sandal in the air. "I had a pedicure to match my fingernails. You like?"

"Great," Boot said unenthusiastically.

"I thought I'd drive by to check out your crib." She extended her hand beyond the awning, catching the drops of rain in her hand. "Is it ever going to stop? It's rained every day."

Boot was already soaked and didn't care. He watched her lick the moisture from her palm.

"Are you going to invite me inside?" She asked. "Or are you going to stand in the rain like something out of a Ziggy cartoon."

"Alright. Why not?"

Boot let her inside and locked the door. He glanced out the window, seeing a police car cruise through the middle of the trailer park. It splashed through the puddles in the road, leaving muddy sprays across its baby blue fenders.

"Are you expecting someone?" Candace asked.

"No one in particular." He watched the police car slow outside his trailer, then continue past.

"Was that the Trenton cops?"

"I think so."

"What did they want?"

"Looking for someone, I guess." He knew they were checking on him, compliments of Detectives Drake and Chau. He pulled down the shade. At least, he could sleep in his trailer without worry of the crewcuts. Everyone wanted a piece of him these days.

She plopped into the chair next to the phone. "Your answering machine is full."

"Who cares?" He opened the official looking letter from the State of New Jersey. Mrs. Ohm was starting eviction proceedings. He had ninety days to pay the back rent or vacate the premises. He took the letter and pitched it atop a pile of unpaid bills near the toaster. He didn't even own a car anymore to live in.

Candace removed her shoes. "What put you in such a great mood?"

He rubbed his temples. "I still get headaches now and then."

"From the accident?"

"Yes."

"It must be more than that. You look worried."

He didn't reply. He moved to the stove and placed the tea kettle on the burner.

She came beside him. She smelled sweet, like when you first break through an orange rind and the mist hits the air. "I hope you have something stronger than that."

"Help yourself to whatever I've got. There's a few bottles beneath the sink. It's pot luck."

She found a bottle of Wild Turkey and poured two tall glasses and placed them on the counter. "This will work."

Boot couldn't remember where the liquor came from. Perhaps it was a gift. He watched her take a shot. "Bottoms up."

"Absolutely."

His glance fell to the petite fullness of her navel and the gold ring piercing the skin above it. A little heart swung inside the loop.

She disappeared into the shower stall and returned with a towel. She reached up to dry his hair. "You really are in a bad mood."

"Bad isn't the word for it."

"It's cool. I like the brooding type. I noticed that about you from the start."

Boot drained his glass. He pictured his life as a car wreck in progress. He needed to find LeBlay and change him into the perfect informant; keep the car from crashing, although it appeared that a collision was inevitable.

"So you're hung up over something," Candace said.

"I don't want to discuss it."

"Hmmmmm. You're trying to turn me on with this dark silent trip."

She took another shot, and he watched her plump and wavy lips accept the edge of her glass.

"Since we're talking about what we like," he said. "I liked your mouth. I noticed it when we met."

"You don't like it now?" She planted her lips on his.

Her kiss was altogether different than Stacy's. He expected that. Stacy generally took cues from him, while Candace leaned into him and clutched his waist, forcing him back into the stove.

Boot reached to brace himself, brushing his hand against the electric stove coil. "Shit!" He threw her forward.

"What?!"

"I have a girlfriend," he said, flapping his hand in the air. "I mean, I burned myself."

She grabbed some ice from the freezer, wrapped it in the towel, and pressed it on his hand. Boot felt the moisture sting his burn.

"I know about your girlfriend."

"We're getting married."

"Then why haven't you made any plans yet?"

Boot was surprised that she knew.

Candace had a devilish grin. "We share the same voice mail, idiot. I try not to listen, but you know, I can't help it. You should really let her know."

"Know what?"

"That you've been out with me at nights."

"That was harmless."

"And that you've been lusting after my mouth." She giggled and kissed him again, this time taking hold of his T-shirt and yanking it from his belt. "It's wet. It's got to come off."

When she tossed his shirt aside, he glanced at it lumped on the floor. He wanted her to take it off, and he didn't feel the least bit guilty. He looked back at Candace, seeing her pull her tank top over her head.

She stood in a bra. "You know, I could be a Page 6 girl if I wanted to."

"Why would you?"

"I didn't say I did."

"No, you didn't." He wanted to see the rest of her undressed. She made it entirely too easy.

"Did you ever take photographs of the girls you did it with?"

"Like Polaroids?"

"Yeah." She reached for Boot's pants and undid his belt.

"You want me to get it?"

"I think I can manage."

"I mean the camera."

"Yeah, let's see how good you are."

He held her by the waist, his fingers reaching into the well of her spine. He felt her tongue deep in his mouth.

She fell back against the wall with a thump. "Ouch! Something got me."

Boot glanced over her shoulder. "The bathroom door handle."

"Is there any place to spread out in here without getting gored?"

"Follow me."

In the back of his trailer, in the bedroom just big enough for a twin-sized bed, Candace removed the rest of her clothes and posed for Boot's Polaroid camera. He flashed a half dozen pictures, as she rolled over the sheets.

He tossed the instant photos on the bed. The tawdry images emerged in the dark, like the sizzling notions in his brain. He wanted her more than he ever did Stacy, and he felt a little sad. Something once dear to him was slipping away.

The storm rattled the ApacheStar's aluminum veneer. Candace sat up and removed her cut shell earrings. She placed them beside the clock on the shelf and blew him a kiss. "Do you think I'll make Friday's edition?"

Boot jumped on the bed. "Not with these shots."

"Can I persuade you?"

She grabbed him, taking command of his movements. She forced him down and brought him back up again. She covered every inch of his body. Boot felt as if he was being chewed up and spit out by her, not an unpleasant experience. He did his best to reciprocate, following her furious pace atop the mattress. At one point, they rolled off the end of the bed and onto the steps leading into the kitchen.

Laughing, she straddled Boot on the top step. She possessed an animal look in her eye, like she did right before downing a shot of booze. "You have a lot of energy for a brooder."

"Look who's talking." Boot caught his breath. His shoulder hurt from where she nipped him with her teeth. "You going to maul me some more?"

"Don't fade on me now, mister."

"No chance."

They finished up in the stairwell, but it would be hours before Candace was satisfied. They repeated the act a few more times with decreasing intensity, and some time after midnight, the battered couple collapsed on the bed, their hearts pumping beneath their bruised ribs.

They listened to the rain for a while. Only their heads touched, like Siamese twins joined at the scalp.

"Oh baby," she said. "I haven't gotten laid like that since college."

"You only graduated in May."

"It's been a long, celibate summer."

"You can say that again, except for the celibate part."

She feigned the batting of her eyes. "So I'm not your only girl?"

"You know who else." Boot found himself thinking of Stacy again. He knew it was over. He only needed to choose the right words to break their engagement. It was time to be the best of all wordsmiths. She deserved an honest explanation.

Candace scooped a pair of Polaroids off the sheets. From his position, Boot viewed them upside down. One was crinkled and ruined from rough sex, but the other remained intact. It showed her on all fours, looking back at the camera.

"Doggie style," she said, "I like it."

"I did the best I could, considering the light."

"Does this turn you on?"

"Woof!"

She slapped them on his chest. "File them under 'C' for Candace."

"You want me to have these?"

"You're not going to do anything with them. Besides, it's easy enough to fake nude photos nowadays. You should know that."

"But I'll know they're real."

"That's the point, honey." She pressed her mouth on his cheek and licked the sweat off, then got up and walked into the kitchen.

When Boot came down, he saw her in the breakfast nook with a can of beer. She wore no clothes and propped her feet on the table, her pink toenails poked in the air. With just a glance, Boot wanted to have her again, on the spongy foam cushions.

"It will be light out in a few hours." He dropped a Howlin' Wolf CD in the stereo, then snatched a cold beer from the refrigerator and slid next to her.

She put down her feet and curled beside him. "I suppose you have to go to work."

"It gets worse than that."

"Tell me."

"I have to find my story source."

"You mean the informer inside the OFJ."

"Yes."

"Where is he?"

"I don't know where to look. He contacts me."

"The Deep Throat type, eh?"

"There's a place in Chambersburg, but he made me promise not to look for him there. He's probably relocated by now."

"I would too, after the beans he spilled on his so-called friends in the OFJ. Where do you think he went?"

"That's not my biggest problem."

"Why not?"

Boot didn't answer. He swigged his beer, staring out at the lights on the Trenton Makes Bridge. He noticed the river flowing higher than ever. It scaled the cement footings of the bridge.

"What's wrong with Deep Throat?" Candace asked.

"He might be phony."

"How do you know?"

"I think he works for Melanie Dove."

"What are you saying?"

"I think he planned to give the OFJ a bad reputation, so Dove could move in on their territory, but I can't prove it."

Candace sat straight up. "No shit."

"I wish it was a joke."

"You think your story source lied about the defectors?"

"I saw the things I saw. They were real, but recently, I suspected he organized a lot of it, if not all of it." For a moment, he followed the ragtime melody of Poor Boy on the stereo. "I think LeBlay runs the defectors. I think it was part of his plan to discredit the OFJ. I was just too stupid to see it."

"Did you approach Melanie Dove?"

"She didn't exactly deny it."

"Whoa. This is heavy."

"Don't tell me."

"When did you first suspect this?"

"You don't want to know."

"Tell me. Maybe I can help."

"When I spoke to Dexter Washington."

"That hard to reach lawyer?"

Boot glanced at her.

"I told you," Candace said. "We share the same voice mail. I heard his secretary canceling your meetings."

"When I finally reached him, he got me thinking. He told me all about my source's past."

"And ..."

"He's a con artist in the first degree."

"Yikes! What did you do?"

"I checked out his former parole officer too. She said he used to be a part of the Dove Network. They appear to have some kind of relationship."

"Deep Throat gets around, doesn't he?"

"Yup."

"Art Fontek let you go with a reference check like that?"

"Not exactly."

"You didn't lie?"

"I wouldn't put it like that."

"What did you do?" Candace placed her beer on the table and turned toward Boot. "This gets messy, doesn't it?"

"Yup." He didn't look her in the eye.

"You haven't told Art about it yet."

"No, I hadn't finished the reference checks. I was under pressure, and the story was getting stale."

"Oh, boy."

"I stalled Art. I told him I spoke to Washington before I did. I figured I'd get to him sooner or later."

"Yikes!"

"Like I said, I wish it was a joke. Now, my source has disappeared off the face of the earth, and he doesn't smell as sweet as he used to either."

"He stinks, actually." Candace drained her beer and looked out the window with Boot. "I wouldn't want to be in your shoes when you tell Art."

Boot let the discussion go at that. He still hadn't decided if he would tell Art. He clung to the thin hope of finding LeBlay first. If this summer brought miracles to Trenton, maybe he'd bag one of his own.

CHAPTER 22
Texas Cadillac

Boot watched Candace mull around the kitchen. She'd showered, dressed, and rooted through the refrigerator by 7:00 A.M. She spread things around the trailer like she owned the place. A leftover container of fried rice, a jar of peanut butter, and a sleeve of marble rye lay open on the counter.

Candace propped her makeup mirror on the window ledge above the kitchen sink. She brushed her short brown hair, taking breaks to sip orange juice directly from the carton. She leaned toward the mirror, wetting her finger to tame the spikes in her eyebrows.

When someone knocked at the front door, she glanced at Boot. "Want me to get that?"

Boot nudged beside her and peered through the window. Two Cadillacs with rental tags were parked behind Candace's Honda. The man in the white Caddy studied the trailer from the front seat, but the burgundy car appeared empty.

"Who do you think it is?" Boot asked.

"You're asking me?"

He pressed his face near the glass. A heavyset man with rounded shoulders and a receding hairline shuffled on the stoop. He gently wrapped on the front door. If he was OFJ, he'd bust it down with a sledgehammer.

"Do me a favor," Boot asked. "Answer it?"

Candace swiped the juice carton from the counter and cracked opened the door.

"Hello," the visitor said.

"Hello." Candace repeated his deep cadence.

"Does a Mr. Booth Means live here?"

She looked at Boot. "Does a Mr. Booth Means live here?"

"I don't know," Boot whispered.

"Identify yourself," Candace said, taking a swig of juice.

"Mr. Charles Goodner," the stranger said. "I've been trying to reach Boot Means."

"I remember your voice from the phone."

"Can I have a word with him?"

Candace faced Boot again. "Did you get all that? It's that guy who keeps calling. He doesn't look like trouble."

"Alright," Boot said. "Let him in."

Charles Goodner clapped his heels inside the trailer. He wore a pigskin vest and a large belt buckle with silver and turquoise inlays. He put his hands behind his back and scanned Boot up and down, as if inspecting a horse for auction. A funny look came over his face. "I'll be damned, if you don't strike a man down in person."

Boot was unimpressed by the enthusiasm, but maybe, this cowboy knew something about LeBlay.

"Sir," Boot said, "have we met before?"

"Not in a long time."

"What's that supposed to mean?"

"This is going to sound strange, but I don't know how to put it gently."

"Put it any way you'd like."

"I'm just going to come right out with it. I think I'm your father."

The air rushed from Boot's lungs, as if Goodner had slammed a fist into his chest. "What did you say?"

"I'm your father."

Candace thunked the orange juice on the counter. "This is too funky, even for me."

"Sorry miss," Charles said. "We haven't been properly introduced."

"I'm Candace. I work with Boot."

"Pleased to make your acquaintance."

"I was just leaving." She dragged her purse off the counter and paced toward Boot. Her lips scrunched like a caterpillar edging across a tree limb. She hooked a finger through his belt loop and whispered in his ear. "He doesn't look like the Acme type."

"What?" Boot mumbled.

"I bet that's a ten thousand dollar wedding band on his finger."

He wondered why she was telling him this.

"Real emeralds and sapphires," she said.

Boot noticed the purse in her hand. He clutched her wrist. "Are you leaving now?"

"Why?"

"I need a favor." He despised asking her, especially in front of Goodner. "I'm a little tight this week. I need cash."

Her eyebrows arched. "How much?"

"What do you have?" His bank account was about as liquid as his credit cards. He couldn't squeeze another dime from them, not legally.

She dug into her purse. "How about forty?"

"Great."

She handed him two twenty dollar bills and left the trailer.

Boot gazed through the kitchen window, watching her sprint to her car. The rain started again, and she covered her head with her beaded purse.

"She's cute." Charles glanced through the screen door. "Girlfriend of yours?"

"Mind closing that for me?"

"I'll get it." Charles pressed the thin door against the jam, until it clicked shut. The noise of the storm quieted.

"I have to say your claim is outrageous."

"Let me explain." The skin on Charles' face appeared leathery from years of sun exposure, and when he smiled, tan wrinkles gathered at the corners of his eyes. "I saw you on the Dove Hour, and I knew. I got the vibe."

"That show?" Boot cringed. He couldn't possibly be the son of a man who watched that crap.

"I know this is sudden. That's why I asked your brother to wait in the car."

"My brother?"

"I didn't want the whole Goodner clan descending on you at once."

Boot glanced out the window. "That man is my brother?"

"Your half-brother, to be exact."

"Half-brother. Your story just gets better and better."

"You have another in Texas. He's hauled up with a broken leg and didn't make the trip. You don't have any full brothers and sisters, if that's your question."

"I wasn't asking a question."

"You must have some."

"Alright then, what's your evidence? Got something better than a hunch?"

"A vibe."

"Whatever. Sounds the same to me."

Charles reached for Boot's arm but appeared to second-guess himself. He put his hands behind his back again. "I'm your father. Lord, just looking at you, I can tell."

"This is a joke, right?"

"I wouldn't joke about this. I've been trying to find you for twenty years."

Boot tried to imagine the person who wanted to test him so cruelly. *This guy's crazy.* "I'd like you to leave."

"I expected you'd say that." Charles paced across the linoleum floor. He stepped halfway to the door and turned around. "Could I just have a minute? I know this is hard."

Boot sized up the stranger who filled his narrow trailer. No, Charles Goodner wasn't a hoax; he was confused. Boot took pity on him. He wanted to hear Goodner's explanation, get a glimpse into why this was happening. "I can give you a few minutes. I've got a busy day ahead of me."

"I don't want to burden you."

"I appreciate that." Boot poured himself a mug of coffee.

"We can take it at your pace."

"Take what?"

"Our introduction."

"You seem very confident that you're right."

"I have good reason to be hopeful."

Boot found it difficult not to look Goodner over. He noticed his full nose and the comfortable bulge of flesh beneath his chin. To photograph him, he'd have to light him from two directions, fill the creases from the side and below. "Are you always like this?"

"Like what?"

"This upbeat."

"I try to be. What did you expect your father to be like?"

"I never thought of it," Boot shot back, although nothing was further from the truth. He'd spent many restless nights, conjuring the notion of his father. He imagined a handsome drifter, a good for nothing louse, even a one-night stand. In each scenario, Boot was an unfortunate mistake, to be returned to the department store like an ill-fitting sweater. Goodner did not fit his imagination.

Boot jiggled the coffee pot. "You want some?"

"That would be mighty polite of you."

"Black is the best I can do."

"Perfect."

Boot filled a mug for Charles, and the men squeezed into the breakfast nook. A heavy rain streaked over the louvered windows, as if a garden hose sprayed the side of his ApacheStar. It rattled the aluminum veneer for a minute and settled down.

Charles palmed his coffee mug. "Your mother and I were young when you were born, younger than you are today." He spoke in bursts, between large gulps of coffee. "I had an addiction. It's not the sort of habit I'm proud of. I gambled away every dollar I had. Lord, I loved the dice."

Boot listened closely, asking Goodner to repeat the facts, waiting for the first flaw in his story, but Goodner's words were precise and candid. They sent a shiver up Boot's spine. It was a true story at least.

"Eventually your mother got sick and tired," Charles said. "She left, and I was too soul sick to follow. You were six months old."

"You just let her walk?"

"I expected Dana to stroll through the door in the morning. Dana, that's your mothers name. It wasn't the first time she'd stormed off for the night."

"But she left for good."

"I should've stayed home, helped raise you, but I was out chasing the vibe. I'm done with that now. I don't gamble anymore. Haven't touched the dice in years."

Boot felt cold inside. There were millions of discarded children in the world. He held an obligation to them. He refused to let Goodner off the hook. "What did you think happened to your son?"

"I believed Dana was hiding you."

"How did you think your son lived from day to day?"

"I tried not to think about that part."

"What was going through your mind?"

"I concentrated on finding you instead. Dana was really mad. She wanted to spite me, and that kept me going. I was in a battle with her."

"Who won?"

"Isn't it obvious? You were missing for most of my life. I thought she took you back to your grandmother's in New York. I thought her mother was in cahoots."

"Did you bother to look there?"

"It's an Indian reservation. Dana was half-blooded. Indians can swallow a secret so deep, even they forget it."

"Did you look?"

"For years I hounded Dana's family. I made a real nuisance of myself. I expected to find you with them, but only recently, I learned important details."

"Which was ... ?"

"Dana dumped you in a department store and left you for the first taker."

Boot's mouth went dry, yet he buckled down his emotions. No, this man couldn't possibly be his father. Of all the crazy things, this couldn't be happening. "How do you know that?"

"I hired a detective to check you out. I know a man who searches public records and whatnot."

"Great," Boot said. Goodner was tailing him too.

"I hope you don't mind. When I saw you, I had to know."

Boot looked away. The rain streaked wavy patterns on the window. He saw the Trenton Makes Bridge in the distance. The rough current slapped the bridge pylons.

"You're a dead ringer for your Uncle Teddy," Charles said. "Let me show you."

Charles removed two photos from his vest pocket and slid one forward. "I'm not yanking your leg. This is Teddy."

Boot glanced at a man in an army uniform, trying not to focus anywhere in particular.

"He died in Vietnam." Charles presented another photo, placing the pair side by side. "This is your mother."

Boot refused to look. "You're wasting your time."

"Just look at them."

Boot prepared to reject the photos, like the balance of Goodner's assumptions, but when he glanced down, the resemblance became immediately clear. It stabbed him like a large splinter piercing the skin, waking him from a lifelong trance. He possessed a similar facial structure to the soldier. He once believed this look was uniquely his own—an assembly of odd parts, like a sketch artist composite in the paper—but here was a blatant contradiction.

"You have Dana's eyes," Charles said. "It's the Indian blood, Mohawk."

He studied the woman. She stood in a pleated skirt and heels, wrapping her arm around a street sign. She appeared carefree and beautiful. Her skin seemed to echo the light of the sun. It looked more honest than half the news photos he'd shot, and he shuddered.

"OK," Boot mumbled. "I've seen enough."

Boot stood up. He was dazed. Goodner's story began to make sense. It felt like an elaborate mind game designed to break him down. "You've got to go."

Charles rose to his feet as well. "Let me add one more thing."

"I'm not sure I want to hear it."

"When I heard your name on TV, that was the clincher. Means was your grandmother's name, Clara Means. You somehow got that name. I just haven't figured that part out yet."

"You can't figure out everything."

"It was in your files, but if Dana just abandoned you, how did you get her maiden name? I suppose that question will remain unanswered."

Boot's temper flared, a seed of rage he'd buried forever. He began tapping his foot on the floor.

"What's the matter?" Charles asked.

Boot didn't reply.

"You're upset."

"I'm alright."

Charles stared for a moment, then tugged down on his vest. "I better let you get back to work."

"That's a good idea."

"I'll leave my card." Charles buttoned his lip and left. Twice, he stopped on the walk but proceeded onward. Boot watched him get into the burgundy Caddy and drive off.

Boot reached into the kitchen cabinet and removed a tattered shoebox from the back of the top shelf. Inside was an old crib blanket made of thick blue and white yarn. A string of pine trees was woven into the material. It was a Mohawk design. Boot knew this. He'd looked it up. The name 'B. Means' was scribbled along the hem. He was found in this blanket as an abandoned infant.

The old material bunched in his fists. So many times he'd imagined his mother penning those letters. Now it was all but verified.

He cleared the kitchen table and started scrubbing the coffee mugs in the sink. His thoughts scattered in several directions at once, and his blood pulsed like a violent machine. He had a family: father, brothers. What a mess. He despised Goodner for no other reason than showing up at his front door.

The water splashed loudly in the steel sink, as the handle of one of the mugs broke off in his hands. He replayed snippets of the conversation. He'd barely kept his emotions in check. He regretted this the most. It ran against several of Pulvermann's rules.

He smashed the broken coffee mug in the trash, pleased by the sound of breaking glass. This was what life did to you. It threw punches when you least expected them. Damn it! He needed to stay on guard, keep his hands up, never let the jabs reach him again.

CHAPTER 23
My Brother the Cowboy

Boot left his trailer to hunt down LeBlay. He felt mad enough to spit. He needed to find the skinny punk, anyway possible. He better put that business with Goodner out of his mind.

A car door slammed shut. The sound rose above the relentless pattering of rain. Boot raised his eyes from the ground, seeing a tall and lanky man coming from the white Caddy by the curb. The man paced up the walk, his gangly arms cutting by his sides. He had sandy blond hair, parted down the middle, and a patchy beard like scuffed leather. He looked at the sky and tossed a brushed suede cowboy hat atop his head.

The man met Boot halfway up the walk. "Morning."

Boot snapped open his umbrella. "Who are you?"

"Pop didn't tell you? I'm Jake."

"Jake who?"

"Jake Goodner."

Boot recalled the second Caddy and who was supposed to be inside. He scanned his half-brother's face. Jake had rugged features and close set eyes. He looked nothing like his father.

"According to Pop," Jake said. "We're related."

Boot ignored him and headed into the street. He huddled beneath his umbrella, listening to the rain tap the taut nylon canopy. He reached the trailer park entrance, hearing Jake's footsteps close behind.

"Your father left already," Boot said.

"I saw him go."

"Can I help you with something?"

"No."

"Then see you later." Boot walked a little farther, but Jake followed.

Boot stopped again. "Are you sure you don't want something?"

"Yes."

"Why are you following me?"

"Have to."

"Why?"

"Pop asked." Jake buttoned up his windbreaker. The navy blue jacket had a fancy gold patch above the left breast. On the opposite side, GOODNER HAULING was printed in gold block letters.

Boot noticed Jake's intense expression. It reminded him of Detective Drake, shameless, devoid of emotion. "Why does your father want me followed?"

"He's worried about the Open something or other."

"You mean the Open Faith for Jesus?"

"Supposed to be a bad bunch."

"He knows about them?"

"He sent a guy ahead to check you out."

"He told me about the detective." Boot immediately thought of the man outside the *Record* building who copied down his Pinto's plate number.

"He wants me with you."

"Do you know what they look like?"

"Short haircuts and tattoos."

"How do you plan on protecting me?"

"Take it as it comes."

"Are you carrying a gun or something?"

"No."

"Do you like following people in the rain?"

"No."

"You just do it because your father asks?"

The rain dripped off the brim of Jake's hat. He folded his long arms, as if nothing else in the world mattered but standing near Boot. "I don't want to be here any more than you want me to, but Pop asked."

"Terrific," Boot said, as cheery as the weather.

"Take it light. He'll get tired of you in a few days and head home, and I'll be going with him."

"Then this has happened before?"

"No."

Boot watched the rain soak the shoulders of Jake's windbreaker. The gold letters began to pucker. "Did you bring an umbrella with you?"

"We can use my car if you want?"

"I don't think so."

"Look, I'm going to be on your ass anyways. We can stay high and dry in the car. You don't look to be flush with transportation."

"You're right about that. I totaled my Pinto last week."

"There you go. Let's get in my car. I'll take you wherever you want. I promise, no funny stuff."

Boot glanced at his camera bag, realizing the struggle ahead to keep his equipment dry. "No funny stuff?"

"I'm bored stiff. It'll be fun to see a reporter in action, if that's what you're up to."

"That's what I'm up to. Promise you won't discuss my business with anyone?"

"Promise. Let's get the heck out of the rain."

They walked back to the Caddy in silence and sat inside. Boot stamped his shoes on the mat, and Jake threw his hat in the back seat. Their breath fogged the big front windshield.

Jake turned over the ignition and glanced at Boot from the corner of his eye. "So this Open Faith or whatnot wants to mess you up."

"They already have."

"Is that what happened to your head?"

"I wasn't kidding about the gun. I wish you were carrying one."

"We won't need it."

"I thought every cowboy packed a sidearm."

"I must have left it home in my stagecoach." Jake threw the transmission into drive. The tires tossed up the wet gravel in the road. "Besides, you're the one with the flippin' cowboy name anyways."

Boot and Jake drove to the OFJ headquarters in north Trenton. Two crewcut goons stood outside the church, blocking the heavy front doors. Boot tried to guess who might be defectors. Who wanted him dead? He stood several feet back, plotting an escape route.

"Could you deliver a note to Paul Andujar?" Boot asked, digging through his camera bag for a pencil and paper, keeping an eye on the men.

The crewcuts held their tongues, refusing to budge. Two more crewcuts crept out of the shadows and joined them. The motley quartet filled the steps, staring down Boot and Jake.

Boot saw Jake looking them over. Jake dug his hands in his pockets and chewed on a toothpick. He appeared fascinated, like a boy viewing exotic animals at the zoo.

"Is this a typical meeting with them?" Jake asked.

"More or less."

The standoff repeated itself at Camp Jesus. Boot watched the crewcuts surround their purple bus in a human chain. They held hands, reciting psalms in a low monastic tone. It reminded Boot of a protest he witnessed as a kid, outside a nuclear power plant on Long Island, except this assembly blended into the general weirdness on Jefferson Avenue. At least they weren't chucking bricks at his head.

Jake spit his toothpick onto the curb. "They don't want to talk to you, do they?"

"Doesn't look like it." Boot grabbed his camera and photographed them.

"I guess they're posed up for you."

"I guess." Boot began to loathe Jake's simplistic narration of events. Was he trying to goad him? "Do you mind?"

"Do I mind what?"

"Could you hold your comments?"

"I figured you were tired of the silent treatment."

They walked to the corner of Jefferson Avenue, where a crewcut distributed purple leaflets to the people entering the street.

Boot scanned the area. The crewcuts' lack of aggression unsettled him. The defectors among them had either split town or were laying in ambush. Either scenario didn't do him a lot of good.

"Let's go talk to him," Jake said. "He's alone."

"Forget about it. It'll be more of the same."

Jake tugged Boot's arm. "Let me give it a try."

The crewcut had a scar that split his right eyebrow in two.

Jake walked up to him and accepted a leaflet, giving it a cursory look. "I'm looking for one of your own."

The crewcut glanced at Boot. "I know who you are. I'm not supposed to talk with you."

"Then talk to me," Jake said.

"I shouldn't, if you're with him."

"I'm not with him, that is, if he had anything to say about it."

"I saw you walking with him."

"I don't know why you don't like him, and I don't care."

"He shamed and slandered our group." The crewcut offered his back, dispensing leaflets in a new direction.

Jake leapt in front of the crewcut. He swarmed like a boxer, crouching down, getting in his opponent's face. "Want to make us go away?"

"Please."

"Where is ..." Jake glanced over the crewcut's shoulder to look at Boot.

"Travis LeBlay." Boot spoke at a distance, taking in the scene. Jake was wasting his time.

"Travis LeBlay," Jake repeated.

"I'm not talking to you." The crewcut turned away but saw Boot and turned back.

Jake pulled a roll of cash from his pocket and peeled off a twenty dollar bill. "Give us a clue where to find this LeBlay fellow, and we'll become as scarce as the hair on your head."

The crewcut snatched the cash from Jake's hand. "He's been ousted from the group."

"Where is he?"

"He stays in Chambersburg," Boot said. "Talito's cousin has a place."

"Not there," the crewcut said. "Travis hangs out at the Stony Hill Inn in Kingston."

Jake looked to Boot again. "Know where that is?"

Boot was disgusted, but he had to take the chance. "I do."

The Stony Hill Inn was a restored colonial roadhouse in the bucolic outskirts of Kingston. Boot and Jake entered the noisy taproom at lunchtime. The place held the musty smell of old wood and mortar. Boot scanned the room. A handful of white collar workers scattered about the tables with glasses of flavored spring water and copies of the *Wall Street Journal* and *New York Times*.

Jake tossed his hat on the rack near the door.

"You going to leave that there?" Boot asked.

"Sure."

"Aren't you worried someone might steal it?"

"No one's going to touch my hat."

They found a table near the windows and picked up the menus from the table. Jake tilted his chair and propped his back against the wall, pulling out a fresh toothpick to chew. Boot watched the street, as well as the steps leading up to the rooms.

Jake signaled the waitress and glanced at Boot. "You want a beer?"

"I guess so."

Jake called across the room. "Two beers please, ma'am. Whatever's on tap."

In a minute, the waitress approached with the drinks. Jake leaned forward in his chair and grinned. "Get a look at this lady. She looks like one of those Open Faithers."

Boot peered over his shoulder, seeing her stutter step halfway across the room. He recognized Kat's dragon tail tattoo. It poked above her crisp white collar.

Kat wasn't as friendly as when they first met behind the purple OFJ bus at Camp Jesus. She grimaced and lifted a glass from the tray. "Bastard!"

Boot put up his hands. "Hold on."

When she flung the drink, Boot ducked. The glass sailed past his head and crashed into the wall.

"Darn." Jake hunched in his chair. "Don't you have any friends in this part of the world?"

Boot jumped to his feet and grabbed Kat's shoulders before she fired again. The tray fell from her hands, and the remaining glass shattered on the floor.

"Get off me!" She thrust her knee toward his groin, but Boot threw his hip, and she missed.

"Slow down," Boot said.

She stamped her foot into his ankle.

"Ouch!" Boot hopped back, seeing Jake lock his long arms around her waist.

Jake lifted her off her feet and threw her over his shoulder, clamping her in place with one arm. Her body draped over him. She kicked and screamed, like a woman rolled up in a carpet.

Lunch in the Stony Hill Inn ground to a halt. Businessmen froze in their seats. Some gripped forks in midair, jaws wide open. Boot shut his mouth and watched.

Jake walked across the room, calmly nodding to the man behind the counter. "We're going to settle this outside."

The bartender stared, kneading his lips.

"She'll be fine," Jake said.

A man in a gray suit stood up and began to speak, but Jake glared at him in a way that made him sit down and swallow his words.

"Jake!" Boot called.

Jake grabbed his hat and popped it on his head, leaving the dark taproom in a wash of sunlight and befuddled expressions.

By the time Boot followed them outside, Kat stood beside Jake on the sidewalk. Red blotches covered the skin on her cheeks. A fat blue vein throbbed on her neck. She sobbed into a white linen napkin.

"She's promised to contain her emotions," Jake said, reaching into his pocket for a fresh toothpick.

Boot descended the steps to the Stony Hill Inn. "Kat, I'm not looking for you."

"Well, you found me."

"I didn't know you were a waitress here."

"What did you expect me to do after you trashed the defectors?"

"I didn't trash the defectors."

"Don't act so innocent. This is your fault. Paul kicked us out of the OFJ, and Si's back in jail."

"I didn't intend for that to happen."

"And when his cousin caught wind, he asked us to leave his house. If it wasn't for Travis getting me this job, I'd be out on the street without a dime."

"Where's Travis?"

"You think I'm going to tell you, after everything you've done?"

Boot approached her, half-expecting her to throw another knee.

"You shouldn't be mad at me."

"It's all your fault."

"Travis ratted you out."

"Yeah, right. Like I'm going to believe that. I'd like to meet the creep who tipped you off."

"Travis did. He told me what you were up to. It was him."

Her eyes widened. The dragon tail pulsed on her neck. "How'd you trick him into talking?"

"There wasn't any trick."

"You're trying to trick me. I've seen you lie. You're good at it."

"It's the truth. Travis approached me first. I never heard of the OFJ before Travis arrived."

"Why would he do that? He had the most to lose."

Boot wanted to shake her. She was as stupid as he had been. "He was running the defectors, wasn't he?"

Kat didn't answer, but the look on her face said everything.

Boot felt sick inside. He'd carried the truth like a secret, never having to face the consequences. "You're part of a terrible joke to make the OFJ look bad. If I were you, I'd run. I'd run as far away from this place as I could."

"Why would Travis do that? Why would he tell on us?"

"He worked for Melanie Dove."

"You're lying."

"I wish I was."

"Don't say that."

"He knows her. He belonged to the Dove Network. Don't you see? He worked for her the whole time. That was the plan."

She shook her head. "You don't know that."

"How do you think I knew about the rail yards and where the guns were headed?"

"I don't know."

"Travis told me, and we're both in trouble because of it."

Jake's lips puckered around the toothpick. "Sounds like a mess."

Boot looked at Kat. "I have to find Travis."

"You won't find him," Kat said.

"Why not?"

"He's gone."

"Where is he?"

"He should be here. He should've bailed Si out of jail already."

"What happened?"

"I don't know. No one's been able to find Travis. Si says all the bank accounts are empty too. I know. I tried to cash a check."

"I'll give you one guess who's got the money."

"Travis," Kat said in a squeaky voice. "I didn't want to believe it, even when Si said it."

"Where does Travis stay?"

"I told you. Here. But he's gone. He left Sunday night and hasn't returned."

CHAPTER 24
Self-Portrait

The big Caddy cruised down Brunswick Avenue. Boot leaned back on the soft leather headrest, planning a countermove against Dove. He thought of following her to Seattle. He wanted to get the dirt on her and smoke out LeBlay in the process. He considered asking Stacy for an airplane ticket, but even with the money to travel, the grand jury summons required him to remain in town. That was his first hurdle. The cops seemed hell-bent on making him cough up LeBlay. Boot tried not to sigh out loud. If he owned just a little more time and money, he'd fix this mess by himself and give everyone what they wanted.

The Caddy merged onto route 29 south. Boot studied Jake from the corner of his eye. The gold emblem on Jake's windbreaker reflected the amber light at dusk.

Boot pointed at the emblem. "What's that?"

"It's the company logo. It's a gas tanker."

"What's it say underneath?"

"Thelonious." Jake shot a glance at Boot, then returned to the road. "Yes, it was a surprise to all of us."

"Why was it a surprise?"

"Pop always said it was an old friend's name. I thought it was somebody he knew way back. He's got it stenciled on every truck bumper."

"Every truck?"

"Yes."

"How many?"

Jake eyed him again. "Couple hundred, give or take."

"So why was Thelonious a surprise?"

"He never told us until a few days ago."

"What didn't he tell you?"

"Heck!" Jake smacked the turn signal and changed lanes. "Figures Pop forgot to tell you. Now I've got to. Thelonious is supposed to be your name."

"My name?"

"Your given name ... if you're who you say you are."

Boot didn't speak. Now, he had a different name. This whole business made him dizzy.

"Yes," Jake said. "Thelonious Goodner. That's your name."

"You can keep calling me Boot, if you don't mind."

"I'd prefer it."

"I never claimed to be your brother. That was your father's doing."

"He's made up his mind about you."

"He certainly has."

"Take his word on it. He's never wrong when he gets the vibe."

"This could be the first time." Boot spoke without conviction. He felt saddled with a family that he never requested.

"You could take a blood test. Who knows? Maybe you aren't his son."

"You'd like that."

"It wouldn't hurt my feelings either way."

"I have bigger problems at the moment."

"I noticed. Got yourself duped by that Travis LeBlay character."

"I wouldn't say duped."

"What else would you call it?" Jake laughed but had the decency to face the road. "If a guy did that to me, I'd whip him. I'd whip him until he wished he never laid eyes on me."

"That's your solution for everything."

Jake fisted the steering wheel. He held a predatory gaze in his eyes. "I just helped you out back there. You could be more appreciative."

"I didn't ask for your help."

"You'd never have found that girl in Kingston without me."

"That wad of cash helped." Boot disliked Jake's arrogance and refused to entertain any further conversation. He sat quietly in the front seat, watching a view of the swollen Delaware River zip between the trees.

When the Caddy pulled up to the trailer, Boot jumped out without saying good-bye and walked inside. He dropped his camera bag on the table, eyeing Jake parked by the curb. His bodyguard wasn't leaving anytime soon.

Boot pressed the play button on his answering machine. Noel Van Dycke left a pair of urgent messages. *Focus Trend* wanted to push forward the story deadline for Christmas, and Van Dycke asked why Boot hadn't phoned yet.

For a second, Boot stood with his hand on the answering machine. Did he want to speak with Van Dycke today? No. He needed to be more certain, perhaps after the grand jury hearing tomorrow. He felt the squeeze, the possibility of deadlines he'd never meet. Could he pull the *Focus Trend* piece together in time?

He opened a beer and walked up to his bedroom. He'd been in jams before but never with as much at stake. He refused to believe in luck, yet the last few days formed an incredible bad streak. He worried about a larger force conspiring to drag him down.

The narrow bedroom at the top of the stairs was pitch black with the shades drawn. Boot flicked on the light, seeing Candace's nude Polaroids neatly arranged on the pillow. He wondered why she'd done this.

Then Boot saw that the bed was made. He glanced the length of the trailer, noticing the cups in the dish rack and the glistening clean countertops. A dreadful feeling swept over him, as a disturbing image of Stacy rose in his mind. She was methodically scrubbing the bathroom and sweeping the floors, working her way toward the bombshell in the bedroom.

Candace's earrings laid atop the creaseless blanket. Boot scanned the crude snapshots, discovering a new entry among the candid Polaroids. Stacy held her middle finger up to the camera. Her mouth twisted like a sick and dying animal. Her hair flew away from her head like the flames off a bonfire.

Boot picked up the phone and frantically dialed her number. It rang a half dozen times before she answered.

"Hello." Stacy's voice sounded hoarse and wet.

"Stacy?"

"Did you find my picture?"

Boot wasn't going to touch that one. He waited for her to rail into him.

"I would've left the ring," she said, "but I paid for it."

"Stace."

"Don't Stace me." She slammed down the receiver. It felt like an ax landing on his neck.

That night, Boot stared at the ceiling, listening to the police car pass his trailer every half hour. The river roared downstream toward Philadelphia, and the ApacheStar creaked in the wind. He drifted in and out of sleep.

In his dreams, someone moved in the kitchen. Boot discovered Eric Pulvermann rummaging through his cabinets. Eric wore his camera vest with the martini glass penciled on the shoulder. He hopped around the kitchen on one leg, a bloody bandage wrapped around his foot. Boot knew that Eric's foot was recently shredded by a land mine in Gaza. It looked just like the picture on his refrigerator.

"Boot," Eric called, dripping blood on the floor. He exhibited no pain. "Make me a drink like I taught you."

Boot found everything he needed below the sink: martini glasses, gin, vermouth, even though they hadn't been there before. He shook and poured a single cocktail for Eric and garnished it with an olive.

Eric put the fluted glass to his lips. "Not bad. Next time, use less vermouth."

"Sorry, I tried to ..."

"You didn't remember what I told you."

"I did. Very little vermouth." Boot stared at the blood seeping though the bandage.

"No, you forgot Pulvermann's 4th Law: be sure of your sources, and when you're not, be damn sure."

"I was going to make LeBlay right."

"Boot." Eric laughed. He pivoted on his good leg, smearing blood on the cabinets. "Look who you're talking to. I, of all people, know what you did."

"I can fix it."

"You better. You're going to embarrass us all."

"I swear I'll fix it."

"I bet my right foot you're gonna screw it up," Eric said, laughing. He looked down. "Oops."

When Boot turned around, Paul Andujar sat in the breakfast nook with Emily Phibbs. Andujar wore a white tunic. His stubby fingers cupped Mrs. Phibbs hands. She was crying.

Boot recalled her dozens of cats, stifling the urge to sneeze. "What's going on?"

Andujar turned his bulbous face, looking at Boot with the utmost disdain. "Her husband's dead. Haven't you been paying attention?"

"I saw it in the obituaries. Heart attack, right?"

"You knew, and you didn't even make a condolence call."

"I meant to."

"Save it, Means. If it wasn't for her, you'd have nothing."

"It must have slipped my mind."

"I'm not surprised."

"I meant to send a card."

"It wasn't important enough, was it? We're only good for five minutes with you, a smattering of ink in the paper, and that's it."

Stacy tousled her hair in the background. Boot didn't have to look. The unsettling noise seized his attention. He turned and saw her standing by the counter. She flipped up her silky locks with the back of her hand, her neck rubbed raw from the motion.

"Stacy," he said.

She swiped the martini glass from the counter. It was filled with Eric's blood. "Entertaining again?"

"Eric Pulvermann was here."

"Cut the crap. I'm tired of the crap."

Boot heard noise coming from the bedroom and tried to ignore it. He already knew who it was.

Stacy glanced at the stairs. "What's that?"

"Nothing."

She sipped her drink. "You know, Boot, what am I going to do with twenty-four dozen wedding favors? Little tiffany bells."

"I'll return them."

"Our names are etched on the side. They won't take them back."

"I'll pay for them."

"With what? A rubber check?"

"I'll find a way." The noise in the bedroom grew louder, leading his thoughts. He heard giggling and the rustling of limbs upon his mattress.

Stacy dangled the martini glass in the air, blood dripping from the corner of her mouth. "Who is she?"

"Nobody."

"Cut the crap, Boot. Who is she?"

"It's no one."

"Go to her. I'm tired of your lies. Just go."

Boot rushed upstairs. Candace sprawled on the sheets, naked, bent over on all fours. He felt a disturbing combination of shame and desire.

Candace blew a kiss over her shoulder. "Was I interrupting?"

When Boot awoke, his heart beat as fast as a newborn puppy's. He rushed to the kitchen, expecting to see people milling about his trailer, but the place stood quiet, except for the sound of his blood rushing in his ears.

Through the window, he saw Jake's Caddy, and he became annoyed all over again.

He slapped on his shoes and stomped out front. The Caddy floated by the roadside like a big white whale. He banged on the driver's side door with his fist.

Jake stirred in the seat and rolled down the power window.

"Go home!" Boot shouted.

Jake appeared half awake. He coughed into his hand.

"Leave me alone. Go home!"

Jake squinted like a cheetah studying prey from the tall grass.

Boot thumped the Caddy's door again, then marched back inside.

The wind and rain kicked up a notch. Boot dropped into the breakfast nook, steaming mad. The thin screen door flapped in the wind. He thumped his fists on the table. He was an entity of one. That's how he saw himself. He was impenetrable, in any situation, no matter what foster home, no matter who called himself the boss. He was an entity of one. People were trying to steal a piece of him, without any rightful claim. He'd thwart their advances, now that he understood their worst effects. They were like ghosts in his head, like barking dogs down the street. He refused to let them grab at him. He was a rock, a true island amid a sea of needy people. He was an entity of one.

CHAPTER 25
What You Believe Will Be Held Against You

Outside the courthouse, Boot noticed several reporters hawking the front steps. The OFJ story had captured people's fancy, and the locals were running with it. He cautioned near the building, spotting a silver truck from Newark TV News. He lowered his head. Damn, he never mentioned his subpoena to Art. His boss was going to learn about it on TV like everyone else.

Boot eyed a straight path to the massive courthouse doors. He regretted sneaking out of the trailer park on foot. For once, he wished Jake was riding shotgun.

A man in a gray double-breasted suit pursued Boot up the stone steps. He was prettier than any of the print journalists, sporting a cleft chin and a smile like the polished keys of a piano. He leapt up two steps at a time, throwing a shoulder in Boot's path. "Mr. Means, Dan Davis from 'Newark All Day'."

Boot attempted to turn away, but Davis lunged forward. His microphone nearly smacked Boot in the lips.

"What do you plan to tell the grand jury?" Davis balanced on one foot, stretching his microphone arm to its farthest extent.

Boot paused, fixing his tie in front of the camera. "It depends on their questions." High intensity lights blared in his eyes, and a handful of journalists enveloped him, throwing elbows and snapping pictures. They smiled like a team of dentists intent on applying their drills.

Davis moved closer. "Will you reveal the people involved in the OFJ smuggling case?"

"I don't know if I can answer that." Boot mounted another step.

"Is Paul Andujar the ringleader?"

"I think I'm not supposed to discuss it." Boot swatted the microphone aside and rushed into the court house.

For twenty minutes, Boot sat on a hard wooden bench outside courtroom 3B, waiting to be called inside. The notion of a grand jury troubled him, and lingering in the hall, hearing the occasional bass tone muffle above the silence, he started to worry about his future. The delay seemed like an endless expanse of time.

When the doors finally swung open, Kat entered the corridor. Her eyes were moist, and black mascara nestled in the folds. Boot watched her turn past him and disappear down the hallway.

"Mr. Means?" The bailiff was a heavyset black woman with purple moles dotting her cheeks. She curled a finger, signaling him forward.

Boot followed her across the dark-paneled courtroom and up to the stand. Twenty-three jurors waited behind a thick oak rail. They looked pensive and relaxed, not tense like him. He felt the weight of their eyes upon him.

The bailiff rested a Bible in front of Boot, and he pressed his palm on the creased leather, swearing an oath with God. The ritual seemed as pointless as any other, although Boot got the point. He must now tell the truth. The trick was avoiding it altogether.

Judge Younghand presided. "Good Morning, Mr. Means."

"Hello, sir."

Younghand acknowledged the cordiality with a quick drop of his chin. "This is a closed inquiry for indictment. We are primarily concerned with the unlawful transfer of firearms, as well as any conspiratorial or unlawful acts by the Open Faith for Jesus. Are we clear?"

"Yes." Boot's neck felt sweaty beneath his collar, and he loosened it with two fingers.

"Let's begin."

A platoon of attorney's from the DA's office were entrenched around a simple walnut table. A woman in a navy blue pantsuit rose from the pack, flipping through the pages of a yellow legal pad. She dropped the pad on the table and approached the stand.

"Good Morning. I'm Melissa Black." Her hair was dyed sunset red, almost orange. She wore clunky costume jewelry in silver and gold. Around her neck, she had a white silk scarf, pinned by a pewter rooster with red stones for eyes. "Good to see you today."

Boot shrugged. He wasn't pleased to see her or anyone else in the room. He wanted to get through this proceeding as fast as possible.

Black tucked a pen behind her ear. It complimented her lousy sense of fashion. "You're a reporter for the *Trenton Record*."

"Right."

"And you reported on the Open Faith for Jesus, the OFJ, and their various activities."

"Right."

"Were you the only reporter?"

"Yes."

"Care to elaborate?"

"It's my exclusive story. I developed it."

"You discovered the OFJ by yourself?"

"I did."

"You have firsthand knowledge of gun smuggling in the Trenton rail yard?"

"Right."

"That's extraordinary."

"I didn't think so at the time."

"Tell us more, please."

"I wasn't sure what I was going to view."

"But you knew enough to investigate it."

Boot saw where this was leading. The very thing she wanted was the one thing he needed to conceal. "I had sufficient suspicion."

"Sufficient suspicion?" Black smirked.

"I thought I should be at the rail yard at that time."

"Do you know how extraordinary that sounds?"

Boot offered her no help. "Sometimes."

"Do you go to the rail yard often?"

"Once in a while."

"And you just happened to be there that night?"

"I had information."

"Someone told you."

"In a manner of speaking." Boot envisioned the lines of communication between Detective Drake and the DA's office. He looked into the empty visitor's gallery, half-expecting to find the burly detective viewing the show.

Black paced in front of the stand. "It's not uncommon for reporters to have informers."

"No."

"You had one in this case."

"I had tips." Boot sensed his vocabulary whittled down to a few words.

"Did you seek entry into the OFJ?"

"I was drawn in."

"Drawn in?"

"I was approached."

"But you're not a member?"

"No."

"And you didn't think of joining?"

"No."

"So someone within the organization approached you?"

"My source prefers to remain confidential."

Black plucked the pen from her ear and twirled it in her fingers like a baton. She looked at Boot, then stuck the pen back in her ear.

She turned to Younghand. "I think I'd like to release the floor to the jury for questioning."

"Are you finished with the witness?" Younghand asked.

"No."

"Proceed."

Black called the first juror, choosing among those with their hands raised.

An elderly man in a tweed jacket leaned forward. He piled his gray-skinned hands upon the railing. "Mr. Means, are you a religious man?"

The question caught Boot off guard. Because of the secret nature of the grand jury, he felt thrown into the middle of a mysterious conversation. He glanced at the judge for help. "I don't see why this is relevant?"

"Answer the question," Younghand said.

"But I don't see ..."

"The jury's been instructed to make a determination of indictment or no indictment. They must consider a wide array of suspects and crimes regarding the OFJ, and I'll allow them a great deal of latitude as to character. Answer the question, please."

Boot faced the juror again. "No, I'm not as religious as some."

"I wonder if your particular faith hasn't clouded your judgment," the juror said.

"My faith?" Boot caught a glimpse of Black whispering to her associates. "My faith isn't the issue. I'm a journalist. I get at the truth. That's the only issue here."

"What is your specific religion?" the juror asked. "Christian? Jewish?"

"I have no religion."

"No religion?"

"Doesn't that answer your question?"

"You don't believe in God?"

Boot recognized the astonishment on the man's face. It scared him a little. When he was a kid, one of his foster parents used to drag him into the basement and whip him with a strap, until he said that he believed in God.

The courtroom waited for Boot's answer, so the man restated his question. "What do you believe?"

Boot held concrete beliefs. He believed in a fresh roll of film and the chance to capture something great. "I believe in my own abilities and strengths. I believe things happen because they're set up that way. I believe that certain talents rise above others."

"How do you feel about the Open Faith for Jesus?"

"They're a cult organization."

"So you assume they're suspicious?"

"They're a stomping ground for ex-cons and drifters, people looking for a home."

"This wouldn't make you think badly of them and want to show them in a negative light?"

"I don't care about the OFJ, as long as they don't ask me for money or knock on my front door."

A handful of jurors laughed.

The next juror was a Hispanic woman. Kinky black hair fell away from her face in waves. "Did you pay your informant?"

"Never," Boot said.

"How did you come in contact with him?"

"I met him at Camp Jesus, Jefferson Avenue." As soon as he spoke, Boot realized he'd inadvertently confirmed the sex of his informant.

Boot noticed Black's interest perk up. She pulled away from her colleagues and approached the stand.

"I've read your columns in the *Record*," she said. "They are very good, highly detailed."

"I suppose."

"Earlier, Trenton detectives testified to that."

"It's a matter of opinion."

"They were impressed with your detail. Your stories alone identified members of the OFJ as suspects."

"Again, it's a matter of opinion."

"Come on now, without your reporting, the OFJ wouldn't be under investigation."

"When you state it like that."

"The detectives believed your information came from a very well-placed source within the OFJ."

"It's a logical assumption."

"Is it true?"

"In a manner of speaking."

"You're being evasive. Is it or isn't it?"

"It is."

"You never mentioned the name of your source in the column, this man you met on Jefferson Avenue."

"Right."

"Would you like to tell the court his name."

"My source has asked to remain confidential." Boot wiped the sweat from his upper lip. He'd give up LeBlay in a heartbeat if he thought it might help, but Boot was the one who created this mess by lying to Art, and he needed to be the one to mop it up.

"You understand the implications here."

"Yes."

"You're required to comply with the grand jury."

"In so far as I need to protect my source."

"By refusing, you're inhibiting an ongoing investigation, and I might add, concealing a vital piece of information. Are you familiar with the term, contempt of court?"

"Are you familiar with the First Amendment?"

"You're very amusing, Mr. Means. You cannot hide behind a free press to protect a criminal act."

"If anything, I've provided the police with their best evidence. You said so yourself."

The jury laughed again.

Black twirled the pen. "Yet you refuse to supply your informant's name. Why is that?"

"I'll supply my notes, unpublished photographs, whatever you want. I wouldn't call that uncooperative."

"But what about your informant. I'm imploring you to comply."

"I must keep my source confidential."

"You mean secret."

"That's your word." Boot felt the impasse so strong, that he might as well be arm wrestling with her.

"But certainly you can see how critical your informant is to law enforcement."

"Perhaps."

"Don't you think that your news story has run its course? You've seized the headlines. Shouldn't you let the Justice Department take over?"

Boot felt backed into a corner. She was trying to make him appear selfish, but he refused to let her know about LeBlay before he covered his own tracks. "I didn't know the Justice Department was in the newspaper business."

Some of the jury smiled.

Black stabbed her pen toward Boot. "It's almost as if you're in collusion with this informant whomever he is."

"Nothing could be further from the truth."

"Then why not help law enforcement close the case. What are you hiding?"

Boot searched Judge Younghand for relief, finding nothing beneficial in his expression. "She keeps asking me the same question over and over again."

"Your honor," Black interrupted, "because he's not answering the question."

"No," Younghand said, lining Boot in his sights. "You're not answering the question."

Boot looked at the judge hovering above him. "You know I can't answer her question."

Black clutched the railing in front of Boot. "You must, Mr. Means."

Boot straightened his back in the chair. The bitch was going to push the issue until everyone in the courtroom was ill. "I believe I have the right to protect my source, under the constitution." *That should fix her.*

"Your honor." Black tossed her hand in the air, throwing back her head for added drama. "I can't go on with this witness. He's obviously stonewalling the court. It's clear he chooses news headlines above due process."

"Mr. Means," Younghand said. "It would be in the court's best interest, including your own, if you answer the question."

Boot didn't reply.

"These are closed proceedings," Younghand added.

Boot held silent. *Yeah, right.*

"I see." Younghand reached for the gavel. "I allow a great deal of leeway with the press. It's a coveted institution in this country, yet by refusing to provide a crucial piece of information before this grand jury ..."

"But your honor ..." Boot interrupted.

Younghand pointed the gavel at Boot. "Mr. Means, I'm speaking now."

"Sorry, sir."

"This is a closed proceeding. Anything you say will be held in confidence up until the time, if that should arise, when indictments are handed down."

"I can't do this, your honor."

"I have to say I've given you every opportunity to explain why you cannot comply with the court."

Boot's reasons for not speaking—LeBlay's fraudulent claims against the OFJ—were more dangerous to Boot than LeBlay himself. "I can't divulge his name at this time."

"The court is frustrated. You haven't shown sufficient excuse for withholding this information. I respect your journalistic integrity, and I want to believe in your noble intentions, but in your refusal to cooperate, you tie the hands of this grand jury. Specifically, you inhibit an ongoing inquiry and investigation."

Boot braced himself for a fine and a slap on the wrist.

Younghand raised the gavel slightly. "Mr. Means, the proliferation of handguns on the street has reached epidemic levels. I cannot allow that to go unchecked. This court requests your cooperation, and it requests it in a prompt fashion."

Boot faced the jury. "I can't reveal my source, sir."

"Is that your decision?" Younghand clenched the gavel.

"It is."

"Mr. Means, I find you in criminal contempt of court. You'll be held without bail until the time you see fit to cooperate. In addition, your records will be immediately turned over to the court." Judge Younghand slammed the gavel into the block.

The sharp sound echoed in Boot's ears. He clung to his chair, struggling to process Younghand's decision. If Boot had money, if he was one of Younghand's golfing buddies, he'd be whisked away for cocktails and laughs at the clubhouse. Instead, he received the full treatment, worthy of any poor boy. He glared at the judge until the bailiff came to haul him away.

CHAPTER 26
Visiting Hours

On his second night in the courthouse prison, Boot was escorted into the visiting room. A transparent divider separated him from the public, but halfway across the room, he paused. The guard prodded him with a shove. He expected to find Art or Candace, even Stacy as a long shot. He never counted on seeing Charles Goodner on the opposite side of the glass. He edged closer to the chair. He had real problems to handle, and Charles' outrageous claims gave him a headache.

A red phone hung from the shallow wall of the booth. Boot took a seat and picked up the receiver. "What do you want?"

"I heard you were in a bind," Charles said. "It's been in the papers."

Boot pictured his name in print. He wondered why Art hadn't contacted him yet. "What are the papers saying?"

"They know that your incarceration involves protecting an informant."

"The grand jury proceedings are supposed to be closed." Boot barely hid his sarcasm. He knew the score. He wouldn't have a job without such leaks. "So much for secrets."

"They aren't worth much, today."

"I guess not."

"The papers are supportive of you. The writers see themselves in your shoes. Sorry you had to spend the night in jail."

"It's not a room at the Hyatt." Boot's back ached from the stiff cell cot. The courthouse prison served as a transitional place for people awaiting arraignments and trials. He barely saw another soul between meals. "I'd rather be outside working."

"I imagine so."

"What else are the papers saying?"

"They think you're being persecuted for uncovering police corruption."

"They must be referring to the officer in the rail yard."

"That's it."

"I didn't even know his name."

"When you pick on one police officer, you pick on them all."

"Did they mention anyone else? Anyone by name?" Boot hoped that another reporter hadn't stumbled onto LeBlay.

"They talked about a few OFJ suspects. I don't recall their names. I'll get the paper for you."

"I'd asked for the local newspapers, but the guards don't pay attention."

Charles tapped his fingers on the ledge in front of the glass." Jake told me about your situation."

"How is my bodyguard doing?"

"He's back at the hotel by the pool. He told me about your informant."

Boot glanced at the guard who was busy trimming his nails with his teeth. "Don't mention him again."

"Excuse me?"

"You don't want to drag yourself into this. You think you understand what's going on, but you don't."

"I know this much." Charles tilted his head forward in a fashion that Boot recognized from their conversation in the trailer. "I've spoken to my lawyer. He claims he could get you out by morning."

"What's he going to do? Blast me free?"

"I'm serious. He hooked me up with some New York bigshot."

"What's the bigshot have to say?"

"He says your incarceration is bogus."

"I agree."

"He can get you out if he goes before the judge. He's done it before."

Boot recalled his one and only phone call with the *Record*'s attorney. The stodgy woman seemed in no hurry to spring him from jail. It made him think of LeBlay's remarks about being on the inside: the feeling of helplessness, the appearance of time stretched to its limit. It wore him down. It made him paranoid of people on the outside and what they thought and did.

"I can get you out," Charles said. "You might've guessed that I have a couple of dollars. It'd be no trouble for me."

Boot considered the offer. It sounded tempting, but it came with too many strings attached, like a father and a family, things with no logical place in his life. Who knew how far the ties might reach? He was an entity of one. He didn't need any more debts, especially with strangers. "Thanks anyway."

"Think about it."

"The paper's attorney is on the case."

"What is he doing?"

"It's a she, and I'm not sure."

"Has she filed a motion with the judge?"

"I hope so."

"Has she given you a timetable?"

"No."

"If you like, I can help. You wouldn't be obliged to me, if that's your worry."

Boot eyed Goodner suspiciously. Everything had a price.

"You'd be doing me a favor," Charles said.

"How's that?"

"Are you familiar with Gambler's Anonymous?"

"It's one of those Twelve Step programs."

"One step is about making amends with the people you've wronged."

"So you think you're doing that now?"

"I owe you at least that much."

Boot just stared at him. It sounded too neat and cozy. Did Goodner want him to step out of his life like it was all a dream? Was he suppose to just leap into his arms? "I don't know what to say."

"Maybe I can explain myself better." Charles closed his eyes for a second. "I know a man who used to play the ponies quite often. It got to the point where he was borrowing from one group to pay off the debts from the other. Neither one of these groups were too friendly."

"Is this about you?"

"I'll get to that." Charles composed his story again. "This man had family with enough cash to pay the marker, but he never asked. Two days before Christmas, trouble from Dallas stopped by and broke nearly every bone in his body."

"So was it you?"

"It's a man I know in GA."

"What happened to him?"

"He got help in the program. He's probably leaning over a car engine somewhere, smoking a Marlboro."

"I thought you were going to say he was dead."

"This was thirty years ago. He still walks with a limp though. He calls it his little reminder."

In the next booth, the man bent toward the divider to kiss his lover good-bye. Their lips pressed against the glass.

Boot was tired, and his temper flared, just looking at Charles got him going. "What makes a woman want to abandon her child?" The question just slipped out.

"You're talking about your mother."

"I'm asking."

"It's a complicated question."

"Then give me a complicated answer, because after all this time, I don't have anything to go on."

"I don't either."

"That's it?"

"You could ask your grandmother, but she'd only turn you against me."

"You must know something."

"Dana was hot-blooded. It ran in her family."

"Go on."

"You should've seen her when she was angry. I guess I got used to it. I never realized how unstable she was."

"Unstable?"

"I can't blame her. We were a lot alike, constantly pushing the limits. At the snap of a finger, we'd hop a junket to Reno and Vegas. Lord, with her arm wrapped around mine at the craps table. I'm telling you, there's nothing like it when the dice roll across that brushed green felt. The whole place draws a breath."

"That's your answer?"

"Make no mistake. Dana loved you."

"Do you ever see her?"

"I don't want to be the bearer of bad news."

"Go ahead. I'm a big boy."

"She was ill with cancer."

"Is she dead?"

"I chased her for a long time, and when I finally came upon her, she didn't have much time left, and she wasn't saying a word about you. Sorry, that was fifteen years ago."

Boot was partly relieved. He'd read about women who gave up their babies, then pulled their lives together and started anew. He always feared some other child might be sitting in his place. "She said nothing about me?"

"She did what she thought was necessary to break free from me."

"You must've been a winner."

Goodner seemed to anticipate this potshot, absorbing it deep inside. "When I look at you, I see how great you are and how much you've accomplished on your own. I think Dana was crazy as me, maybe crazier. I should've stopped her from leaving."

"By what you've told me, you couldn't even control yourself."

"I have my regrets, even though I think most things happen for a reason."

"You've said that before."

"I believe it. I didn't know what I was gambling until I lost you. I needed to learn that."

"And what was I supposed to learn?"

"You didn't deserve this. That's why I'm here. To make it right. It was a miracle that I found you."

"It seems pretty miraculous from where I'm sitting."

"You're making a joke of something amazing."

"I find it ..." Boot was about to say overwhelming, until he remembered his promise to himself. He strengthened his resolve to remain guarded. "I find it hard to believe."

"You found the Jesus of Trenton. That's a blessing. Did you ever think He came for you too?"

"For me?" Boot waved his hand at Charles' assumption. "I've seen the mumbo-jumbo. Hell, I wrote a good part of it in my column. Don't think you can sell that stuff to me."

"Then at least think about letting me help you."

"You really want to help me? Leave me alone."

Charles pulled back in his chair.

"Maybe this is the right way." Boot employed Charles' divine logic against him. If a journalist knew anything, he knew how to twist words, better than a politician. "Did you ever think we were separated for a reason?"

"That's ludicrous."

"Who's to say? Maybe God wanted us apart."

"That can't be ..."

"Leave me alone. That's the help I need right now."

Charles didn't move. He gripped his side of the counter.

Boot felt mean and ugly. It composed the most discrete part of his emotion, a bottomless pit of energy. "Let's say you are my father. I'll live with that, although I'm not scared of being alone. I'm not scared of a jail cell either. Go back to Texas and don't bother me."

"If that's what you want." The words seemed to choke in the big man's throat.

"That's what I want."

"Then I'll honor your wish."

Boot hung up the phone and left his chair. Charles was more than he could manage, although Charles had no right to know that. He had no right to anything.

The guard moved from his post to escort Boot back to his cell. Boot strode past him and stepped into the hall. He refused to look back. He didn't need to see Charles' face. He didn't need that image burned into his memory.

CHAPTER 27
The Best Publicity

In the morning, Boot paced in his cell. It had beige walls, a beige floor, and a beige toilet and sink. The claustrophobic accommodations offered all the pizzazz of a public restroom with a board for a bed.

The guard deposited a tray of pancakes and watery eggs at the door. Boot sat on the beige flannel blanket and placed the tray across his knees. At least, he was getting regular meals, but the guard didn't utter more than two words, no matter how hard Boot tried to spark a conversation.

He downed the lukewarm food and bided his time. The more he thought about his predicament, the more it appeared to have a single solution. He'd never be able to scale Dove's ivory tower and bring her down, and that feat seemed easier than finding LeBlay. He dropped his head in his hands. Jesus, just one chance. He needed to tell Art the truth and take his lumps. Art might show pity and guide him clear of this mess.

When the guard returned, Boot stood up. "I'd like to use the phone."

The guard held the cell keys on a rubber cord, which he swung around his wrist. "No need."

"What do you mean?"

"You're free to go."

"Free to go where?"

"Judge Younghand's releasing you."

"Did he say why?"

"That's not my department."

Boot gathered his possessions from the safe and hit the street running. The sky was overcast and gray, as sheets of black rain dotted the pavement. He ran across town without an umbrella. He didn't care that the rain soaked his clothes. He needed to reach Art at the *Record* building.

Two blocks from the office, Boot spotted a *Trenton Times* news box in the street—OFJ INDICTMENTS HANDED DOWN. He slipped some change in the box and pulled out a copy. Several members of the OFJ were facing weapons charges. Boot dropped the paper in the street. Someone in the OFJ was talking.

He started running again. A handful of picketers in neon orange rain ponchos marched outside the *Record* complex. Boot burst through the line and into the main building.

The newsroom appeared moderately busy. Boot saw the back of Art's wide shoulders through the glass wall of the editor's conference room. He sat with two senior editors, Faith Runyon and Thomas Nesko.

Boot shuffled toward the conference room, planning his opening words to the paper's top staff, but as soon he drew near, he noticed Candace sitting among them. Her curvy lips hovered above a coffee mug. She was talking non-stop to a short man with kinky hair. Boot froze just outside the door. Paul Andujar was in there too.

Suddenly, Boot's world spun in a new and unfavorable direction. He took a step backward. He'd rather attend another luncheon with

Drake and Chau, than spend a minute with this crowd.

Art pivoted in his chair and waved. His words rumbled behind the glass. "Come on in, Boot."

"That's alright." Boot glanced at the bright red exit sign above the newsroom door. "I'll come back later."

Art's voice grew louder. "I think now is the best time."

Boot dragged his feet into the conference room. Candace and Andujar stood up immediately and left. Boot tried to read Candace's face, but she refused to look him in the eye. Things were worse than he expected.

He sat down and focused his attention on the trio across the table. Runyon brushed her hair behind her ear, studying a note pad full of scribbles. Nesko eyed Boot's wet clothes and frowned. Art pushed a half-eaten bagel and coffee aside and cleared his throat. Boot recalled the same inquisition at his job interview. His resume and portfolio were light, but he impressed them by handling their rapid-fire questions for over an hour. He looked for a repeat performance, his very best yet.

Runyon glanced at Art. "Where are we going with this?"

Art reached for his coffee but put it back down. "Let's give Boot a chance to speak."

"I'd like to hear what he has to say." Nesko twisted a piece of plastic strapping around his fingers, as if fashioning a noose for fun.

"Good morning, Boot," Art said.

"Hi." Boot didn't like Art's tone. Art seldom balanced reserve in his speech. Boot appreciated Art's forthright style, where he blasted you, dumping his thoughts in your lap like a bucket of acid.

"Sorry, I'm late for work," Boot said. "I've been detained the last couple of days."

The joke sailed over Art's head. He cut to business. "I spoke with Dexter Washington this morning."

Boot realized the game was finished. He saw a demotion on his immediate horizon and drew a deep breath. He envisioned a career of shooting Miss Record portraits for Page 6. "You got Washington on the line?"

"That's affirmative," Art said. "It's bad news."

"How bad?"

"I think you know."

"I have an idea."

"There were two things I didn't like about my conversation with Washington. One, the interview wasn't quite what I had anticipated, and two, I discovered you only spoke with him on Saturday night. Is that true?"

"Not exactly."

"Is it true?"

"It's true." Boot watched Runyon close her eyes and shake her head.

She took off her glasses and massaged the bridge of her nose. "On one hand, this might only be a misrepresentation of the facts to us, but you understand that the trouble goes deeper."

Boot sat up, leaning into the table. "How so?"

"Candace Hohl alerted us to an oversight in your reporting."

Boot felt the sharp edge of the knife in his back. He wanted to slap Candace, but she'd probably enjoy it. "I didn't know about LeBlay until recently."

Runyon shook her head again, peering down her nose. She was the embodiment of disapproval. "Think of your journalistic principles."

"It's still a solid story."

"Let's look at your situation like a news story. The basic questions are: who knew what, and when did they know it? Are you familiar with those questions?"

Boot loathed her sarcasm but lapped up the abuse to redeem himself. "I studied them at school."

"I'm asking myself these questions about your conduct. What did you know and when did you know it? And I'm not hearing the answers I like."

"I admit I was fooled, but I've been trying to verify LeBlay's past ever since."

Nesko chimed in, tossing his plastic strap on the table. "That's putting the cart before the horse, isn't it? But then, you've already put the cart out there without the horse, haven't you? There are editors at this paper for a reason."

Beneath the table, Boot dug his fingernails into his palms. "Why are you doing this? The OFJ has been indicted."

"Not every member," Art said.

"That's irrelevant."

"Because you failed to perform the proper journalistic procedures, you've misrepresented the entire OFJ organization, and you've made the paper look bad."

"Sloppy," Nesko added.

"Wait," Boot cried. "LeBlay's a bad guy. We all know that."

"You've got that part right," Nesko said.

"He convinced members of the OFJ—ex-cons, I might add—to commit illegal acts. How is that a misrepresentation?"

"Listen to me," Art said. "That wasn't the whole story, at least not the story we printed, and it certainly wasn't the course that I instructed you to take."

"I did the best I could."

"I asked you to check LeBlay's references, and you led me to believe you had."

"I was being practical." Boot was on fire, although he resisted saying the things he really felt. He could take aim at each of them—coward, creep, has been. "This paper needed a break. You said we were on the brink of folding. I went with the facts as I saw them. I went with my instincts."

"That doesn't give you the right to skip procedures."

"Is that what this is about? Procedures?"

"If you had given yourself a little more time, you may have established the link between LeBlay and Melanie Dove. That was the story.

You missed it. That was the reason why this happened. As it stands, you've probably lost that link."

"Give me more time. I know I can do it. I can close the gap."

Nesko pointed his finger at Boot. "This is the conversation we should have before the story is printed, not after it's placed in the public domain."

The editors ceased talking. They sat quietly for a longer period of time than it takes to read Page 6. Runyon scribbled on her pad, making check marks in the margin. Nesko glared at Boot. Art sipped his coffee and gazed out the window. The silence unnerved the young reporter.

Art put down his cup. "Give us a moment, Boot. Go sit in the newsroom, and we'll get back to you."

Boot left the conference room and headed down the corridor toward the water cooler. His throat felt dry, and sweat beaded along his hairline. He spotted Paul Andujar sitting with Teresa Ringley in her cube. Just one glance from Teresa said that she knew everything. Boot found it hard to bear the look on her face. She seemed disgusted.

"Boot?" Teresa shuffled behind him. "Where are you going?"

"To get a drink of water."

"What happened?"

Boot glimpsed into the conference room. The editors were arguing. Nesko waved his hands in the air. "They're deciding how to punish me."

"You screwed up."

"That's tomorrow's headlines, right?"

"You should've consulted with me. You were very close. You know I would've helped."

"Just call me golden boy." He yanked his pants pockets inside out. "I think I have my horse's ass trophy in here somewhere."

"It's not funny."

"Who's laughing?" Boot scanned the newsroom. More than a dozen people tapped the keys on computer terminals. "I thought you were on strike."

"It's defunct."

"I saw people picketing out front."

"Rico will go on forever, but a bunch of us decided to return."

"What does the union say?"

"The union's busted up. Storch saw to that."

"And you?"

"I needed the paycheck."

Boot turned his shoulder. "Looks like I'm not the only one who's been compromised this morning."

"Don't let your emotions ruin your chances."

"Look at me." Boot feigned a smile. "I'm overjoyed."

"We all get setbacks."

"You call this a setback? It's a lynch mob in there."

"Nesko can be a bastard. Just ride it out the best you can. I know you've been going through a lot lately."

"You don't know the half of it."

"You look like you've been through a meat grinder."

"And it's not over yet. So if you don't mind getting out of my way, I've got to save my ass."

"Hold on. Someone wants to talk with you."

"If it's not Travis LeBlay, I'm not interested."

"Andujar's in my office. He might have a few answers for you."

"What are you doing with him?"

"Interviewing him for Sunday's People section."

"Is he giving you a picture?"

She looked down.

"Then what's he want with me," Boot said, "besides a chance to knee me in the groin?"

"Just talk to him."

Boot saw Andujar sitting on the stool in Teresa's office. His face appeared pink and puffy, like a newborn baby. His short legs dangled above the floor, and he tucked his feet behind the metal bar that braced the chair legs.

"Please." Andujar waved his stubby fingers, beckoning Boot forward. "You have nothing to fear."

Boot walked into Teresa's cube and dropped into her chair. "You have something to say?"

"I forgive you for what's happened."

"Great. I can sleep now." Boot moved to get up, but Andujar pushed down on his knee.

"I know you're angry because your fortune has turned," Andujar said.

"Why does everyone think they know what's going on?"

"I know more than you think."

"What are you doing here?"

"Art Fontek invited me. They wanted to apologize and work out an agreement."

"What sort of agreement?"

"An agreement to put an end to this problem. I think they call it a retraction."

"There won't be any need for that."

"I wouldn't be so sure."

"You're not as clean as you pretend to be. The defectors still set up shop under your nose."

"You ought to let go of that." Andujar folded his hands in his lap, pushing his tunic top between his legs. "This story had to end sometime. You know much of the hoopla will disappear with the Jesus sign gone."

"Where did it go?"

Andujar offered his ugly turn of the mouth. "I remember what it was like to be in jail. Even after a day or two, you miss so much."

"I didn't hear anything about the Jesus sign being gone."

"Jesus has left Trenton." Andujar snapped his fingers in the air. "Gone, just like that. Someone poured gasoline over the sign and scorched it beyond recognition."

Boot felt himself losing grip of every aspect of his story. "Good. I was starting to get tired of it anyway."

"You ought to be."

"I'm surprised the building lasted as long as it did."

"I thought you'd be the least surprised. Your boss owned the building."

"Yeah, right. Art Fontek bought the Anderson Box building as an investment."

"Sheldon Storch did."

"That's ridiculous."

"You didn't know? His holding company purchased it this summer. I think he has plans for a movie theater now."

"And you know this because ...?"

"Art Fontek told me. I guess Storch thought it was his best chance at keeping Camp Jesus alive, so he bought it. Fontek said you sold a lot of papers with that story."

Boot stomped his foot on the floor. "Those bastards."

"I see why they kept it from you. You remind me a lot of myself at your age."

"Excuse me, but we're nothing alike."

"You feel like a loner, like you have to battle the world alone."

Boot searched Andujar's black eyes, finding an eerie kind of compassion lurking inside. "You're the oddest person I ever met. That includes Dove and LeBlay."

Andujar appeared invulnerable to insults. "There's a pair of names."

"You should be familiar with both."

"I was suspicious of LeBlay for a while, and thanks to your reporting, I put everything together."

"You could've been more cooperative with me, and maybe this wouldn't have happened."

"I pointed you in the right direction, but you didn't want to see. You were caught in LeBlay's spell. Getting popped in the head by one of his men didn't even wake you."

"LeBlay was a good talker."

"Like Melanie Dove, but phony to the core."

Boot understood the same woman that Andujar described, but he'd never admit it. "I guess you feel the same way about Dove as she does about you."

"I pity her."

"I'd figure you hated her."

"That would be like hating a cardboard cutout of an actual person. She's two dimensional, a veritable hypocrite."

"She's said the same about you."

"I have nothing to hide, but within her house you'll find many lies. She can't even be honest about her girlfriend. Excuse me, her assistant."

"I assume you mean Julia Sherowich."

"How would she explain that relationship to her conservative fellowship?"

"It's not my problem who she sleeps with."

"It shouldn't be a problem, but it is for Dove. In the Open Faith, we accept everyone. Jesus loves us all. Loving within the same sex is not a sin or a sign of weakness. Commitment and responsibility is valued far above those things, and forgiveness is tops."

"Have you forgiven the defectors? I heard you kicked them out."

"I had no choice."

"Who told you about them? I know LeBlay wouldn't."

"We're a tight group. Once the rumors started bouncing around, word came back to me. We can take care of our own."

"Where is LeBlay?"

"He's no longer my concern."

"You wouldn't ..."

"I wouldn't harm him, but he knew when to leave town. He wasn't stupid."

"Which leaves me holding the bag."

"Travis was a pro. He could fool the best of them."

"I suppose."

"You weren't the only one. Kathy Scott would agree with you."

"Kat?"

"Yes, her."

"Was she the person who told you about LeBlay?"

"Not at first, but eventually she helped clear the air. She came to me, and I brought her to the grand jury."

"Damn."

"She cut a deal with the DA to help out Simon Talito."

Boot felt the pinched nerve between his shoulders begin to twinge. "I don't know why you're talking to me. Right or wrong, the things I wrote damaged the OFJ."

Andujar twisted his expression again. "Today, crime is the best publicity."

"I think Art tried to tell me that once." Boot disliked that Andujar was right, but the little man nailed down one salient point after another. He remembered that about his brochures.

"The Open Faith will recover. Thanks to you, four times as many people know about our mission. So don't worry about us. I see the membership roles expanding in the future."

Teresa poked her head in the office. "Boot, Art wants you in the conference room."

"Here goes nothing," Boot said.

Andujar extended his hand. "Good luck."

Boot stared at Andujar. He felt stupid. He'd done something he hated in other people. He judged Andujar by appearance. He shook Andujar's hand. "I don't completely get you."

"Some day, you'll understand."

"I'm not so sure."

"You're very angry with yourself at the moment. Forgiveness must begin there."

Boot quickly released Andujar's palm, unable to deal with the naked honesty. "Thanks, anyway."

When Boot entered the conference room, he found Art alone at the table. Art's necktie was pulled down, the first two buttons of his shirt undone. A gray tuft of hair poked through the opening.

"This is not a happy moment for me," Art said.

"I screwed up," Boot replied. "I lied to you and the paper."

"I've been around this business for a long time. I've seen every type of journalist. Each man has his own style."

"I thought you liked mine."

"There are many things I can accept, but a lapse of integrity isn't one of them."

"What has the editorial hit squad decided for me?"

"I fought to get you this much."

"Great. Let's hear it."

"You can type a single retraction. It will include your journalistic assumptions and errors. This is basically your fault."

"I understand."

"And if you ever want to work in this industry again, I suggest you take the righteous path with this."

"What do you mean, if I ever want to work ..."

"You don't actually think you can go on writing here?"

"I'm fired?" Boot expected a demotion. At worst, he anticipated a brief stint as a copy boy to prove his salt, but with the news staff slimmed down to a minimum, he never saw this coming. They needed him.

Art scratched the mole on his nose. "Storch wanted to send you packing without an explanation, but I wouldn't let that happen."

"Shit." Boot still couldn't believe it.

"After Nesko calmed down, we agreed to bury the fact that you lied to your chief editor. That's a break for you. We took your inexperience into account, and I feel partly responsible for what transpired."

"But you get to keep your job."

"We're giving you the opportunity to type a retraction."

"An apology, you mean."

"It's not so much an apology, as an extension of the facts. You need to say how you were conned by LeBlay. Of course, this comes with your resignation."

As Art spoke, Boot thought about talking his way back onto the *Record*, but the hard news started to register. He was fired, finished at the *Record* for good. It had happened as fast as flicking a light switch.

"I know it's embarrassing for you," Art said, "but it's better than making it public. You wouldn't work in this country again. There are too many journalists out of work."

"Including me."

"Journalists have been known to resign over issues."

"I don't know what to say."

"I'll give you a reference, but I'd be careful about who else you ask. Word about this will get around."

"It already has." Boot stood up before the trap door opened beneath his feet and he was ejected into the parking lot with Rico and his gang of rebels.

"I'm sorry for you, Boot."

"Right."

"I still think you'll make a decent journalist one day."

CHAPTER 28
The Safest Sex

Boot typed his retraction and sent it along the computer network to Art. He stumbled about his office in a daze, packing up his things. He stuffed old news clippings and photos into a paper bag, until he realized there was nothing worth saving. He reached into the bag and shredded a small stack of photos, hurling them through the frosted glass windows of his loft. The big presses stood silent, and only a few pressmen looked up to watch the fragments float to the cement floor without a sound.

The street looked almost empty, as Boot walked outside the *Record* building. He recalled his pride on his first day at work, even though the *Record* was the least read paper in town. Now, he created an embarrassment for them. He pushed through the handful of picketers by the curb, ready to slug the first man who cut a remark, but no one offered a word, not even a nasty glare. He wondered if they already knew.

The rain fell out of the sky in buckets. Boot tugged his collar to his neck and headed for the waterfront, reviewing his desperate finances. He was unemployed. He had less than ninety days before getting evicted, and his savings account wouldn't cover living expenses for more than a week. He'd rob a bank but lacked the funds to buy a gun for the holdup.

It occurred to Boot that the article for *Focus Trend* might still be possible. He dug into his coat for Noel Van Dycke's business card. *Focus Trend* didn't have to know about his trouble at the *Record*. Perhaps he still had time to pull his career from the fire.

He found a phone booth on Warren Street and pleaded with Van Dycke's secretary to get her boss on the line. She put Boot on hold for ten minutes, as he pumped the phone with every bit of change in his pocket.

Van Dycke coughed into the receiver. He sounded annoyed. "Where have you been?"

"In jail." Boot tried to make light of his absence. "Maybe you read about it?"

"My secretary told me. Tough break."

"When do you want my work?"

"Two days ago. Why didn't you call?"

"You only get one phone call in the slammer."

"I see." Van Dycke drew a sustained breath which muffled in the receiver. "You're in luck. Yoshii's been in Chile longer than expected. He's going to be late."

"Yoshii?" Boot knew Yoshii from *Newsweek* and *Time*. He'd get noticed for sure next to a pro like that.

"But I know he'll deliver."

"I'll deliver too."

"This is your last chance."

"I understand."

"Get a story outline and picture proofs on my desk by noon tomorrow. Can you handle that?"

"Yes."

"That'll be a step in the right direction. I won't tolerate another delay."

"Yes, sir."

"Send me what I need, and I'll get back to you." Van Dycke hung up the phone.

Boot stood with his hand on the receiver. The rain washed through the gutters, carrying cigarette butts and old lottery tickets down the street. He watched the garbage collect atop a sewer grate on the corner.

Three crewcuts in leather jackets waited beneath the awning of a pawn shop. Boot recognized two defectors from the rail yards. All three men were studying the phone booth.

Boot headed back into the rain. He brushed his hair away from his forehead and over his head. The water ran down the back of his neck and gave him a chill.

Turning onto State Street, Boot passed Smythe's Diner and peered through the corner windows. The crewcuts were tailing him, gaining ground with quick steps. The largest man studied Boot with a peculiar grin. Boot wiped the rain from his eyes. The crewcuts weren't coming to say hello.

A reflection of the capital building painted Smythe's dingy windows in brown and gold. Boot jogged toward the statehouse, planning to scare off the crewcuts inside the official confines. He pushed inside the quiet foyer, surprised to see two of the crewcuts still following. They strutted past the guards, like a pair of oddball tourists.

Boot picked up the pace, trying not to panic and lose his knees. He marched past the bust of Woodrow Wilson and mounted the steps to the senate gallery. The crewcut's voices echoed in the stairwell. Their boots clapped the hard marble like synchronized hammers.

Boot jogged through the southern wing, listening for the defectors. He turned the first corner, hearing their footsteps fade. He turned another corner, then another, losing himself inside the massive complex. He stood in the center of a narrow hallway, with only the sound of his chest rising and falling.

Down the hall, a red exit sign led onto a fire escape. Boot walked softly toward the door and nudged the metal bar. A wave of fire alarms sounded off, as if every siren had engaged in the city.

Boot fled down the fire escape and into the alley. He took two steps before spotting the third crewcut on State Street.

The zealous defector blocked the mouth of the alley. He dropped a chain from his sleeve and spun it in the air. "Have you ever read the Bible?"

Boot recognized the gruff voice from the phone threats to his trailer. He swallowed hard. "It's a thick black book full of words."

"You should give it a look. It has helpful hints during troublesome times."

"Is this one?"

"Might be."

Boot gathered his courage and charged. He refused to be trapped in the alley. He rushed straight at the whirling chain, like a half-baked kamikaze, screaming out loud.

The crewcut planted his feet. "Come to papa."

Boot lowered his shoulders, tucking his chin into his chest.

The crewcut raised the chain over his head.

At the very last moment, Boot dashed to the side. The chain whizzed past his ear, like the spinning blade of a helicopter.

He ran harder. He entered the street, unsure of his direction. The crewcut remained on his heels.

Boot bolted past the twenty-four hour exterminator, the late night check cashier, and the bodega between the boarded up crack house and the quickie gun seller. In the rain, the streets looked sparse and lonely. Deep puddles splashed beneath his feet. His heart pounded in his chest. If he ran himself ragged, no one would notice until rush hour.

The train station stood down the block. It looked like an ugly pit stop on the road to someplace worse, like a welcome center for the Gulag during the spring thaw. Boot raced for the entrance and slammed the glass door in the crewcut's face.

The big man clutched his nose.

Boot sprinted across the terminal, bursting into the last set of stairs. He headed for the lower level, hoping to lose the crewcut in the yard.

The stairwell darkened as he dropped. His hands were moist with rain. Halfway down, he lost grip of the railing and landed on his backside.

"Well if it isn't snapshot." Christine stood over him. She wore skintight leggings and a tank top with dayglo stripes.

"No time. I've got someone on my ass."

"Who?"

Boot stood up. "Defector. OFJ."

"One of those assholes?"

"Yup." He stepped past her, but she locked her arm around his elbow and swung him around.

"Wait up." She pushed him into shadows. "Take off your jacket."

"My what?"

"Go ahead."

Boot stared at her, feeling the cold wall against his back. He heard the stairwell open on the main concourse above them.

Christine heard it too, and her eyes rolled upward. "It's now or never."

Boot took off his jacket and watched her toss it into the corner.

"Drop your drawers, snapshot."

"No way."

"Yes, way. I know what I'm doing." She reached and undid his belt in a second.

"Hold it."

"Shut up." She yanked his pants and underwear below his hips.

He wanted to stop her, but she gripped his penis in one hand and squeezed.

She dropped to her knees.

He grabbed her head and grit his teeth. "Ooooh, stop it."

"Shut up, snapshot."

"You're hurting me."

"Shut your trap, or I'll squeeze harder."

The crewcut clipped down the stairs, but in the low light, Boot couldn't be certain until the big man was only several feet away. It was hard to make out anything except for Christine's dayglo stripes and the chrome links of the chain wrapped around the crewcut's wrist.

Christine jumped to her feet and blocked the crewcut's progress. "If you're gonna watch, it'll cost you twenty."

"Twenty?"

"Yeah, same as him."

The crewcut seemed embarrassed and confused. "Did you see a guy?"

"Does it look like I'm guarding the stairs?"

"I suppose not."

Boot shivered, his pants undone, his penis hanging like a sausage in the farmer's market.

The crewcut jangled the chain on his wrist, trying to get a closer look at Boot. "I'm looking for a man in a dark jacket."

Christine produced a razor and brought it to the crewcut's neck. "You see this."

"Hey!" The crewcut stepped back.

Christine pointed at the scar on her face. "You see this."

"Yes."

"This shit's gonna happen to me only once. You better just be fiddling with that thing on your wrist."

"I got no problem with you, sugar."

"At the moment."

"Just passing through."

"Then can a lady get space to work, please?" Christine asked, although she hardly posed it like a question.

"Amen."

"Get lost."

The crewcut continued down the stairs, turning back, squinting in Boot's direction.

They listened to the crewcut's steps retreat. When he reached the lower door, the stairs filled with light, then faded to black again.

Boot zipped up his pants. "Thanks."

Christine held out her palm, stabbing it into Boot's midsection. "That'll be twenty."

"For what?"

"I could be working right now."

Boot reached into his pocket and counted his net worth in front of her. "I have eleven. That's it."

She swiped it from his hand. "I suppose."

"I owe you." Why not? He owed everyone else.

"That's right, you owe me." She slipped the cash between her breasts. "Safest sex you'll ever have."

At the trailer park, police barricades blocked the entrance. Boot saw yellow flashing lights at a distance. One of the barricades was pushed aside, and water gathered about its stiff wooden legs.

Boot looked across the property. Pockets of water covered the grounds, extending up from the river in an uneven patchwork. No lights burned inside any of the two dozen trailers, and Mrs. Ohm's house appeared darkened as well. He assumed the police had chased everyone out because of the rain. At least, Jake's Caddy was nowhere in sight.

He spotted Stacy's red Corvette parked out front of the ApacheStar. Dirty brown floodwater touched the edge of its shiny mag rims. He waded through the ankle high water to check it out.

Stacy sat on the steps beneath the awning. She wore a bright green raincoat and hat, and her Doc Martin boots were untied at the top. A bottle of Wild Turkey rested between her legs, and as the water swept below her feet, she looked like a stranded boater drifting downriver.

She grabbed the bottle neck and swallowed a shot of booze. "I swore I'd never come back here."

"How did you know I was coming?"

"I called the office. They said you were no longer employed by the *Record*."

"I'm on a roll today."

"I heard about your prison stay too. I figured you had no place else to go. Am I right?"

"Right."

She glanced over her shoulder. "It's a mess in there, and I'm not cleaning it up."

"Nobody asked you to." Boot recalled the bench warrant to search his trailer for OFJ evidence. He'd seen the police in action. They turned places upside down in fifteen minutes. He hoped they missed the hiding spot for his photographic negatives. He needed those for the *Focus Trend* piece, his last shot at salvaging his career. He resisted the urge to rush inside and check.

Stacy pulled the hat from her head and wiped her forehead on the back of her wrist. Her silky brown hair was cut short and spiky. She resembled an OFJ candidate. "All this rain, and it's still hot as hell."

"Your hair, what did you do?"

"I wanted a quick makeover."

"You did it alright."

She leveled her sights on Boot. "You really pissed me off."

"I know."

"You lied to me."

Boot didn't reply. She'd echoed the day's theme. It felt like a dull thump on the head. He stood in the rain, his clothes soaked, his soles squishing in the mud. The stitches in his head were wet and sore.

Stacy drank the same Wild Turkey that he and Candace shared three days ago. Stacy had purchased the bottle on a whim last winter. "Who was she?"

"No one important."

"I knew you'd say that."

"It only happened once."

"You weren't ever going to marry me."

"Don't go there, Stace."

"You weren't, were you?"

"I intended to."

"Intended to?"

"I didn't know it at the time, but to answer your question, no, I wasn't going to marry you."

She looked up and toasted the sky. "Let the rain fall."

"How much did you have to drink?"

"Not nearly enough."

He stepped closer. "It's not like you to ..."

"To what? Get cheated on? Get dumped all over? You're just one in a long, long line, and I'm not only talking about boyfriends. I can build you a list."

"I'm sorry. I wanted to tell you myself."

"I got your message, loud and clear." She swigged from the bottle. She looked glassy-eyed, and her speech began to slur. "The trouble was I thought you were different. I looked up ... I admired you, everything you came from, what you accomplished. I'd never be able to do what you did."

Boot had no place in his brain to file her remarks. He rarely accepted compliments from people. Instead he sloughed off all forms of praise, believing people would change their minds as soon as they knew him better. Stacy was a perfect example; Art Fontek and Teresa Ringley too; even Paul Andujar in a way.

"What happened to you?" Stacy rose on the porch, wavering.

He didn't answer, concentrating on her precarious balance.

"Even after everything you did," Stacy said, "I'd take you back. Isn't that pathetic."

"Don't do this."

"I know you're a good person. I'd take you back, if I'd give you the chance. You'd be able to fool me, make me think you love me, which you don't. I know that, so that's why I have to leave. I don't want to give you the chance."

Boot understood her drunken ramble. It sounded as clear as words in any textbook. He could lie to her some more. He felt guilty enough to repeat the same mistake ad nauseam. He hated knowing that about himself. It made him feel weak. He was glad she was leaving.

Stacy splashed her boots into the water. "You never talked a lot about being an orphan. I know you don't like to bring it up."

"What's that have to do with anything?"

"It's everything. I always thought that I could love all those missing years back into your life."

"I don't think ..."

"Shush Boot. I'm trying to make a point. It's me here. I'm not as good with words as you."

"Go ahead."

"I thought I could love back those missing years, but maybe no one can. Maybe you don't want it to happen. Maybe you like the emptiness." She stepped toward her car and slipped in the mud, clutching onto her car roof for support.

Boot lunged for her, until he saw her right herself. "Let me drive."

She pushed him away and opened the door. "I'll make it."

"You're a little tipsy."

She gave him a hard stare. "You don't have to save me anymore. I'll make it without you."

He let go, watching her drop into the seat and shut the door.

The Corvette started up and pulled away. Water shot from the fenders like a speedboat cutting through the ocean. He hoped she arrived home safely and slept until morning. He hoped she never stumbled into the desire to call him again. If he had one wish for her, it was that she would wake up in the morning with him completely wiped from her memory.

CHAPTER 29
The River Doesn't Care

Boot stepped inside his trailer. Every cabinet, drawer, and container appeared to be turned over and gutted. Pots and dishes were piled on the counter. Food from the kitchen cabinets lay on the floor, and dry cereal and coffee grinds coated the sink. His filing cabinet leaned against the bathroom door, its contents scattered like disheveled mail. Clothes were strewn about the place like a plane wreck. He never realized how much stuff he'd tucked into the corners, until he saw it disbursed across the ApacheStar.

Kneeling on the floor, Boot tugged at the carpet covering the bedroom steps. The rough fabric unhinged from its velcro fasteners. He pried open the steel panel within the second step and removed an airtight strong box. The contents shifted inside, and his adrenaline soared. His archives of photographic negatives, his last chance at success, remained intact. With the *Focus Trend* piece in print, he'd forget his insurmountable bills, the tiny trailer, and his disastrous career in Trenton. He'd relocate to New York City where he belonged, rubbing elbows with the big boys.

Boot cleared the kitchen, kicking his clothes aside, piling the larger items in the breakfast nook. He needed space to string the dry line, set up the enlarger, and lay out his developing trays. The rest didn't matter.

The rain continued outside, pinging the ApacheStar's aluminum veneer like pails of change dumping out of the sky. Boot tacked black felt over the windows and screwed the photo safelight into the overhead socket. He stood in the kitchen, letting his eyes adjust to the dim red glow. The Delaware River raged outside. It sounded louder than usual, faster, angrier. He heard a siren wailing along route 29.

He dropped a Willie Dixon CD in the stereo and started with the negatives. He developed proof sheets of the OFJ at Camp Jesus. When he first saw the crewcuts, he wrote them off as freaks and thugs. He remembered thinking how stupid they looked in their dark clothes and tattoos, although in the end, he was the fool. LeBlay must have been waiting for Boot to arrive, choosing the right moment to pounce. Boot wondered if Dove scripted their first meeting, move by move, word for word.

The developing chemicals smelled sweet beneath Boot's nose. He labored for several hours, proofing his recent catalog, until the dry line became a montage of Trenton's summer with Jesus. He found news shots intermixed with candids of Trenton residents. He saw poses of Stacy and Candace as well. He took a step back, shocked by the uneven quality of his work. His portraits were superior to his news photos. He should've expected that, but in his shoot and run lifestyle, he'd forgotten what he enjoyed the most: a subtle, well-composed picture of a human face.

He scanned the dry line again, looking to make sense of his work as a whole. He saw people from every walk of life: cops and cons, the employed and unemployed, the holy and unholy. He needed an angle for *Focus Trend* and considered discussing a variety of rituals in his article. There were union protests, a line of police cars, a street man salvaging aluminum cans from the garbage, commuters jamming the train platforms at rush hour, the secret life of the OFJ, and the staged ceremonies of the Dove Network. But as he stared at the diverse images, they appeared less like a story and more like a collection of dangerous tradeoffs. Every photo had exacted a cost: a bump on the head, a lost job, a broken relationship. He'd paid for them all with blood. If he nailed the *Focus Trend* piece, then maybe it was worth the pain.

When the last proofs were exposed and set, Boot flicked on the lights and shuffled upstairs with his laptop computer. Candace's nude photos remained on the shelf beside the bed. Boot picked up the stack and laughed out loud. The cops must have liked her poses; two were missing. He shrugged. Oh well, she said she didn't care.

He plugged in his laptop and typed an outline until two in the morning. The wind gusted through the trees, and water slapped along the trailer's wheels, beating a hypnotic rhythm. He stared at the flat computer screen, until his eyes felt strained and tired.

As he reached to press the Save button, the lights flickered and died. He heard Willie Dixon croak on the stereo.

He stumbled downstairs and stepped into a calf high puddle of water. "Shit!"

Sloshing through the cold water, he groped for a flashlight. "Shit, shit."

He grew frustrated and ripped the black felt curtain from the rear window. The mansion across the river employed tiny Christmas lights, detailing its grand framework like an obnoxious sign for vanity and wealth. He stared at it in disbelief. Nothing but water laid between the mansion and his trailer. Dark hulks of trees poked up through the surface, as the Delaware River churned wildly downstream.

The ApacheStar groaned, listing to one side. Boot splashed for the front door, but it wouldn't open. The outside water pressure sealed the flimsy passage shut.

He heard a gushing sound behind him. Water squirted from the bathroom door. It burst open and flooded the kitchen. Loose clothing piled against his legs. His knees quivered. His pulse raced. The frigid water reached his hips, as swollen books gathered around him. He threw his shoulder against the door, but it refused to budge.

The trailer shifted, shimmying, squeaking, pulling away from its cinder block supports. Boot comprehended the moment. The Delaware River had crested, the distant unbelievable threat come true, rising over its banks, drawing his trailer into the mainstream.

The ApacheStar picked up speed, spinning with the current, tossing him around like floating debris. He slammed against the breakfast nook. The table edge chopped into his kidneys, sending a shock of pain up his spine.

He shook it off and regained his footing. He clawed along the countertop, fighting his way for the kitchen window. His winter coat blocked the shattered glass opening. The saturated goose down expanded like a sponge.

By the time he pulled the coat free, water lapped against his chest, pouring through the window at a severe angle, sucking the ApacheStar toward the muddy riverbed. He grabbed the window frame, slicing up both hands as he yanked himself clear.

The choppy water swirled around him, rushing into his mouth. He treaded water, spitting and shivering. He tried to gain his bearings in the river. The trailer's roof bobbed in and out of the current, and the stone columns of the Trenton Makes Bridge raced toward him in the moonless night. He reached out for the foundation, but the awesome force of the water pushed him past. He only dragged his fingernails over the mossy stones.

The trailer collapsed against the bridge. The horrible noise of twisting metal barely rose above the thundering river. He watched his photo enlarger fly through the imploded roof and sink beneath the whitecaps.

He swam for the shore, straining in the swift water, gaining little distance, if any. The Route 1 bridge swept overhead, and he struggled to keep his head above the swells.

His waterproof camera bag floated close by. Boot managed to grab hold of it, but when he threw his arms on top, he tumbled over and swallowed more water.

Coughing, freezing, Boot thrashed his arms and legs. His muscles momentarily cramped, and he slipped below the surface, pulling himself back up by the broken camera bag strap. He'd seen the same drama on the TV news. He'd seen the rescue workers cast ropes from bridges and shores in vain, seen the victim bob like a cork in the ocean, felt the hope of survival. One time he'd go under and never resurface. He knew that. After hours of floating aimlessly, it might come as a relief.

He held his breath, going under once again. He didn't feel defeated. It was strange; he felt resigned. He pumped his arms. His palms burned from the open wounds. He came up again, gasping for air. How many more times?

Several feet away, he saw the vinyl cushion from his breakfast nook. He recognized the wine stain from Stacy and the cigarette holes from when he used to smoke. It was funny that he knew such a cheap thing so well. He tried to get near it, but his strength abandoned him. He concentrated on keeping his head above water instead.

Minutes passed, and remaining afloat seemed an endless and unmanageable task. The vinyl cushion bounced closer, but he no longer cared. The river was a much larger force, with an angry and unswerving temperament. He stared at the cushion, until he went under another time.

He clutched the strap with the last of his will. He wished someone saw him drown. Sure, he'd make the news for only a day, but a record would be left behind. He deserved at least that much. He refused to disappear into the anonymity from which he was born. There had to be a witness. He needed a witness.

Kicking his legs, he fought for the surface, uncertain if he'd make it this time. He swallowed the brackish water, growing nauseous. The relentless river demanded to be inside him, and he cursed it. Gone were his negatives; gone were his opportunities, yet of all the things lost, he thought only of the photograph, the old snapshot that Charles left behind. He thought of his mother, her bright skin, her crazy smile. She knew something but wasn't saying. She had a plan that he never quite grasped.

The river wrapped around Boot, sucking him inside like a cold womb calling him home. He needed to see his mother, speak to her once, feel her touch. He admitted it to himself, to her. He understood nothing about the world, and he pushed his arms down, calling out to her. He was sorry. Wherever she was in the universe, he was sorry. He hadn't lived up to expectations. He wished he'd done so much more.

CHAPTER 30
Texas Sun

Boot stopped outside Charles Goodner's ranch. In the desert, the sun shone down so bright that it bleached everything shades of white. The rocks in the distance rose like disintegrating columns, like forgotten Roman ruins. They appeared to stand within a short walk, but Boot knew they might be twenty or more miles away.

After the flood, Boot had awoken in a Philadelphia hospital. He began to piece together his night in the Delaware River. He must have gotten a hand on the vinyl cushion from his trailer. He remembered hacking up lungs full of water, clinging onto that dirty old piece of foam like a lifeline.

A stranger had pulled Boot into a small boat with an outboard engine. The man would forever stick in Boot's mind. He possessed a terrible lisp, but Boot understood every word. The stranger never explained why his boat was on the river that night. He simply patted Boot's head and passed him to the rescue crew on shore. Boot didn't even know his name.

When Boot left the hospital, his hands were stitched up like his head. He spent two days wandering the streets of Philadelphia, sleeping in shelters, grabbing the odd meal in soup kitchens. He felt thin and used, like an old leaf sliding to-and-fro in the wind.

He tried to locate the man with the lisp. He found the rescue squad that transferred him to the hospital, but they didn't know the man's name or address. Boot hitched short rides up the Delaware, making inquiries along the way. No one could satisfy him. It was as if the man with the lisp never existed.

Boot needed a new plan. His total wealth amounted to the clothes on his back and the contents of his camera bag. He found a used camera shop in Bristol and hocked all but his Nikon and the wide angle lens. His chance with *Focus Trend* was gone. He felt relieved to be out from under the pressure of stories and deadlines. Somewhere in the cold Delaware River, he'd found a kinship with his mother. He was on the run. He could do anything, go anywhere. He decided to gather up his cash and buy a plane ticket for San Angelo.

In Texas, outside the Goodner property, Boot scanned the horizon. A dusty road led up to the sprawling ranch house. His search for the man who saved his life led him to Charles Goodner's door. Maybe there were no accidents. Charles had spent a load of time and money trying to find him. His father deserved better than a short good-bye and a swift kick in the ass.

But it was more than that. The picture of Boot's mother still resonated in his memory. He wanted to know more. He wanted to get behind the two-dimensional image and compose the whole story, and only one person held the missing clues.

Boot pressed the bell at the gate. He wasn't sure how long he might stay, although he believed the decision belonged to him. He raised his camera and framed the house in the lens. What could he learn about this part of the world? What did it have to offer? He squeezed the shutter release, hearing his camera slice another moment in time.

As a physicist for the space program, CHRISTOPHER KLIM worked on satellite planetary exploration, until departing for the commercial sector to help develop cutting-edge communications technologies. Traveling throughout the country, he's also worked as a bartender, a freelance photographer, and an assistant to a master chef. He lives with his family in New Jersey, and he knows that God exists. This is his first novel.

www.ChristopherKlim.com
ChristopherKlim@erols.com